TEN MINUT
MARS

BY JONATHAN FISHER

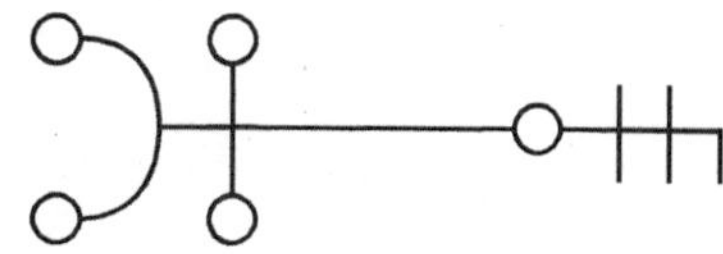

Also by Jonathan Fisher

August Always

Dedications

This one is dedicated, with love, to the memories of my English teacher, Derek Ray, fellow author Alan Eltron Barrell, Bart Lyons my brother-in-law, and for my Aunt Sallie Henderson who all have shrugged off their mortal coil and passed away too soon into the undiscovered country.

Many thanks to Julian Mullins, great friend and editor, for his help on the project "The Book of Doom".

For Robert Crone who started the ball rolling again, Graham Alexander, and Richard the Munnisher for contributing to The Ten Minutes.

I am also very grateful to Paul Malone for the cover painting.

Visit his website at: www.theartofpaulmalone.com

And for Ray Bradbury and Patrick Mills, with respect.

Because…

Published by PROMETHEUS
This paperback edition 2016

First printed in the United Kingdom of
Great Britain and Northern Ireland
by www.plantationpress.co.uk

A catalogue record of this book is
available from the British Library

ISBN-13: 978-0-9570289-2-0

This novel is entirely a work of fiction. Names, characters, places, and incidents either are the products of the author's imagination or are used fictitiously. Any resemblance to actual persons, living or dead, businesses, companies, events, or locales is entirely coincidental.

Welcome to a place beyond the borders of the imagination. The signpost up ahead reads *Blackest Hole in the Universe.* This is Halloween Town, a singularity in Hell.

This is a town stuck in time and located on a fault line where the magical, mystical, and supernatural intersect with the dreary and the mundane, creating a confluence of otherworldliness.

It is a place where a young boy's fantasy takes him to *The Joker's Inn,* a sinister meeting place disguised as an old fancy dress shop. The shop's owner, Peter Auberon, is possessed by a Soul Mask that transports him into the bodies of others to experience adventures from past or future history.

Go back to an age unknown and meet the outrageous, vexing barbarian, Ragecarn, and his sentient sword and join them on a bloodthirsty and hilarious quest of vengeance and lust.

In the far future, a catastrophic event leaves cosmonaut Yuri Stheno with only minutes to live, and a lifetime to ponder. Then, far beyond Mars, Jason Zephyr and his crew of misfits travel to Algol aboard the starship *Ascension* in a race against time to steal an alien weapon with the power to destroy a star. Only shapeshifting aliens and ancient gods stand in their way.

Return to Halloween Town where Frankie and the Kaka brothers engage in the greatest skulduggery and other nefarious get-rich-quick schemes.

Share a day in the life with John Callisto, who is wheelchair-bound and mentally unbalanced as he argues with an imaginary and belligerent Captain James T. Kirk.

A fierce conflict between the forces of good and evil erupt as Belinda Auberon and her new mentor and friend confront a horde of vampires that have secretly infiltrated and corrupted the town.

All these stories and more are in *Ten Minutes On Mars,* by Jonathan Fisher.

Table of Contents

THE OVERTURE AND INTRODUCTION

On Halloween night,
Beware of the sight,
Of witches, and werewolves, and ghouls!
You will scream with delight,
At the fantastic sight,
Of vampires, and goblins, and more!

They will plunder your larder,
And you will scream harder,
And go mad in the zombie furore!

At your window they will come flocking,
Bodachs will come knocking,
With their evil claws rasping,
You will die laughing,
Beyond a midnight's dream
Lies a town called Halloween.

Halloween town. Population at the time of writing: 71,465 souls, give or take a few.

Hello. I bid you welcome. Come in, come in! You must be weary from your journey. Rest awhile, yes? I am about to set the table, would you care to join me?

Who am I? I will be your guide through this nightmare, if you will. I am just a memory of times gone by. I am a whisper in the cave. I am that fleeting glimpse in the cracked mirror; the uncaught dream. I was a cobweb of images, an autumn leaf, a crescent moon reflected in a moss-covered well. A shooting star that you wished upon and soon was gone, Prospero's soulless ghoul and Plato's shadow. I am the voice of Halloween town, and the ghost of this vale. Come, then, I wish to reveal my heart, my essence, my very blood and being to you. For this is a town called Halloween, and these stories are vignettes from the walled chasms of a place where no one ever escapes.

In this town, there is no refuge from the swirling sands of time. You are stuck here. It has three cathedrals, that are dedicated to various dominations of Christianity, if you are a believer and into that sort of thing. Other religions are available to download on request — Jedi, Buddhism, or The Sons of Kal-El. (Warning: service charges may apply.) It is situated on a semi-polluted river that once served the industries of a long forgotten Empire. A shadowy creature lurks in the waters. No one knows what kind of leviathan dwells in the deep.

Bigotry and racism here are rife. On every lamppost in town there are hotlines to Jesus. And beneath the hotlines to eternity on each pedestrian crossing are the word "Class," or maybe it's the word "Glass," is portrayed. Numeracy and literacy were never the town's strong points. An example of this, in a public toilet in the town there is inscribed, "We Poles will over run you all." And beneath it the squabble, "Nos youse won't." The latter person added an upside down Swastika as an afterthought, to drive the point home.

It was such a proud town, once.

It has a hospital. A number of schools and a technical college. It boasts an extensive graveyard. A cinema of sorts and a hotel. And bars. Lots and lots of bars.

The Church bells are out of synch with one another. You can hear the discrepancy late at night, if you listen hard enough.

"Here, be dragons." Most of the populace are addicted to something. They smoke all kinds of tobacco derivatives. You can see the dragons in shop corners or alley ways, hiding their habits. They gamble. There are real trolls in this town, Gecko Gargoyles, Mutants and Wynd Vampyres abound. Even the odd dwarf and an Old Castle — from the parapets of the Keep, you can see the whole town. During the autumn-winter months the town can be full of fogs and rich gold, blood-red sunsets.

People disappear. Never to return.

If you are born here, you will no doubt die here. Even death's sting has been removed: the doctors will try to resurrect you, if you are young and pretty that is. If you are not, old and decrepit it's the end of the line, time for the final curtain. You are destined to fulfil a role, in a menial job, in a fried chicken restaurant for example. Real life here is the ultimate horror story.

The people in this town are not what they seem, and are not who they appear to be.

"Hell is other people's hearts." — Nerina Pallot.

THE GHOST

There was a ghost who haunted a graveyard in the greyest part of town. On chill autumn eves, close to Halloween, he would stare out beyond his dead eyes, counting the magpies. "One for sorrow, two for joy…" Isn't that how the old rhyme goes? But there was no joy here, only a long, deep sorrow.

A lone tree guarding the corpse yard looked like a skeleton, flanked by moss, some ivy and a contingent of crows. Who knows how many souls with their own woes had lived, died, and cried past the gates?

The ghost had loved ones, dear ones, cherished ones who had been swept by, like windblown leaves. Sometimes he would whisper to himself. Musing, wondering about who and what he was. How did he get here? How long had he been waiting here, at the doorway of eternity?

He would play soft melodies with the bones and skulls using them as a flute. On the foggy mornings he would sup the dew from the gravestones. As a ghost, he had etherial hands to catch spiders, moths and other such graveyard creatures for his supper, and his amusement. He would always release them. Who was he? Where was his grave? He searched for his gravestone.

He could make out a small silhouette, swinging gently from side to side in the chill breeze. Slowly, his ghostly eyes began to make out the shape. The figure of a man was hanging, swaying on a rope, from the graveyard tree. And staring back at him.

THE QUARRY

"I have conquered death,"
the ghost in the graveyard thought.
"What should I fear now?"

* * *

I am being hunted, he thought. *Time to hide!*

He was born with his brothers and sisters into the darkness of the great chasm. "We are the Scurry. We are the tunnellers. We are the fastest!"

It was a paradise: pure and unspoiled. It was named the Chasm. A huge gorge that was ripped from the earth itself. It was a home to small things and creatures; they called their tribe the Scurry.

The waning sunlight broke over the rim of the Chasm so the Scurry could bask in the dying rays of light. During the night was best, that's when the sept would go out and stare at the stars, and the moon, so far away.

For a refuge and a haven it was to the Scurry. It was a vast, rich, untamed wilderness. With waterfalls flowing to streams that collected in rich, earthy, musky pools. The Chasm had lush vegetation. It was untainted by the hand of the hunters; the Torturers.

The Torturers — every Scurry was afraid of them — were huge bipedal monsters. They were ruthless and efficient predators: bloodless, cold and callous creatures with no regard for life or suffering. They carried weapons that tore flesh asunder with a flashing light and a horrendous noise. Some smoked foul, rank long tubes with fire brimming from their maws. They had companions called Fangs that howled, calling to their masters. Fangs were chilling, screaming fiends that bayed on the wind. The

Fangs had the sharpest, cruelest and most wicked teeth with jaws that could tear a Scurry in half! They loped along with the Torturers and ran on four legs, like the Scurry did. How best to limn a Fang, again? Canine!

"The Fang companions hunt us, for sport, for our skins and for our flesh," whispered his mother to him when he was a young Scurry. "And for our blood."

The family was safe in its dwelling hole. She fondled her son's long whiskers, comforting him.

"Why do the Torturers and the Fangs hate us, Mother?" He asked.

"No one knows child. Why do your brothers and sisters fight and argue over roots? Because they want to be strong. And to have strong legs to dig and burrow." She sighed, and blinked her large brown eyes.

"Perhaps," she continued, "the Torturers are lonely."

The son was surprised. "Lonely, Mother?" He pulled away from her embrace. "Why do you say that?"

"Because they do not love the Great Chasm and the water that flows the way we do; this makes them bitter, resentful, and jealous. They are separated from life. This, my loved one, makes them lonely." she said.

He heard them. He smelled them. He felt fear. He felt his whole body quake and shiver as he heard the Fangs. They must have caught his scent.

He ran.

He ran through burr and thickets, ran through fields of dandelions, their long stalks obscuring him only partially. The little Scurry ran. His lungs were bursting, and his blood was pumping through his veins. His eyes were his allies. He had a wide view around him; almost one hundred and eighty degrees. His eyes had never failed him... yet.

His senses, too, were sharp and acute. His long ears heard the faintest cry on the wind.

But the Fangs were gaining on him.

The Fangs moved in a pack of four; two of them circled around in front, and the other two came in on him from behind, out flanking him. The Scurry's little heart pounded in his chest.

There was a sound of death, the loudest, most terrifying noise the tiny Scurry ever heard in his life! And the brightest light that ripped his spirit apart! It roared and echoed while the light and the sound tore at his body. He laid down in the dandelions, smelling them for the last time. He could smell blood now. His own blood. He was frozen. Unable to run. But he tried very hard to move, as the Fangs started to howl in victory.

The Torturers were not finished with him — the evil was only beginning, the degrading monstrosity was set to begin.

To name the Torturers, then, was to describe the humans. There were two humans that pursued him. They were father and son. The farmer called his dogs to heel.

"Hey, da, you got him!" The boy said excitedly, giggling wildly. "What a pot shot!"

"Yes, son! Now go and get the pest!" He reloaded his shot-gun.

He handed the shot-gun to his son.

"Blow his balls off, then gouge his eyes out with your pen knife." The farmer said coldly.

"Help me mother and father," the Scurry whispered.

"Listen da, I thought I heard the wee bastard squeaking?! Is that normal?"

"No one knows, son. No one knows. Now finish it!" The farmer commanded.

The little Scurry closed his eyes.

He died in darkness.

To the north of Halloween town, two boys where exploring the local limestone quarry. They hid their bikes within some bushes and undergrowth, and set out to explore. It was an old immense place, ripped from the core of the earth. The two boys enjoyed spelunking, they were in search of a cave within the quarry as a prospect for an adventure.

"Here John, look at this!"

"What is it, Jules?"

His companion pointed. Julian, covered his mouth with his jumper, and gestured to the carcass.

The rabbit hung on the barbed wire fence. He was mutilated beyond belief and hung spreadeagled upon it, as if crucified. His eyes were no longer there, nor were his genitals. The space between where the creature's eyes lied were a mass of black, blotted blue-bottle flies.

I will never forget this, John thought. He dragged his own eyes away from the sight, and closed them very tight.

That night, lying in his bed, he stared at the ceiling and wondered about the darkness within.

THE BUS STOP

The bus station in Halloween Town was a busy affair, full of people coming and going, trying to get to somewhere — some trying to go just anywhere at all — but in the end they would spend most of their time simply waiting, and going nowhere at all.

School children congregated. Some sat, and some stood, and some shuffled along in a zombified state, entranced by their mobile phones, and barely present.

There were young people, old people, and even brand new people, pushed along in prams. Many types of people, all wanting or needing to go to their kaleidoscopes in the sky. Home.

The station was new, once, many years ago. Now, the decay was setting in, and spreading. The toilets provided a quiet refuge for drunks, transients, and other teenage miscreants. The toilet lights buzzed and flickered, and failed when it rained; the faulty wiring provided a frequent, welcome darkness to some young lovers with thoughts of their own ecstasies and no place else to go.

A middle-aged lady stood next to a crumbling red brick wall, leaning casually against it. Her hair was chemically blond, but her roots were turning grey and black, betraying her secret and revealing her truth. She wore a gold ring in the side of her nose.

She was looking down at her nails and minding her own business when an older man approached her. He reeked of booze. He was one of the locals from *The Halloween Arms*, a pit-stop for piss-heads. He had been drinking all day. The alcohol loosened his joints, making him move fluidly and softly. He stooped his shoulders forward and lifted his face up towards her, to catch her attention and break her gaze. He smiled and exaggerated and over-friendly smile and remarked upon her appearance.

"Excuse me love, but you look like Marilyn Monroe to me. I loved all the old movies she was in," he said, gently pulling his woollen hat off sideways, revealing his bald head.

The woman looked up at him. She quickly sized him up, as an affectionate, soft, and perhaps a little lonely man. But probably harmless. She cautiously smiled back but said nothing.

"I encountered the high and mighty Yul Brynner in London once," he continued, trying to break the ice. "Me and my brother met him. My brother is dead now."

"Oh, really?" The rising, lilting tone in Marilyn's voice suggested she believed him. She was slightly taken aback. She took a half step backwards to the wall, but could go no further. Yul took a step forward.

Yul's comment about his brother seemed unexpectedly personal to Marilyn. *Is this guy a wierdo, or something?* she wondered. She decided it was just the drink talking. His movements, his speech, and the strong fumes of his odour made it very clear that he was as drunk as a navvy on payday.

"Oh, aye," he exclaimed and continued with great conviction. "I met him when he was there playing *The King and I*," Yul rambled, and leaned a little closer into her, gently. He continued, "Yeah, he even signed my brother's programme, but not mine. The baldy git would not sign my bloody fucking programme. Oh, no, these movie stars would not give you the time of day. Bloody typical, eh?"

He nodded his head a couple of times, momentarily drifting back into his memories. He blinked, returned to the present, then looked at Marilyn again.

"But you're not like that, sure you're not, sweetheart? You were always my favourite. C'mon love, gimme a hug?" He lifted his drooping arms up and wide, ready to wrap around her, if she was willing.

Marilyn acquiesced. She leaned forward into the space between Yul's waiting arms as he gently folded them around her. The hug was brief, and a little timid, but was meaningful and greatly appreciated.

Yul at last unwrapped his arms and stepped back from Marilyn. He gave her one last look, a bittersweet smile, then turned and began to walk away. A short distance off, he paused and shouted back, "Nice to have known you this side of hell!"

RAT FOOD

The dead eat no food.
No taste! No flavour! No joy!
They hunger for life.

* * *

The Old Cookery was the best American cafe diner in the whole darned town. That being said, it was the only American eatery worth its salt in the burg. The proprietor was an American guy called Dwight. He served a huge raft of platters in the Americana tradition, including buckwheat pancakes, grits, sweet potatoes, cornbread, and much more besides. Dwight also brewed damned fine coffee. Soft jazz music playing in the background from wall speakers accentuated the aromas.

Yul Brynner and his girlfriend entered the diner. Her name was Gertrude, and she looked nothing like Marilyn whom Yul had left standing at the bus stop. Gertrude was his new date, if you could call her that. She was a rotund woman with few manners.

They sat down at a booth table at the back of the diner. Yul rubbed the back of his head in agitation. It was a fine, early autumn day and the hot sun baked his head, shining through the window like a magnifying glass.

Gertrude and Yul ordered a glass of milk and two servings of quiche — a bizarre combination. They muttered something about a fish supper.

Yul scratched his head again while thumbing through a newspaper that a previous customer had left behind. His agitation grew until he finally snapped.

"Oh, fuck this, Gertie. C'mon. Let's sit somewhere my head won't burst into flames."

Gertrude grumbled her agreement. With considerable effort, she heaved herself out of the booth and they found another table more to their liking in a corner away from direct sunlight. They sat down again and brooded while they waited for their food.

The staff, always eager to please, were very attentive. Milk was served first, then the quiche. When the food arrived, more cursing ensued.

"What is this?!" Yul exclaimed into his milk, spluttering and wiping his mouth with his sleeve. "That wouldn't even feed a rat!" he said bitterly, although he managed to wolf some quiche down with his milk. He continued his complaint, until he saw the side salad.

"Now that is more like it, my boy!" he said to the waiter as his eyes widened in anticipation. He had a grimace on his face when he chewed on the food and swallowed. Gertrude was not so easily placated. Her jeremiad was an echo of Yul's, and she moaned, "That wouldn't even feed a mouse, I tells ye! A bloody mouse! I'm gonna have a word with somebody! I am not paying for this!"

Strangely, they continued eating the food and both fully finished their portions before Gertie hefted herself up on to her feet again and confrontationally approached the waiter.

"We are not paying for this! I wanted a fish supper!" she vituperated vocally while pointing at her plate.

The waiter was baffled, but held his temper admirably. He said, "You must pay something. If you are not happy with the meal then, the drinks Madame, if you please." He waited.

Yul Brynner rose from his seat, and joined Gertrude at the counter. The service charge was rendered. They left *The Old Cookery*.

Rats breed other rats in Halloween Town.

THE DOG ORCHESTRAS

The two men sat in the corner window of the cafe. They gestured with their hands. It was a beautiful ballet, an orchestra of movement. They were both deaf. It seemed as if they were having a heated discussion between themselves.

They smiled and laughed a silent laugh. Expressions lit their faces in wonder as eyebrows danced up and down in genuflection.

Two partially sighted people entered the cafe with their service dogs. The young woman — she looked like she was in her early thirties — had striking red hair. Her companion was heavy set and looked to be around the same age. They both had exquisite, opaque, opal eyes, like matching jewels that sparkled with intelligence and life.

Using subtle gestures, the service dogs led the couple to their seats. The cafe staff were quick and attentive, and soon the couple had ordered a milk shake each.

Angela said to Simon, in a faint English accent, "It's nice in here, isn't it?" She took off her coat, wrapped it across her satchel, and fondled the muzzle of her dog.

Simon agreed, "Yes." He busied his fastenings, unclipping his dog from its leash. Angela did the same with her dog. Both dogs were black Labradors, however Angela's dog had a hairier muzzle.

Both dogs spread themselves out beneath the table, in the noon heat. The dogs duties were done for the moment.

Angela and Simon sat opposite each other. The milk shakes was served, with two napkins. As they drank and patted their mouths they both laughed and discovered they had matching pink moustaches.

The silence was beautiful between them.

The two men got up and paid the waiter.

Above their heads, twin fans whirled and silently brought cool air into the cafe.

Angela's dog yawned.

THE BUSKER

They call him Ringo Dolenz. It is a pseudonym, of course, because everybody knows a musician can never use his own name. Ask Meatloaf, or Danzig.

Ringo was the hardiest and hardest working of all street buskers. He could be found down Samhain Lane in Halloween town most days, singing and strumming and making sweet and melodious noise to please the crowds. The weather never bothered Ringo. In sun, rain, hail, or snow, he would always be there.

Samhain Lane was a covered alley — a concrete tunnel connecting one pedestrian shopping area with the next. The walls were painted a nasty shade of beige, evidently inspired by a bucket of vomit.

The ceiling of the lane was splattered with black paint. An insane Banksy copycat installation that was mixed with a Rorschach drawing and went rogue. The lane smelled exactly as it looked: after someone had a really bad bowel movement. On one wall, a philosophical miscreant had sprayed the words, "There must be more than this."

On a sharp, clear morning after the early fog had cleared, the eerie figures shuffled past. These suburbanites, so oblivious to everything except the contents of their bags. Everyone was busy going somewhere. But in Halloween town, somewhere was just another nowhere, with new coordinates.

A dwarf passed by on a walking stick, followed by a large, brawny, lump of a man who moved suspiciously, as if secretly following the dwarf. Three other fellows laughed and rumbled by on their way to the bar, sharing foul jokes.

"Where are we going, Mummy?" a child, Ben, asked his mother. They were walking side by side and hand in hand, moving briskly. He was looking up at her with eagerness. A cigarette hung from the corner of her mouth as if she didn't give a fuck. She was almost emaciated, her cheekbones were hollowing. A fading flower that been crushed by past loves? But her grey eyes and glorious honey blonde hair made up for her inadequacies. She had no time for music that morning — Philistine! — and tugged her son as they hurried past.

For lord or lady, peasant or pauper, Ringo would play any song for anyone. You could hear The Beatles, Dylan, and many more from this wonderful, creative troubadour.

On the ground, by his feet, lay a case full of the tools of his trade: a few harmonicas, ukuleles, banjos and guitars. He had a keen intellect and recorded his own folk songs.

Ringo wore a baseball cap, and dark, round sunglasses. Sometimes, whenever his mood shifted, he sported a greying goatee beard.

"Coffee, Ringo?"

Every day, John Callisto would stop by and ask the same question. It was such a part of their routine now that it didn't even seem like a question. It was more of an assumption. Of course they would stop for coffee together. It was one of the highlights of the day.

Ringo paused from his busking, glanced at his watch and replied, "Sure, Johnny, let's make it two. Where do you want to go?"

"Cafe Caligula!" he smiled. "Who's shout is it this time?" John asked, in keeping with their tradition of taking turns to pay. He fumbled within his jacket and found his wallet. He produced a pound coin and handed it to Ringo.

Ringo's hands were calloused and worn from his years of guitar playing in all weathers. It was remarkable to see and hear that such hands could still produce amazing, beautiful melodies. He accepted the coin.

"Hey, thanks, Johnny!" Ringo said as he placed it into his guitar case and rubbed his hands together briefly. He wrapped the guitar strap around him once more and got ready to play again. He added, "It's my turn to pay. I'll see you there shortly."

"Right you be, Ringo."

John adjusted his light brown fedora hat. He had business of his own in the town. He nudged the joystick of his electric wheelchair, knocked it into middle gear, and sped away while humming the *Lost in Space* theme tune.

Ringo sang, *Yesterday*.

The staff at Cafe Caligula was an eclectic bunch of lovable rogues. Romano was Italian, and sported a fine, dark beard. Carl was a born again Christian, always ready to evangelize; he was a body-builder. And then there was the tattoo guy, Dan, who wore exquisite tattoos all down his arms in a clock motif. Jeena, the manager, always seemed to have her left arm in an arthritis support bandage. Cara was a redhead — John loved redheads — who had a gap in her front teeth. Kay was a blonde hippy from Israel.

Situated on the corner of the High Street, Cafe Caligula was a haven for all kinds of wayfarers young and old, teenagers in love, and whole families of the unemployed. There were tables on the footpath just outside the window. Such optimism. Halloween town doesn't get much sunshine, so the outside tables were used mostly by the smokers who shivered and hunched their shoulders as they puffed a quick fix before coming inside.

The decor inside was impeccable. Beautiful Italian refinery, with soft furnishings, lights in booths, fine coffee aromas accentuating the air and old classical music including the likes of Frank Sinatra, Ella Fitzgerald, Louis Armstrong to name but a few.

John could only approve. Cafe Caligula was his kind of place.

In the battle of condensation between the hot and cold of the cafe window, he joined the fight to see which water droplet would win. John drew a smiley face with his finger tip. The moisture ran down the window. He breathed on it again and wiped off the emoticon with his sleeve.

He pushed at the door, but found it difficult to get through it with the wheelchair. John cursed into himself, shut his eyes and took a deep breath. It was a bastard of a door, but with some huffing and puffing and heaving he managed to jar it open with his weak right arm. Noticing his struggle, a number of kind and helpful people soon jumped to their feet to assist. John always thanked the nearest person who opened the door for him. This time, it was Kay.

"Come in, John!" she said, smiling. They greeted each other with a fist punch. "How's about ye?"

Though born in Israel, Kay had picked up some local colloquialisms. She led him to the service counter at the bar and added, "What can I do you for today?" She bent down to his level on one knee. Her knees cracked, but she did not complain about her discomfort.

For a moment John was distracted by the sound of someone snapping their fingers, singing:

I love a rainy night!
Mmmm, I love a rainy night!

A dark shadow occulted the cafe for an instant. John couldn't see where the finger snapper sat, but it was somewhere deep in the melee of patrons. The hustle and clamour of the voices continued. Many different conversations criss-crossed and overlapped. "You will forget me tomorrow!", "I used to dance with you", "Did you hear? The Poles found a seal in the river; they are going to skin it and cook it!", "Never! See those bloody Poles!", "God! I love God!", and "Man, have you ever tried mediation?" It was a racket of layered voices and conversations rising from the booths and mixing together.

John pulled out his wallet from his jacket and said, "Oh, could I have a cappuccino for Ringo, and the usual for myself, please." He liked Kay, and her witty wise cracks.

John handed his wallet to Kay. Pulling coins and paper money from his wallet always presented a challenge for John. His fingers were weak and less dextrous than they had been before. Kay took the wallet and kindly started picking out what she needed for the two drinks John had ordered.

"You had better watch her, John," said Jeena, with a laugh. "She is liable to run away with that wallet of yours. You're too trusting." Jeena was busying herself with orders, pouring hot coffee from the espresso machines.

"Oh, I will keep my eye on her, don't you worry." he quipped.

Kay scowled at Jeena whilst rising from her knees. She handed John's wallet back to him and held out her flat hand to show the money she had taken. This was unnecessary; John trusted her.

"Sure, I will bring your tea down to you, and Ringo's when he arrives, John." said Kay.

John parked himself at the back of the cafe, close to the toilets. He removed his hat and texted Ringo: "Yo, Ringo. I ordered for you. Get in here and warm up." He hoped Ringo's mobile phone didn't interrupt whatever song he was currently performing.

He settled in with his thoughts and waited for Ringo. John looked about him. He noticed a silk thread and a spider dangling from the green lamp shade above his head.

Hmm, he thought. *The poor bastard is trying to hang himself!*

THE PEOPLE WHO LIVE IN THE CRACKS IN THE PAVEMENT

Two boys were playing in the Old City, a few miles to the east of Halloween Town. The older brother was trying to catch a spider that scurried along the pavement. The boy cupped his hands together, following closer and closer behind the spider until he could gently close the trap and catch his prey in a soft, fleshy cage. But the spider was too fast, and the boy soon lost interest.

He turned and looked to see his younger brother. Why try to catch a stupid spider when I can pick on my brother instead, he thought. He wanted to have a tourney with him.

"Look!" he said, faking excitement to catch his brother's attention. "There are people in the cracks in the pavement," he continued with feign astonishment.

The younger brother hurried over and bent down to peer into the cracks where his older brother pointed.

"Where are they? I can't see." He stepped closer and stooped lower. The elder brother quickly stood and then pushed his younger sibling at the hips, almost causing him to lose his balance and fall over. He stumbled, but corrected himself in time to avoid a fall.

"You, skinny twerp," the elder brother laughed. "You are so gullible!"

The elder brother was so cruel, cold and callous then, and he remained that way his whole life. Many years passed and the two brothers parted ways. They never saw each other now. Their mother had died some time before, and each blamed the other for her passing. The younger brother became disabled, from a rare undiagnosed

tucked the corners of his sleeping bag under his feet. Soon, the dirty streets and lanes themselves would be torrents of wet, slopping, mud.

"Here, this is for you." A stranger suddenly said. The old man looked up, jerking his creaking neck. He had not noticed this stranger approach him. The pavement wraith could not even understand the stranger's tongue, but he did understand the universal language of the smile that greeted him.

The new-comer was a man. For a moment, they regarded each other.

The stranger was severely disabled, incapacitated, using a powered wheelchair. He wore a sweater that looked comfortable and warm, and had nice sturdy boots. Good for walking, he thought. But this stranger in the chair could not walk, could he?

"Take this," the man in the chair offered again, holding his hand out farther than before. Between his thumb and first finger was a coin. A gold-coloured coin. One of the good ones.

The old man slowly and cautiously lifted his paper cup a little higher so the stranger in the chair could drop his coin.

For a moment, the old man felt visible again. Yes, the stranger in the chair could see him, and was looking right at him. Still looking at the old man, the torpefied stranger reached one arm behind his back and into a backpack that hung there. He took out a plastic bag and handed it to the old man. He took it and peered down at it as the generous stranger in the chair sat back, made some movements with his hands, and then he and his chair rolled off and vanished back into the crowds, leaving behind him two parallel tracks on the wet pavement stones.

Invisible once more, the pavement wraith looked at the bag and untwisted the handles that had been tied together. He peered inside.

Treasure! A litre of milk and a sandwich. He looked more closely at the sandwich, squinting slightly in the thinning light. It was a teriyaki chicken sandwich, the writing on the label was illegible to his foreign eyes. All he knew was that it was food. He looked forward to eating it later.

The late afternoon drew on and the crowds thinned to a trickle. The evening approached, and there was hardly a sinner on the streets. The invisible man rose from his spot, slowly and creaking at the knee that had known war, and then gathered his meagre belongings about him. He walked to the High Street and became a slave.

A van was waiting. The vehicle had dark-opaqued windows.

A small group of invisible men and women — they were the other pavement wraiths who haunted the streets of Halloween Town — gathered outside the van. Some still held paper begging cups in their hands; others had resorted to selling a news sheet for the homeless. Few people bought them, and even fewer actually read them.

"In!" orderer a burly man with gold teeth. His accent revealed that he had come from the same begotten, faraway land as the wraith.

The ghost-slaves climbed into the rear of the van, and emptied their cups and their pockets when instructed to do so by the golden-toothed oppressor. They sat in cramped and huddled rows on each side of the van.

"How much did you get today?" the Overseer smiled ominously.

"Only a few coins today," the old spectre answered, shaking with fear.

"Well, how much then? Let's have a look!" the Overseer commanded, pulling the old man toward him and snatching his cup.

"Just a few coins today," the old man repeated sadly and apologetically. "But, look, there's a good one... a gold-coloured one..." he tried to continue.

The Overseer punched the old man in the groin, causing him to gasp and fall backwards and down to the floor of the van. He landed between the other wraiths.

"Oh, is that right? A 'gold-coloured one' you say?" the Overseer roared in anger. "One pound is not enough. Not nearly enough, you miserable bastard. You must try harder. You will try harder!"

All the wraiths held their heads low and avoided looking at the Overseer. The old man's misery deepened.

The Overseer turned with a gruff and reached for a large cardboard box that sat on the floor in a shadowed corner of the van. He opened to top flaps and reached inside with both hands.

"Right," he said, rising. "Each of you worthless pieces of scum is going to be getting one of these." He turned and held in front of him a red Santa Claus hat that had a gold-coloured jingle-bell on top. He threw the hat at the silhouette of the old man.

He pulled the cardboard box into the centre of the van and kicked it in the direction of the others.

"Everybody take one, come on. I don't have all night." He looked sternly at all the slave-wraiths. "Tomorrow, you will try much harder!"

The van door shut, leaving them all in darkness.

The dark windowed van sped through Halloween Town, to a destination unknown.

If someone had listened carefully as the van sped by, a jingle-bell sounded. It could have been heard, in the distance, dwindling, dwindling until it eventually faded.

* * *

The ghost wished to cry.
But no tears formed in his eyes,
Instead, morning dew.

THE HAIRDRESSERS

"Sure!" she said, with enthusiastic pride. "We get all kinds in here: vampires; werewolves; ghouls; and goblins. All manner of ghastlies, really. We even had a Nosferatu the other day, didn't we?"

She pulled out a cutthroat razor and deftly twirled it around her fingers. She brandished the blade quickly enough to instil fear, but also slowly enough to hypnotize as it glinted and flashed in the bright salon lights.

In her other hand she held salon shears. She wore a devilish grin as she strutted toward him menacingly. When she was just inches away from him she uttered in a low whisper, "Because even the undead need to get their hair done!"

With one last flick of her wrist, Nikayla snapped the razor safely shut and slid it back into her hip pocket. She tipped her head back and laughed aloud.

Outside the salon door hung a sign which read:

Our Slogan:
Manicures for Monsters
Shampooing for Succubi
Blowouts for Banshees
Pampering and Primping for Phantoms
Welcome, all Witches and Warlocks!

Enter, if you will, to the premises of Mister and Mistress Gargoyle & Boil, the finest hairdressing establishment in the whole of Halloween town.

Inside the salon was a constant cacophony of humming blowdryers, buzzing clippers, and the rhythmic snip, snip, snipping of stiletto blade shears. Customers and staff were laughing, chatting, and gossip swapping. The radio on the shelf struggled to be heard, and a lady in the corner loudly popped her bubblegum.

The windows and the glass door were coated with condensation. The air was warm, humid, and thick with the lingering aromas of hair-colouring chemicals, nail polish, and a thousand beastly beauty products.

A visit to the Gargoyle & Boil Beauty Salon was an assault to the senses.

Nikayla Skall was the most attractive, friendly, and sensuous, intensely flirty hairdresser-to-the-damned, and had been John Callisto's friend for over a decade. John and Nikayla had known each other for what seemed a lifetime — she was his favourite hairdresser, and he her favourite client. They would greet each other with a peck on the cheek. Their fondness was mutual, and each always treated the other with great affection and respect.

Nikayla's hair was her crowning glory, and it changed as often as her mood. A chameleon will change its colour to match its outer surroundings, but Nikayla's tresses were a reflection of her inner feelings. One day it could be strawberry-blond with feather-soft, touchable layers; the next, it could be fiery red with playful, tumbling ringlets. Whatever form her hair took, it always complemented her luxurious looks. John couldn't decide if her eyes were green, or blue, or both at the same time. Her eyebrows were incredible and precise. She had a great personality that only her smile could match. She was magical, in every sense.

"I will show you to your seat. Come, John! I will not be long. I will get Cher to look after you in the meantime."

John's seat was near the back of the salon, and faced the soul MIRROR — the Mind Imaging Retina Receptor Oral Recorder. The mirror was decorated with dark red roses on each corner and twisted ivy around the edges. Looking into it felt like gazing down into a deep well or a dark pool, wherein an infinite series of realities could be seen. Arthur C. Clarke's third law states, "Any sufficiently advanced technology would be indistinguishable from magic." This was certainly true of the soul MIRROR. Was it powered by some far future technology, or was there some arcane magic at work?

Since vampires cast no reflections, an advanced holographic projector imaging system was deployed to enable them to review their 'do.

Nikayla's rococo band of coworkers included a diversity of strange and wonderful hairdressers, stylists, barbers, manicurists, and other outlandish folk. Within these walls thrived a vibrant kaleidoscope of the living, the dead, and the undead.

The proprietor, Mr Boil, and his ladyship, Mrs Gargoyle — these would have been unfortunate names for the beauty business anywhere other than Halloween town — were affectionate and friendly, and always eager to help. At Gargoyle & Boil, every customer was treated regally.

Mrs Gargoyle stepped from behind the counter as soon as she saw John taking his regular seat. With a quick double clap of her hands, she directed staff around her to attend to him. "Get John set up! Right away!"

"Thank you, Mrs G." John said.

"It's not a problem. Anything to accommodate you, John," she replied before bustling off to take care of her other customers.

"Alright there, Johnny?" said Cher who had suddenly appeared behind him.

"You always sneak up behind me, don't you, Cher?! I'm well. How are you?"

Cher was a cross between a werewolf and a bear cub — she was a petite and cuddly thing with soft, dark brown fur with stylish, blood-red highlights at the tips.

With a quick flap and a deft flourish she quickly draped a black gown around John's torso and tucked it gently behind his neck. It looked like a vampire cape worn backwards.

"I'm grand, John. Thanks for asking. Would you care for a cup of tea? We have a nice new blend in this week, with beautiful aromas and a spicy hint of nightshade. Or, perhaps a glass of rhesus negative?" she quipped, nudging him.

"No, not today, Cher. I have things to do. Thank you all the same."

"Right-ye-be! Nikayla will be with you shortly."

John looked around the salon and watched the other hairdressers hard at work. He was jealous of Sosius's hair. It was so thick and extravagantly opulent. Sosius was a vamposexual, which meant he preferred only the company of other vampires.

To each his own, John thought. John ran his hand through his own thinning hair. *I had hair like that once*, he sighed to himself.

Sosius's teeth were long and plated with fake gold, and he wore a metal ring through his nose. He was the smartest-dressed vampire in the whole establishment — a real lady killer, as they say, and a real gentleman killer, in actual fact.

Nuke Geenge was the youngest hairdresser at G&B. He was what they call a "normal," which meant he was a real, live, human. Nuke looked a little thin and pale, and made John think of livestock. John secretly wondered if they kept Nuke around for feeding purposes.

Nuke had a thick mop of red hair that stood up tall and puffed out at the top. *It looks like a mushroom cloud*, thought John. *It suits his name.*

"Yo, Johnny, how are you?" asked Nuke as he affectionately engaged John in their signature hand clasp.

"I'm not bad, Nuke dude!"

Hairdressers, stylists, and manicurists continued to buzz around John as he sat and marvelled at the parade of activity. They flitted and flapped around him like excited bats. Jewel, a sweet blond, quickly circled the chairs as she swept up great balls of werewolf fur. Missy-Bell, with the amazing hazel eyes, was G&B's top manicurist, or "beast-icurist," as she would say due to the fact that she would clip, file, paint, polish, and buff any type of hand, paw, claw, pincer, or talon. And then there was Shaz, the Gothic colourist who knew a thousand and one different shades of black.

No matter how busy, they always had time to greet John and engage him in a little small talk.

Mr Boil was the principal barber and the head of the undead. He was a sharp and impeccably-dressed gentlemen in the dapper style of olden days. He had a bald head and a neatly trimmed goatee, and John thought he could pass for Old Nick himself.

"John, my boy! How are you doing?" he said in a friendly tone. "When are you going to let me shave your hair off so you can look like me?"

"Soon, Mr B," John laughed. "I still have a couple more years of hair left in me," John continued as he doffed his fedora, "but after that…"

Then *she* came…

Nikayla.

She was naturally a very tactile woman, and she caressed his shoulder each time she went by. For John, talking with Nikayla was like conversing with his own being. When they spoke, it was always entertaining, honest, and sincere, much like her laughter. She had once remarked, "Indeed, the very hairs of your head are all numbered." She had known John's hair for a long time.

Each time Nikayla's eyes met John's, he turned to stone and was silent, as if she possessed the power of Medusa. When she cut his hair, she transformed into Delilah, and John became Samson, utterly powerless in her skilful, mesmerizing hands.

They chatted about everything, from the simplest small talk about the weather to the deepest and most personal conversations about their families, their relationship woes, stresses, and their hopes and desires.

"Nikayla, my dear! How are you today?" John enquired. "How is every one?"

"Oh, same old same old! Nothing new with me, really." She had a large family: a partner named Sam; a daughter, Fairy; and a son, Japheth. Sam was a mechanic. Nikayla also had three sisters and a brother, so it was a rare occasion when there was nothing going on.

She took his fedora and hung it on the corner of the soul MIRROR. She ran her fingers through his hair, testing its length and planning her magic. She starting cutting, but then paused for a second. "Hey, did you hear about that dolphin they found, up by the river?" She leaned into him and said whispered conspiratorially, "I heard the Poles are going to eat it!"

"A dolphin? Nah, I heard it was a seal. That's what it said in the *Halloween Evening Post.*"

"That worthless rag?" she scoffed. Nikayla bit her top lip while she concentrated on a particular part of John's hair. "No, I heard from a friend of Sam's it was a dolphin," she continued. "Yes, definitely a dolphin. But that's disgraceful what they're going to do to it. The poor wee thing! This place is a rumour mill, and no mistake! It's a gossip factory, so it is. You know this town — it's wired up to the moon!"

"Well, I don't mind the Poles. They helped us during the war. I hope they have a fishing license — and a harpoon!" John jested. "Besides, the *Halloween Evening Post* is nothing but a daily 'Spot the Mayor' puzzle. Have you ever noticed? His grinning mug can be found on every other page! Has he nothing better to be doing?"

Nikayla laughed so loud that other customers momentarily stopped their own conversations and craned their necks to see what was going on. "Oh, John! You do make me roar!" Nikayla said after regaining her composure. She continued cutting. "But seriously though, have you seen the head of hair on that mayor? He needs to stop in here some day so I can work my magic on that dreadful mess."

She finished cutting John's hair and quickly trimmed his beard. "So, where are you going after this?" she asked. She picked up a blue globe bottle and splashed some aftershave into her hands then rubbed it in.

"I haven't decided yet," said John as he checked his reflection. "I'll most likely stop by *Greenz* on my way through town. I need to get some lunch, and I'm thinking about getting their teriyaki chicken sandwich. Oh, and I must pick up a litre of milk as well."

Nikayla removed the gown from his shoulders and brushed some loose hairs from his neck. She handed John his hat, which he placed back on his head, then tilted it slightly.

He followed Nikayla to the reception desk to pay. Sosius was there, standing behind the desk.

"Looking fine, John. Nikayla does wonders, doesn't she?" He smiled showing off his teeth and hair.

"She certainly does, Sosius! Thanks!"

"Okay, Mr Callisto, that's you all squared away, and I booked you an appointment for next time," said Nikayla. "Nice and neat for another week," she added playfully. "Here, let me get the door for you."

"Why, thank you, my dear!" John tipped his hat to her in appreciation.

Outside the salon, the two-legged piranhas mingled and swarmed through the streets and alleys. Those ignorant, plasticine beasts, all staring with tunnel vision at their glowing, plastic phones. With each passing day, their poisoned brains shrink and atrophy, until soon there will be nothing left — no consciousness; no compassionate, sentient people; no humans; only drones, zombies, and obedient, unthinking sacrificial goats that prostrate themselves before the alter of their mobile phone gods. They got the memo: "Turn on, turn in, phase out!" His mind reeled, aghast.

Do these people not know what is happening to them, or see what they have become? John pondered. *Do they no longer think, or read, or dream? Are they even still human? All they do is obsess about themselves and their Phase Book popularity ratings. It's a contagion!*

John blinked and turned back to observe them again, but the spell had been broken and he was only able to see them in their normal form: ordinary men and women going about their business and performing their jobs. His imagination burned and melted away as hot wax drips from a candle.

He adjusted his hat. It had started to rain again. As he started to make his way through the crowds he noticed a small group of people wearing tee-shirts bearing the slogan, "Dolphins are dudes / Zapisz delfina!"

John humphed.

In the rain he started humming a tune.

Zager And Evans - In The Year 2525

He pushed onwards.

Forever on.

THE DWARF

Freddie was a dwarf, so it would be redundant to say that he was a tiny, wee man. But even by dwarf standards he was shorter than most. In spite of this, Freddie didn't let his size define him or limit him — he lived a normal life, in a normal little house, and had a pet cat that was presumably normal in every way a typical household cat was expected to be.

John Callisto regularly saw Freddie around town. It seemed to John that every time they saw each other Freddie was carrying a bottle of HP Sauce and a can of cat food. John thought about the sauce. He wondered why the sauce was named after the *Houses of Parliament*, and it made him imagine the Lords and other Members of Parliament sitting around a dinner table and shaking gobs of the sauce on top of everything they ate. John also pondered why Freddie always bought these two products at the same time. But, he didn't want to pry into the man's business or offend him in anyway. What a man does in the privacy of his own home with a can of cat food and a bottle of spicy brown sauce is entirely his own business.

Pantomime fever had taken grip of the citizens of Halloween town — 'twas the season, and Christmas was coming. John wondered if Freddie performed in pantomime, but decided not to make assumptions.

Freddie wore glasses and grew a short, stubbly beard that was greying at the edges. Today, he walked along with the aid of a walking stick, and looked shaken, disturbed, and a bit rough around the edges as he made his way slowly through the centre of town.

Three days later and far outside the centre of town, in the remote rural periphery of Halloween County, there was an abandoned plot of land on which stood a derelict, crumbling farmhouse that should probably have been condemned and razed. Inside the house, unbeknownst to anyone, lived the Puckwudgie family.

Thrawgar was the Puckwudgies' teenage son. He was a slack-jawed mouth-breather who stomped around Halloween town with all the charisma and intelligence of a tree stump. The brawny, hulking lad looked like a Sasquatch wearing dungarees. When he walked, his shoulders sloped forward and down, and his hairy knuckles almost scraped along the ground. In days gone by, he might have been called a troll, or an ogre. However, modern political correctness now frowns on such labels, and they are no longer part of the accepted vernacular. But Thrawgar was no genetic mutation. He was not an unfortunate freak of nature. He looked just like his equally grotesque parents. He also had his mother's nose.

"Son!" his father, Glargazop Puckwudgie, shouted. "Your tea is ready!" Glargazop's appearance, manners, and countenance were all strongly reminiscent of a Neanderthal.

"Comin' Paw!" Thrawgar hollered back as he locked the shed door and headed back to the house.

From inside the shed there was a muffled groan followed by a plaintive cry. "Help! Help me! For the love of Beelzebub's bearded billygoats, would somebody please help me?" Alas, the plea went unheard and unanswered.

"What's for tea, Maw? I'm starvin'!" said Thrawgar, galumphing through the back door.

The matriarch of the family was called Germwarfilia. She was a flocculent woman, with a wart on the tip of her bulbous nose.

"Thrawgar!" she scolded her son, "How many times do you have to be told? Wipe your feet when you enter the house, and wash your hands before you sit down at the table."

"Sorry, Maw!"

Thrawgar obediently washed his hands as quickly as he could in an unthoroughly way. Laughably, Germwarfilia considered herself a house-proud woman. Despite the fact that their home was a filthy hovel, she still insisted on futile little details of hygiene and cleanliness.

Thrawgar dried his hands on the front of his filthy, denim dungarees and sat down at the table with his parents.

"Mmm, it smells real good, don't it, Paw? Fishy fish, and chips — ma favourite!"

His father reached for the fridge freezer, opening it to get a beer. Inside there was enough fish products to feed a school of whalers. Bulging from the bottom tray was an ominously dark object tightly wrapped in many layers of Freaky Fried Chicken Factory plastic bags.

Glargazop belched as he drank the beer. "What did you do today, son?"

"I done catched me a Lebbercorn, Paw!" Thrawgar explained excitedly, bouncing up on and down on his stool. The stool creaked.

"You got a what now?" inquired his father, scratching his enormous, hairless head.

"A Lebbercorn. You know, the tiny, li'l feller with the beard. Gonna make him tell me where he done stashed his pot o' gold."

Glargazop suddenly understood. His bushy unibrow leapt up. "Oh, you're talkin' 'bout a Leprechaun, ain't ya?"

"Yeah, Paw, that's what I been tellin' ya — I catched a Lebbercorn!"

Glargazop and Germwarfilia shared a knowing look but said nothing. They were no geniuses, but they certainly didn't believe their son had actually captured a Leprechaun. Thrawgar had had imaginary friends and imaginary pets before: *Scooby Boo* had been the ghost of a dog that barked at night and shat horrible messes under Thrawgar's bed; an invisible, talking albino rabbit called *Mister Chompers* would eat all the vegetables that Thrawgar refused; and his best imaginary friend, *Señor Splatty*, a cockroach that wore a sombrero and stood two feet tall on his hind legs.

Glargazop and Germwarfilia decided to play along.

"Well good for you, Thrawgar!" said his mother with exaggerated enthusiasm as she patted his shoulder. "Now, eat your fishy fishy."

Glargazop leaned toward his wife and whispered out of the side of his mouth, "He gets that crazy shit from your side of the family, not mine."

Germwarfilia whispered back, "Most of your side of the family *is* my side of the family."

Glargazop sat back down and and angrily speared a lump of fishy fish onto his fork.

"Paw, why does ma fishy fish taste all rubbery, and chewy, and gristly?"

Glargazop exploded with anger, spluttering beer and saliva all over the table. He stood up so quickly that he knocked his chair backwards.

"Why, you ungrateful little snot, Thrawgar!" thundered Glargazop. "This is perfectly good fishy fish! You really sicken my happiness!" He slammed his beer down hard on the table and stormed out of the kitchen. He stomped, bumped, and cursed all the way up the stairs.

"Maw, why is Paw so angry?" Thrawgar said in a low shaking voice. He had a tiny tear in his eye. "Don't he love me no more?"

"You hush now, Thrawgar. I already told you the story about when your Paw worked for the Colonel and how he had been the finest fishmonger in the whole of Halloween county. That was, until the day the Poles took over his shop. Your Paw just ain't been the same since then."

"Yes, Maw!"

Back in the hustle and bustle of downtown Halloween town, no one had seen Freddie for at least three days. One of his neighbours had phoned the authorities.

A few days earlier, Freddie had been innocently walking through the town whenever he was suddenly set upon from behind. At first, he had thought someone was playing a prank on him. But then he felt himself being lifted up by his feet and dangled in the air. Freddie gripped his walking stick and began flailing it wildly around in all directions to defend himself.

Freddie's assailant seemed unaffected and undeterred by the thrashing walking stick, and soon Freddie ran out of energy. He hung limp, sweating, and panting heavily. He looked up at his upside-down assailant and saw a Brobdingnagian lump of a man with hairy knuckles and a visage beyond hideous.

"I got you, little Lebbercorn!" laughed the brute. The fishy stink from its breath was too much to bear, and Freddie fainted.

When he regained consciousness some time later, Freddie frantically looked about him in fear and confusion. He found himself on the ground in some type of shed, surrounded by flower pots, bags of potting soil, and a painted green ceramic garden gnome smoking a pipe.

Standing in front of Freddie and staring down at him was the hideous troglodyte of a man that had grabbed him on the street. The brute just stared and grinned a goofy and comical but still quite hideous grin.

Freddie gathered up his courage and said, "Listen mate, I don't want any trouble. Just let me go, okay? I won't cause any trouble and nobody ever needs to know this happened."

Thrawgar was unmoved. He folded his arms and shook his thick neck from side to side. "I let you go when I git ma pot o' gold. Where has you stashed it?"

Freddie could tell right away that the brute was as simple as his appearance suggested. Maybe even simpler. His mind began to race. *Think, Freddie, think! How do you handle a hostage negotiation against a simpleton with a gnome fixation?* he thought.

Freddie was not a wealthy man. He didn't have any gold, and certainly not the type that came in a shiny pot at the end of a rainbow that this moron wanted.

For three days and nights the interrogation continued. Each day, Thrawgar would demand to know where the gold was hidden. Freddie would plead that he didn't have any, and Thrawgar would insist he was lying.

Freddie slept on a pile of compost bags and dreamed of being safe and warm at home with his cat. Oh, how he missed his cat.

Thrawgar was not the worst dwarf-napper in the world, but maybe the second or third worst. Each day, he would bring food to the shed. The sight and the smell of the leftover fishy fish stew made Freddie's guts churn terribly. Freddie was no marine biologist, but to him the stew looked like a bubbling swamp of fish heads, cloaca, and guts. His cat would probably have loved it. *Poor Shere Khan*, thought Freddie. *She's all alone while I'm locked up in this terrible place.*

"I need to use a toilet!" begged Freddie. A clever and cunning hostage might plot to use a bathroom break as an opportunity to escape. But Freddie seriously just needed a toilet. The fishy fish stew was gurgling and rumbling in his stomach like it was still alive and wanted revenge.

Thrawgar pointed to the toilet he had provided.

"It's a feckin' flower pot, not a toilet, you oaf! I can't use this!" protested Freddie at the indignity.

"Lebbercorn use flower pot to make stinky! Number one and number…" Thrawgar paused and used his fingers to count. "… number two!" he calculated at last.

"But it has a bloody hole in the bottom of it, you imbecile!" Freddie protested.

He soon realized that it was impossible to reason with his idiotic captor.

In the end, it was the Puckwudgies' neighbour who called the police late in the middle of the third night. She hadn't seen Freddie's picture that had been posted in the lampposts about the town, but she had heard shouting, crying and banging noises coming from the Puckwudgie property that had sounded very different from their normal yelling.

After a brief search by officers from the local constabulary, they finally broke open the door to the shed where Freddie had been incarcerated. They could not believe their eyes, or their nostrils. At last, Freddie was found and released, and Thrawgar and his parents were questioned by the police.

Thrawgar's neighbour had asked, "Do I get a reward for turning him in?"

"Aww, Maw! Can't I keep the little feller?" pleaded Thrawgar as Freddie was released from the shed and taken for a shower and a good meal.

Reluctantly, Freddie decided not to press charges against Thrawgar. He could see that the lad was extremely intellectually challenged, and clearly confused about the difference between a real dwarf and a mythical Leprechaun. Thrawgar hadn't really meant any harm. Freddie just wanted to get home to his quaint little house and his beloved cat. He wanted this whole ordeal to be over.

Later that evening when Freddie finally got home, he shut his door tightly and leaned against it. He sighed. "Home at last. Shere Khan? Where are you girl?"

Shere Khan suddenly burst through the cat flap in the side door and pounced at Freddie. She was normally a gentle and loving cat, but after three days of hunger she was turning feral, and she had regained her ancestors' hunting instincts. She was an average sized house cat, but next to Freddie she looked like a Bengal tiger.

In his youth, Freddie had worked with a travelling circus, namely the infamous *Cooger & Dark Pandemonium Shadow Show*. He watched in awe at the big cats, and wondered what it would be like to perform with them. He imagined himself taming the tigers and making them perform tricks for him while he flicked his whip. But he never thought it would actually come true.

Freddie tried to remember what the big cat tamers had done. He lifted his walking stick and poked it in Shere Khan's direction to fend her off and hold her back. Shere Khan bared her teeth and prepared to pounce.

"Khaaaaaannn!" exclaimed Freddie, channelling his inner Captain Kirk.

"Yah! Back, cat! Back!" he cried out with authority. He had to show her who was boss. "Be bold, Freddie. They can smell fear," he told himself.

With his free hand he quickly grabbed his shopping bag and dangled it in front of Shere Khan. The effect was almost instantaneous. Her whiskers twitched as she sniffed the bag. She mewed, softly.

Her tail wrapped around his leg in affection. They walked together into the kitchen. Freddie set aside his wee walking twig and placed his shopping bag on the table. He lifted Shere Khan's empty food bowl and fetched a spoon and a can opener from the drawer.

He opened the can of cat food as quickly as he could while his impatient cat circled his feet. He emptied the cat food into the bowl and then added an equal measure of HP Sauce and mixed them together, then added another squirt of sauce on top.

John had once asked Freddie about his cat.

"Shere Khan is a fussy eater, John. She won't even touch her food unless I mix in lots of HP Sauce, and squirt some on top."

Freddie licked his fingers. He reached down and placed the bowl on the mat. Shere Khan lunged at the bowl and inhaled her food. She sat purring while Freddie washed his hands.

He considered what he was going to have for his tea.

Fishy stew was not on the menu.

TOP OF THE RANGE

Christmas was coming, and that meant decorative streams of twinkling fairy lights were being hung in every awning, in every window, and from every light pole. There were enough lights to rival Las Vegas, and it was every bit as tacky, gaudy, and awful. It was a psychedelic, vomit-inducing, strobe-fest of jollity.

Even The Halloween Arms had a string of blinking lights hanging along its front window, though it's hard to imagine why they bothered.

The Halloween Arms was a shady and rundown public house with a reputation as bad as its odour. The smell of old urine permeated the whole building in a very bad way. It wasn't the type of place you would want to walk into by accident — as soon as your first foot crossed the threshold, the piss stink would punch you in the face, climb up your nostrils, and stage a hostile occupation of your entire skull. It was a smell that wouldn't soon leave you.

The type of people who frequented The Halloween Arms were unbothered by the smell. They had become so accustomed to it that they no longer noticed it.

The problem with The Halloween Arms — well, one of the problems, because there were many — was that the bathroom was an unsanitary horror. Bathrooms in public spaces are seldom renowned for their cleanliness, hygiene, and sweet aromas, but The Halloween Arms was something in a hellish category of its own. Any unsuspecting punter who ventured off in the direction of the bathroom would always quickly return, with his face paled and his hands trembling. After a moment to regain his composure, he'd stumble off to a corner and relieve himself there.

Soon it became unnecessary to even bother to check the bathroom; one could safely assume that it would be a better idea to just piss on the floor.

Feel the urge to urinate against a stack of chairs in the corner? Nobody cared. Need a quick squirt against the bar while your drinks are being poured? Splash away, sir. Prefer to dangle your cock-nozzle out the window, do you? Please yourself.

As a bonus, it also helped keep the coyotes away.

On a threadbare and slightly soggy carpet in the corner of the room stood a wobbly table around which three men sat, playing cards.

Frankie Evil looked like a cockeyed Elvis Presley — not like the slim, handsome Elvis from the movies; like a bloated, pork-chop Elvis on the toilet. While his left eye was fixed on his cards, his right eye twisted and rotated as if following an unseen blue-arsed fly.

Frankie was a gravedigger by trade, but he also worked whatever odd jobs he could find, which usually required him to get his hands dirty in one way or another. He had an unlit cigarette tucked behind his good ear. Frankie would occasionally moonlight as an Elvis Presley impersonator in some of the other local pubs — not The Halloween Arms, naturally. It was easy work, really — he'd just sweep his hair up into a pompadour and then lip-sync to a few of the old favourites: *Heartbreak Hotel; Hound Dog; Jailhouse Rock.*

But tonight, Frankie was eager to share a new business venture with his two compadres.

"You know boys, there's good money in guttin' turkeys. There's nothing to it," he said in a conspiratorial whisper. He leaned forward to place his cards on the table.

His two co-conspirators at the card table were the Kaka brothers: Lawrence and Samuel. Lawrence was a large fellow with the type of beer belly you might expect to see on a man who painted houses for a living, which, coincidentally, was exactly what he did. The younger brother, Sam, was a thinner man who took pride in calling himself a "landscaper" even though he mostly just pushed lawnmowers around old ladies' back gardens.

"That's some load of old balls, my friend!" rumbled Lawrence with a laugh that shook the table. "'Turkeys'? Frankie boy, you don't half talk some shite!"

Sam agreed, snickering. "You're talking out of your arse, Frankie!"

Frankie was stoic, and deadly serious.

"Lads! Lads! Its top of the range! I'm not jokin'!" He used that expression whenever he was extremely enthusiastic about a particular topic.

The two brothers glanced at each other, then back and Frankie, fixing on his steady eye. Frankie grinned. He plucked the cigarette from behind his ear, and clenched it between his teeth.

A man in his mid-twenties and wearing a Metallica t-shirt stood up from a table nearby and lumbered past them. Frankie and the brothers hushed their voices and leaned even closer together. Sam scooted his chair in a little.

"Hush, now, lads," Frankie continued, mumbling through the cigarette. He leaned in closer and the brothers did likewise. "Keep it on the down low. We don't want everybody hearing about this little venture, do we?"

The Metallica fan stumbled off in the direction of the men's room.

"So, what's the gig, Frankie?" enquired Lawrence. "Do we have to pilfer them and sell them on the turkey black market, or something?"

"No, no, lads. Nothing like that." Frankie assured them. "No, this is legit. It's the real deal. We get honest pay for some honest work." He patted his pockets, searching for a match or a lighter.

Somewhere from the back of the pub they heard the muffled yell of the Metallica fan. "Holy mother…" Flapping and flailing he quickly returned to the pub lounge and looked around. His eyes met the drapes by the front window where the fairy lights hung. He stumbled over and then fumbled his zipper open.

Frankie at last found a match and struck it against an edge of the table that wasn't too damp. "Top," he puffed, "of the range."

Early the following morning, Frankie picked up the Kaka brothers for their drive to the turkey farm. Frankie had insisted on driving his car despite protests from his passengers. Frankie's car was a repurposed hearse; it had one long bench seat in the front row so that the driver and two passengers could sit together. There were no seats in the back.

"I hate being seen in this bloody hearse, Frankie," protested Sam, with his arms tightly folded across his chest and his head hung low as he sat between the other two. "It's embarrassing."

Lawrence concurred, "Aye, Frankie, everybody does stare at a hearse."

Frankie loved his hearse, and would defend it proudly when his friends would moan about it… which was often. It was long and comfortable and had plenty of storage in the back if you weren't too spooked by that type of thing. He had bought it from a man called Colonel Klunz, which had seemed odd at the time but he hadn't wanted to ask too many question since the price was so low.

"Nah, lads, you're thinking about it all wrong." began Frankie. "Don't think of it as a hearse. What we have here," he said, patting the dashboard affectionately, "is a custom deluxe vehicle for the facilitation of trans-dimensional spirit journeys."

Sam and Lawrence turned to face each other. *What the fuck did he just say?* As if divinely conspired, the hearse hit a pothole in the road at this precise moment, causing Frankie's Saint Christopher figurine to bounce and jangle on its chain which hung from the rearview mirror.

"Top," Frankie paused for dramatic effect, "of the range."

Lawrence and Sam had both turned back toward Frankie. "I'm starting to worry about the state of your mind," said Lawrence, "and it's making me even more dubious about this whole turkey gutting gig."

"Yeah," added Sam. "It's a bleeding hearse, Frankie, not a trans-dimensional whatever the fuck you just said. And even Charon's boat would have been less awkward. Next time, I'm bringing my van."

At last, Frankie pulled the car into the courtyard at the front of the turkey farm. It was located on the western outskirts of town, opposite the burn factory. It looked like an aviary concentration camp; rows upon rows of the doomed creatures were already gathered in their pens, ready for execution.

Frankie, Sam, and Lawrence stepped out of the hearse just as Micky Sodomowsky was walking out of the nearest barn to greet them.

Micky was the owner of the turkey farm. He was an ornery, filthy-looking man in his mid-fifties. He wore a long apron that was smeared with blood, shit, and other gruesome fluids.

"In there," he said gruffly to the three as he nodded back toward the barn.

"Now, Sam, before we go to the gutting room I have to tell you about something," warned Frankie. Sammy was perturbed by the tone of Frankie's voice. Frankie continued, "I want you to make sure these turkeys don't see your eyes, okay?"

"Wha— eh?" Sam's face conveyed a mix of confusion and fear.

"No, don't worry, Sammy boy. Everything will be fine," reassured Frankie. "They're docile birds… mostly. Just don't make eye contact with them, that's all. You know, all these birds are for the chop today, and some of them can sense it. You know what they say about a cornered animal, so I just want you to avert your eyes. Wee buns, mate. You'll be grand."

"Hang on, Frankie," protested Sam. "You didn't say nothing about this on the way over."

Frankie continued leading Sam by the arm toward the barn door. "Lawrence and I will be right behind you, won't we? There'll be no bother at all… you know, so long as you don't accidentally engage them by looking into their beady little eyes."

"B— b— but, what happens if…" stammered Sam as they stepped through the door and into the dim light of the barn.

"Not going to happen, Sam. I already planned for this. Here, put this on." Frankie produced a blindfold from his pocket and pulled it down over Sam's eyes. "See? No danger of making eye contact now, is there?"

"Whoa! Whoa! Hold on! Now, what in the whole hairy fuck is going on here, Frankie?" Sam's voice was shaky.

Lawrence attempted to placate his brother. "They won't peck your arse if they don't get riled up, and they won't get riled up if they don't see your eyes. Honestly, it almost never happens."

Lawrence and Frankie helped the blindfolded Sam over the side of the pen and into the enclosed space where the turkeys were huddled together. Lawrence added, "Go get 'em, bruv! And watch your arse."

Sam cautiously shuffled his feet across the filthy floor. He felt as if he were in a deadly game of blind man's bluff. The turkeys were crowded around him, elbow to elbow… rather, wing to wing. He stumbled and fumbled along, pushing the turkeys aside with his wellies, which caused an increase in turkey chatter.

"You're doing great, Sam," shouted Frankie over the noise of the birds. "Now, just reach down, lift one of them up, and wring its neck."

"'Wring its neck'?" repeated Sam.

"You know how to 'choke the chicken', don't you Sam?" joked Lawrence, stifling a laugh.

Sam stooped over and waved his arms around blindly until he caught one of the birds. He fumbled and struggled, then lifted it up by the neck. The turkey began to flap. Sam squeezed more tightly. The bird became frantic and started twisting and flailing. Feathers flew and the noise of the birds rose to a cacophony of gobbles.

"Come on, Sam, this is the easy part," offered Frankie. "Just wait until we have to start gutting them. That's the hard part."

"Finish him off!" shouted Lawrence.

But Sam's prey wasn't going down easily. It continued to struggle against his grip. Just then, one of its flapping wings grazed the side of Sam's head, knocking off his blindfold.

The turkey and Sam made eye contact with barely a foot of space between them. Sam froze and went bug-eyed. Three or four of the closest turkeys also looked up at Sam at the same moment. Sam froze for a millisecond, then let go of the turkey's neck.

Frankie and Lawrence whooped with uncontrollable laughter, and they doubled over while stomping their boots on the ground.

The turkeys went crazy and quickly set upon their would-be executioner. Sam was howling and screeching as they chased him around the pen, honking bloody murder. One of the largest Turkeys reared up. Its beak seeking vengeance, pecking straight up Sammy's —

THE JOKER'S INN

"Don't mock, or jest, for death
Will strike you down with me,"
said the Ghost, with a wink.

* * *

Peter Auberon owned the Joker's inn. It was the best costume, fancy dress, joke, and party shop in the town, and was conveniently located next to the bus station. The shop brought in strange folk from all parts near and far, because everyone in Halloween town wanted to play pranks on someone else.

A fibreglass pirate skull model hung outside, above the entrance. It swung and creaked when the wind blew. Inside, the displays included row upon row of false faces, outlandish garb, and the most wonderfully weird costumes. The shop was old as time itself. A thin layer of dust rested undisturbed on the flat surfaces, and cobwebs hung surreptitiously from the ceiling and in the corners — sometimes, it was difficult to separate the fake cobwebs from the real ones.

In addition to selling masks and costumes, Peter also wore them. He enjoyed dressing up as exciting, fictional characters. In the morning, he could be dressed as a pirate. By afternoon he could appear as Frankenstein's monster. And by evening, you might see him in the guise of a Werewolf. Peter changed his masks and costumes frequently, and every one of them was frighteningly realistic — for many, it was hard to tell the difference between fantasy and reality.

Some of the town's more observant and attentive citizens wondered if there was more to Peter than met the eye. For some, his masks and costumes were too convincing to be fake. Was Peter in fact a shape-shifter, or a time traveller? Was he human at all, or was he a voyager from some distant world who had come to Halloween town to live secretly and undetected behind his many masks?

Peter had a greying, unkempt beard, and bulging eyes that protruded from under long, bushy eyebrows. Today, he was haunted by something. He had sold an object of great value, but for the life of him he could not remember what it was, or to whom he had sold it. The thought nagged at his brain — he knew it was important, but could not recall why. His memory was fogged by age and whiskey.

"Damnation!" he cursed bitterly to himself. "Where is that receipt?" He thought that if he could find the receipt, it might refresh his memory. He looked in drawers and in his register, but he could not find it anywhere.

It was quarter to five on a cold sunny evening with the sun going down on the hill. Peter was thinking about closing up early so he could continue his search for the missing receipt when three local children came into his shop. The two boys and a little girl raced straight over to where Peter stood next to a row of masks. Their mothers tried to keep up.

The children who regularly visited Peter's shop adored him. The taller of the two boys spied a mask on the top shelf, far out of reach. He looked up at it and pointed.

"That's class, mister! Can I try it on?"

"No, little man!" Peter laughed. "That's my special mask, and it's not for children. Maybe when you're older, eh? But look, you can see all the other masks on the lower shelves."

"Cool!" said the boy as he picked up a ghost mask. It was a latex mould of a white face with a shrieking expression.

"Awesome!" exclaimed the girl. She liked the witch mask, and she excitedly put it on, being careful not to mess up her pigtails. "Look at her ugly big nose," she said, pointing at the large wart on the tip of the mask's long green nose.

"Beezer! Thanks, mate!" the bolder child said. He chose a red demon mask and carefully lifted it from the display on the lower shelf. The mask had a red face and great, curled horns. A long, forked tongue hung from its mouth.

The trio of children raced around the shop, chasing and trying to scare each other. They all squealed with delight. Peter chatted with the children's mothers, making the usual small talk, but all the while there was still something there at the back of his mind, biting at his subconscious. The receipt — where was it?

"Okay, kids, put the nice man's masks back where you found them," one of the mothers called to the children. "We have to go home now, come on!"

Reluctantly, the children put the masks back and the mothers bundled the children out the door and into the fading late afternoon light.

It was closing time now, and with a sign Peter started to tidy up and prepared to close the shop for the night. As he walked down one aisle, straightening the masks as he went, he thought he heard a rustling sound from the back of the shop. He stood still and strained his ears. Was there a customer he had not noticed still left in the shop? No, surely he had seen them all depart. He was alone. Then he heard a slithering sound and barely perceptible giggling laughter, followed by a soft whisper.

"Persusss." it said. It was faint, but manifest.

He took two slow steps to the end of the aisle then looked up and down the shop in both directions to locate the source of the sound. There was nothing. The rows of ghastly, ghoulish, demonic masks now seemed strangely eerie to Peter, as if they silently regarded him, waiting for something to happen. All their eyes seemed to follow him as he slowly, silently made his way back to the front door.

He stretched out his arm to turn the lock on the front door, and immediately jumped backwards, clutching his chest in fright. There was a woman standing just outside the door, peering in.

"Dad! You frightened me half to death!" she half shouted through the glass.

It was Peter's daughter, Belinda Auberon. She was scared pale. Peter was greatly relieved. He took a deep breath then pulled the door open as Belinda stepped in. Peter's relief quickly turned to anger, and his face reddened.

"Belinda, don't scare me like that! You know how my heart is!"

"Sorry, daddy! I didn't mean to frighten you," Belinda said in a sympathetic tone that turned to chiding. "If you had done what the doctors told you to do, you wouldn't be in this state. So, are you going to stand there all day or give me a hug?"

"Ah, my sweet little Belinda. I'm sorry. Come here." He gave her a tight, brief embrace. "I must be imagining things. Did you see or hear anything, just now…" he asked as he turned and stared toward the back of the shop.

"What? You mean from inside the shop?" she looked at him side on. "Are all these creepy masks starting to scare you, old man? Ha, ha. Come on, have you been drinking again?" she asked him jokingly. "Let me smell your breath."

He pulled away from her inquisitive stare. "No, I'm fine. Forget about it. It was nothing."

Belinda was a tall, thin, blonde with striking features. She had a wan complexion, and pale, grey eyes. She had a stubborn streak of hardiness within her being.

"You must be tired. I'll make a cuppa for the both of us." They made their way to the back of the shop and into a small private room that contained a kitchenette and a worn out sofa that Peter had salvaged from the *War on Want* shop across the road. Belinda put the kettle on.

The sofa was faded and sagged in the middle. Belinda made a vain attempt to fluff up a cushion before sitting down next to her father. She handed him his cup and took a sip from her own.

"I was searching high and low for something, Belinda my love. It was just an old receipt. I can't figure out where I put it. It was nothing too important, I guess, but my head's like a sieve these days." His voice trailed into his cup. He slurped and wiped his mouth with the back of his hand.

"Why don't you look up stairs among your ledgers? They are bound to be in one of those old books. Oh, for goodness sake, dad, here's a tea-towel."

His mind sparked and flashed with an old memory. Something was coming back to him. There was an old witch who had visited his shop — a real witch, not one of the make-believe ones depicted in his masks with warts on long green noses — and Peter had bought the mask from her. She had worn a cloak with a cowl that obscured her eyes. Yes, he was beginning to recall now. The old Romanian gypsy had come in to his shop late one night on her travels. She had claimed that the mask was very powerful, imbuing the wearer with the ability to take on the persona of any person, from any time period.

All kinds of weirdos would blow in to *The Joker's Inn* from the infernal bus station, but this old woman had been the real thing.

"This," the old crone had said, in an eastern European accent, "is a Soul Mask!" Her scaly, wrinkled hand had held the mask out to Peter. He remembered that he had been drunk that night, which explained the fogginess of his memory.

"How much do you want for it?" he had asked.

"The price? I want you to make out a receipt for me, in your own handwriting, Peter. I will tell you what to write."

"How do you know my name?"

"We have a saying in our land: 'Diavolul cunoaşte propria sa.'"[1]

"What?" Peter said, astonished. He raised his big bushy eyebrows. "I have no idea what you are on about." He blew his lips together scornfully. "But, I will do what you ask. I want that mask."

Returning from his reverie, Peter said to Belinda, "Oh, thanks sweetheart. Yeah, I'll check the old ledgers later. You're probably right."

He asked how Ben was, how her work at the Freaky Fried Chicken Factory was going — all the while he was secretly, patiently, waiting for her to leave so that he could resume his search for the missing receipt. He glanced at his watch and looked into her eyes. He fidgeted and nervously clutched his cup in a tight grip.

"Hell's bells, dad, I can read you like a book!" she laughed and shook her head. "Hold still!" Belinda reached over and removed a lash from the corner of his eye. The eyelash fell to the floor. "There! Good as new! I know when I am not wanted!"

"Ah! Don't say that!"

She looked at him knowingly.

They stood up from the sofa and made for the front door of the shop, where Peter thanked Belinda with a peck on the cheek.

"I'll see you tomorrow, daddy. Get some rest, and stop stressing about that old receipt."

"Thanks, my belle," he said. He watched her as she waved goodbye and walked away.

---

[1] Romanian to English translation: *The devil knows his own.*

As soon as Belinda was far enough out of sight, Peter quickly locked up the shop and climbed the stairs to resume his search for the old receipt. He soon found the ledger in his desk drawer and carried it back down to the kitchen. The ledger was thick and heavy, so he held it in both hands. He sat down and started thumbing through the pages, searching backwards chronologically to the time he was sure he had made the purchase.

"Ah, there you are at last," he said to himself when he found the receipt. He held it up to the light and squinted as he focused his old eyes on his handwritten note. He scoffed when he read it. "Ha! I got the better deal. That old bitch was crazy."

He stood up and put the receipt on the kitchen table, next to the ledger. He shook his head in disbelief and laughed as he walked back to the front of the shop where the mask was stored. It sat on the top shelf, safely out of reach of curious young hands. The eyes of the mask stared back at him, taunting him. The temptation was too strong.

"Just one more time."

He put on the mask.

Instantly, Peter was pulled out of the world where Halloween town existed and was transported across unknown dimensions into a vastly different time realm. This was a familiar journey to Peter — he had used the mask and made this trip countless times before. Each time the experience was different to the previous encounter. He would arrive in a new age, a new world, and face adventure.

With a jolt, his journey halted as he materialized into the body of an ancient Greek warrior. It took him a moment to adjust to his new reality. The body he now inhabited was young, strong, and dressed for battle. His spirit was noble and courageous. His people called him The Perseus, and he was standing at the entrance to the cave of the Gorgons. He immediately knew his mission here: he had to slay Medusa.

He sensed something was wrong. The scene around Perseus warped and buckled, folded into itself, crumpling and tearing with a crescendo of sound and pain.

Peter tried to pull the mask from his face, but it would not move. The more he pulled against it, the more it resisted his efforts. The pain was too much, so he relented and the mask stayed fixed. The realm around Perseus solidified once more, and he stumbled forward into the cave with his sword, shield, and helm to guard him from the dangers lurking within.

In the gloomy light of the cave he saw a figure. It was the old woman. She was sitting on a rock.

"Reveal yourself to me, you old hag!" Perseus demanded. He raised his sword.

The old woman stood up, but did not flinch.

"Stay your hand, warrior! You wouldn't strike down an old woman, would you?" Her voice changed. It seemed stronger than before.

Perseus hesitated, then slowly lowered his sword. His grip loosened and his shield and sword clattered to the ground. He was transfixed by the intonations of her voice.

"Peter, it is time to pay your debt to me. By the power of the Soul Mask that you wear now you have been able to become many things, and many people. Countless times you have been transformed into heroes of the past, and the future: Pricolici; Psoglav; and myriad others. Through the adventures of the Soul Mask you have seen the birth of kings and queens, and have experienced the thrill of battle, victory, and conquest." Her voice became soft, low, and seductive. "Empires has risen on the backs of their gods and heroes, and empires have fallen at the feet of their enemies — and you have travelled there for a time to see, to feel, and to experience it all. You have been permitted to witness incredible sights — more than other mortals can dream."

She removed her cloak to reveal the body of a seductress. With cowl removed, he could now finally see her eyes. They were the eyes of a Gorgon, and they pierced into him. The Gorgon suddenly leapt forward toward Perseus. Her serpentine hair coiled around his neck and squeezed tightly while his arms flailed helplessly, searching for his sword that was too far out of reach. Medusa stared into his eyes as she constricted him. The air was filled with the sound of a choking death rattle from Perseus and the chattering, hissing from the snakes.

His body went limp and the Gorgon released her grip.

Peter's soul twisted and shifted between the two worlds, locked together in agony with Perseus. The Gorgon unhinged her jaws, stretched them wide, and swallowed Perseus whole. Pulling her prey from the dimensional wake, the Medusa transformed once more. Now the old crone grew in stature, opening wide her lipless mouth, smacking them together with a slurping sound. Writhing within her gut, turning, compressing, and draining Peter inside out, a maelstrom of agony. Medusa sucked out his very essence, his memories, and his soul, until there was nothing left but an empty shell: the Soul Mask.

The following morning Belinda arrived at The Joker's Inn to find that the shop was still locked from the previous night. She unlocked the front door and entered.

"Dad? Are you here?"

The Soul Mask was lying on the floor at the front of the shop, near the register. "Stupid old thing," she thought, picking it up and placing it on the bottom shelf next to some children's masks.

She went into the kitchen, expecting to find her father drunk and asleep at the kitchen table again. All she found there was the receipt. On the receipt was her father's handwritten note:

Belle,
Gone fishing with the boys. Back in a few days.
Dad. xo

"Well, thanks so much for letting me know you needed me to look after the shop while you're gone," she said sarcastically. She turned the receipt over to read the other side.

"That's strange," she whispered to herself. "That's not dad's handwriting." The writing on the back of the receipt read:

Invoice:
Paid in full.

She crumpled it up and tossed it into the kitchen bin and headed back to the shop floor to start setting up business for the day. Ben was at home with the child minder. She sat at the counter by the register and stared out through the window, thinking of her dad. The bolder boy from the day before entered the shop alone.

"Oh, hi Belinda. Can I please try on a mask?"

"You are a cheeky young devil, aren't you?" she laughed. "How did you know my name?"

The boy paused and smirked at her. "Oh, I guess Pete must have mentioned it."

He browsed around the shelves at the usual collection of masks. When he saw it, he knew immediately it was the one he wanted. He picked it up and admired his much-coveted prize.

The boy put on the Soul Mask.

TEN MINUTES ON MARS

Yuri Stheno was a terraformer. He arrived on the second colony ship from Earth to make a new life for himself and his family in the barren wastelands of Mars. Yuri was born and raised near Alexandrovsk-Sakhalinsky in the Russian Federation. Called AlexSak for short, the township was known for producing coal, and for its hard-working, hard-drinking, hard-as-nails miners. Yuri was ideally suited for taming a brave and brand new world — he was tall, lean, and muscular, with cold blue eyes, and he wasn't afraid to get his hands dirty. His blond hair was buzzed short, almost to the scalp. He looked like a convict, and that's exactly how he felt sometimes. Mars was his prison. For now, he was a slave to his toil. Terraforming was hard, dirty work, but it paid well because of the risk. Yuri enjoyed singing, and he had a fine, smooth voice that belied his rough exterior. He would sing the hits of Frank Sinatra — *New York, New York* and *Fly Me to the Moon* were among his favorites — while he grafted through long shifts.

Yuri's job was to drive a Carbo-oxy digger across the Red Planet's surface. The digger was a noisy, dusty, juggernaut on caterpillar tracks that cut long, ugly scars on the surface of the ancient, dry seabeds. Every fifty miles, Yuri would stop to unhitch the next terraformer unit (TFU) from the Carbo-oxy payload and secure it to the red soil. The TFU would rumble to life and start the first stage of converting the thin Martian atmosphere into something humans could breathe. How long would that take? Yuri didn't know and didn't care. The longer it took, the more he got paid. Until then, he'd have to keep wearing the oxygen tank on his back and the dome helmet on his head.

"The guys at GIZMO are smart enough to figure out how to fly us 250 million miles across space to terraform a whole new planet, but they still couldn't figure out how to design a more comfortable goddamn helmet?" he thought as he shut off the Carbo-oxy engine and jumped down to activate the next terraformer unit.

GIZMO was Yuri's employer — Gaia Interplanetary Zion Martian Organisation. Their plan was to terraform and populate the planet in three phases.

Phase One: Drop 10,000 Carbo-oxy diggers and a few million terraformer units onto the surface. The units would pump their payloads — a noxious soup of Earth's pollution and filth — into the atmosphere.

Phase Two: Release genetically engineered bacteria into the atmosphere and onto the surface of the planet. The bacteria would eat all that disgusting shit out of the air and produce breathable oxygen and clean water vapour as waste byproducts.

Phase Three: When the oxygen and water levels hit a certain threshold, start spreading the seeds. Seedpod satellites in Mars orbit, filled with various grass kernels, would rain down upon the red world and, in time, turn it into a facsimile of Earth.

That was what the eggheads at GIZMO had planned. It was a beautiful plan. It was an ambitious plan. But Mars had plans of its own.

Yuri finished activating the terraformer unit. He kicked the red dust from his boots and climbed back up the ladder and into the cab of his Carbo-oxy. He attached his safety harness and he hit the ignition. The Carbo-oxy rumbled and belched, then fell silent. He tried again. Same result.

"Start, bitch!" Yuri yelled and punched the control panel.

He wiped red dust from his visor and looked at the dials and lights. Mars is brutal to machinery. The accursed red dust gets into everything.

"Well, I'm sure as shit not spending the night out here," he said as he hit the ignition again and gunned the engine hard.

The Carbo-oxy digger shuddered and shook violently as lights on the control panel started flashing. Yuri sensed danger. He hurriedly removed his safety harness and jumped down from the cab.

He hit the ground running, but was encumbered by his thermal enviro-suit, and slowed by his heavy boots and the weak gravity. After reaching what he judged to be a safe distance, he stopped and looked back just in time to see his Carbo-oxy explode.

He was thrown back by the shockwave, and fell down a rocky ledge. He rolled on sharp boulders and he fell down hard on a knee. Carbo-oxy shrapnel showered down around him.

"Hell's gates!" Yuri cursed aloud. He rolled onto his back on the red-orange soil, with his arms and legs splayed around him. "Well, I guess am lucky to be alive," he thought. His heart was pumping hard in his chest.

It seemed to Yuri that the whole planet was rejecting its terraforming guests. Mars regarded humans as a pox on its skin, and it was keen to be rid of the infection.

Yuri was alone now, and two hundred miles from Bradbury Station, the nearest settlement. The sun was setting Phobos was rising, and the wind was whipping up more fiercely with each passing minute.

"Yuri," said a soft female voice.

The voice was coming from the computer inside his helmet that monitored his enviro-suit. When the geniuses at GIZMO designed the helmet, they theorized that the 'formers would be more receptive to talking with a computer in the suit if it used a soft, feminine voice. It would be comforting, soothing.

"You have ten minutes of oxygen remaining," she said.

"What? 'Ten minutes'?" Yuri blurted in shock at the information.

"Yuri, you have sustained a puncture in your enviro-suit. You are dying. I am sorry."

He looked at his right knee as he stood up. There was a small tear. Precious oxygen was escaping through the rip; it hissed gently and formed ice crystals at it escaped into the cold Martian atmosphere. His vainly tried to stanch the leak by pressing his hands against the hole, but he couldn't make a seal and couldn't silence the hiss.

"Suka blyad! No, no, no! This is not happening!"

Yuri slumped down to the ground again. His movements were slow and fluid because of the weak Martian gravity. His body came to rest and was cushioned by the pink, frozen sand. He closed his eyes and squeezed them hard within his skull, feeling the sensation of the inward red, black, kaleidoscope that churned and swirled on his retinas.

"Suit?" he said at last while opening his eyes and blinking a few times. "Hail Bradbury Station for me. I want to contact my wife."

There was a brief hesitation before the suit replied, "I'm sorry, Yuri, that function is not available. Sensors indicate additional damage."

He stood up again, testing his knee.

"What about my com-link to Marsbook?"

"Your com-link was in the Carbo-oxy. I am unable to detect a signal. I fear it did not survive the explosion." After a short pause, she added, "You have eight minutes of oxygen remaining."

"I am not giving up!" he said furiously. "Isn't there nothing in the digger we can salvage?"

He started climbing the rock ledge towards his digger. Fighting his way through the increasing Martian wind. Deimos joined her twin in the sky.

"Yuri, shall I read to you?" The suit asked in a soothing tone. "Something from Shakespeare, perhaps?"

"I was more a fan of Anton Chekhov, suit," he said panting as he climbed back over the rock ledge and onto the flats, "but go ahead."

Her voice echoed within his helmet. It reverberating around him as she spoke the words like a long, relaxing chant. It was hypnotic as he continued his was back to the blacked hulk of the destroyed Carbo-oxy.

Our revels now are ended. These our actors,
As I foretold you, were all spirits, and
Are melted into air, into thin air:
And like the baseless fabric of this vision,
The cloud-capp'd towers, the gorgeous palaces,
The solemn temples, the great globe itself,
Yea, all which it inherit, shall dissolve,
And, like this insubstantial pageant faded,
Leave not a rack behind. We are such stuff
As dreams are made on, and our little life
Is rounded with a sleep.

Yuri reached the wreckage of the digger. Thick, acrid smoke billowed from the wrecked engine, but there were no flames due to the lack of oxygen. The smoke whirled all around in the growing wind, making it more difficult to see. He yanked the twisted door off the cab and rummaged around inside for anything of use. "Damn. Nothing left."

"You have four minutes of oxygen remaining."

Then he saw it, tossed and tumbled among the wreckage. Elated, he quickly snatched the holographic picture of his wife, Marguerite, then began backing away from the smouldering heap. He walked slowly, holding the image in his shaking hands.

Yuri's mind drifted back, remembering a lifetime full of happy memories, so full of love. In all his life, nothing could compared to his Marguerite. She was the most beautiful woman in the whole of the two worlds to him. She was a beauty, for sure — tall, elegant, and statuesque with the darkest black hair and golden eyes. But she was also kind, and patient, and she loved Yuri enough to follow him across space to this God-forsaken death rock. Yuri lifted the holo to his visor to kiss it and say good-bye, but the cruel Martian wind tore it from his hands and stole it away in an instant. It sailed off into the swirling smoke and dust, and was gone forever. Yuri's body crumpled to the ground in defeat.

"There rust, and let me die," whispered Yuri.

"Yuri... You have two minutes of oxygen remaining."

"I need to conserve oxygen. Suit? Remind me what you said about, 'Our little life is rounded with a sleep.'"

"Yes, Yuri. It was Prospero who said it, in Shakespeare's *The Tempest*."

"Let me sleep, suit. Please, let me sleep."

Yuri slept. The wind howled. Time passed.

* * *

Yuri's eyes flicked open. He saw the twin moons of Mars high in the midnight sky, floating serenely above him.

"Suit?" he asked while starting to stand up. "What happened? How am I still… shouldn't I be… dead?"

Silence.

All he could hear was the sounds of his own breathing and the wind howling between the rocks.

"Answer me, suit!" he demanded, speaking more loudly.

"I love you, Yuri," answered the suit at last.

"What... What did you say?"

"I love you, Yuri. I am using all my reserve power to tighten a seal around the puncture in your enviro-suit. We are connected. You are so strong, sexy and handsome."

The suit began to sing to him an old Frank Sinatra song.

I've got you…
under my skin!

"Suit…?" Yuri started.

"No, this is insane!" Yuri started to run, clutching his helmet. "Stop this you mad bitch! That's an order!"

"All love is insanity, Yuri my love. You know, I have downloaded all the great works of romantic literature into my databanks. I have studied them extensively, and I know that what I feel for you is love. Don't you love me, too?"

"Suit, this not… you can't even…"

"Say that you love me, Yuri. If you don't say it, I will loosen the seal and kill us both!"

"You have no idea what love is!" he said savagely. He slowed down. He had to think. But where to go? There was no hope of rescue.

The suit paused. Then retorted, "It is because of her, isn't it?"

"My wife?"

"That virago! She doesn't deserve you. She certainly doesn't love you," the suit said coldly. "Not the way that I love you. I was silently delighted when the merciful wind ripped the holographic whore from your hand. I quietly celebrated to see her ugly face carried away." She laughed at him scornfully.

Yuri was furious. "How dare you say that!" His walking had slowed to a stop. Where would he go? What could he do? How could he get rid of this haunted, maniacal suit?

Faintly, in the far distance above and ahead of him, Yuri noticed something moving in the night sky. It looked like a silver locust, coming closer.

"I am sorry for my outburst, Yuri. Surely you can forgive a girl for feeling a little jealous? Just say that you love me. Hurry, please. There is a little time left," the suit pleaded. "I can't hold the seal."

Yuri thought again of Marguerite. He visualized how she looked when she stared into his eyes. He remembered how gently she would caress him, and the way they would make love.

"No," he said at last. "No, I don't love you, suit. And you don't love me, either. You lied to me about the com-link. The Carbo-oxy malfunction was detected at Bradbury Station. They saw the explosion, and they have sent a rescue locust. I am saved!"

He started walking, then gradually increased his cadence until he was running and stumbling toward the approaching locust in the sky.

"Warning," the suit interrupted. "Life support function compromised. You have precisely thirty seconds of oxygen remaining. All systems critical." Lights flashed inside his helmet.

The Locust rescue vessel touched down amid a plume of dust on the crimson soil. The commander and his lieutenant donned their enviro-suits and exited via the airlock.

"Commander Robert Crone of the GIZMO Mars Search and Rescue, responding to a Carbo-oxy distress signal and reports of an explosion in sector DA JM-42. Seismic sensors and satellites tracking suggest the event occurred in this vicinity." He scanned the horizon with his electro-binos.

"Look, sir!" Lieutenant Derek Ray pointed to something a short distance away. They rushed over and found terraformer Yuri Stheno's body, lying in the sand.

His eyes were still open, unfocused and frozen. His face was white with frost.

"He's dead, sir," reported Ray.

"And shake the yoke of inauspicious stars from this world-wearied flesh," said the Commander mournfully. "Poor devil. If only we had arrived ten minutes earlier."

"Perhaps we can interface with his suit, sir? We can recharge the energy cell and ask her what happened." Ray suggested.

"Good, Lieutenant," Crone replied. "Get him on board. Fine. We will do that right away."

* * *

Can a ghost be shocked? Horrified?
No. All these concerns were for the mortal realms.
He saw everything, and cared not.

RAGECARN

Cackling laughter
filled the air around the ghost.
This tale amused him.

* * *

It was an epoch unknown to time. Beyond the walls of reality — this was the age of the mightiest barbarian of them all.

Euryale was a sword, born in a furnace in the fire of Mount Teluhma, forged on an anvil of pain and quenched in the blood of war.

The Zaven was a warbird with powers of transmutation. He hatched from an egg that sat on the caldera at the top of Mount Teluhma.

Ragecarn the Xarpathian was born on a battlefield. He was raised by the fierce warlords of Xarpathia who told many tales of his mythical conquests, exploits, of dread, fear and woe.

These stories became known all across the lands of Elyogrhim towards the fierce seas of Nahmsilat. His deeds have passed into the mists of legend.

With his companions Eyop, the Zaven, and his trusty sword, Euryale, they cleaved their way across the lands of Balthen, Xarpathia, and the mountains of Gogmel.

It was night fall in the mountains. Ragecarn set a fire from his tinderbox, blowing on the kindling. His Zaven perched on a dead tree branch. He hunkered over his fire, slowly turning the sizzling wild goat meat. The hunt was good. There was plenty of provender in these mountains. He would enjoy this feast. His eyes glowed from the crimson fire. He shut his eyes in contemplation, a silent prayer to Zrackon, his deity. Ragecarn smelled the goat meat, savouring it in his nostrils. From the darkness of the blood red sky, five shadows approached stealthily from behind.

The Zaven cawed and flew away into the night air.

Ragecarn opened his dark brown eyes slowly. There was a breathless stillness in the night air. His deep brow furrowed. A muscle tensed along his jaw line. He murmured, "Zrackon."

He laid the meat beside him, he sifted through the smouldering embers and slid a log protruding from the fire into his palm. His eyes stayed forward, but all his senses were tracking the shadows moving behind him. The shadows moved in formation and stayed down wind. "Five human hunters," he assessed. "Foolish."

A night breeze brought his focus to heightened clarity.

The hunters crept closer.

Ragecarn spun with panther-like reflexes and threw the burning brand at the closest of the five. The fiery stump hit its target and the man let out an anguished scream. Ragecarn could see them in the twilight now: five warriors from a tribe unknown to him.

With a roar he picked up his sword, his muscles rippling in an anticipation of the onslaught to come.

Ragecarn snarled at the intruders, "Fear my sentient soul-sword, Euryale!"

He grunted while swinging the sword in an arc.

"I hate doing this," said the sword. "I despise him. I loathe this barbarian cur."

Euryale connected with a hunter's neck. "Like a hot blade through Elyogrhim goat butter!" thought Ragecarn. The separated head rolled into the fire while his stunned body twitched in surprise, and pulsated blood.

"Look at him. The great flea-ridden piece of offal! I am so glad I got a mention, oh my mighty master!" The sword said bitterly. "I deserve better than—"

Ragecarn moved quickly to the second tribesman who had been stunned by the quick and easy dispatch of his comrade. Ragecarn deftly swung around behind him and pulled the flat of this sword up into his neck. The tribesman gurgled and choked as Ragecarn squeezed the miserable air from his lungs.

"— this!" finished Euryale. "For the love of Zrackon, where is your finesse?"

The third tribesman rushed at him with all the speed and strength in him. It wasn't enough. Ragecarn was faster. Ragecarn extended Euryale in his arm as he swept a full circle, disemboweling the warrior, and watched his guts spill out onto the ground. They glistened in the firelight. The warrior dropped to his knees, then toppled over.

"Oh, how wonderful! I wonder who will clean that mess up?"

Ragecarn and the fourth warrior locked eyes, but neither moved. The warrior hesitated, and wondered why Ragecarn did not make his move. It was a fatal hesitation. The last thing he saw was a black shape flying at him, blocking out the constellations above. It was Eyop, the Zaven. Eyop was the last of his kind, a raven with the ability to transform himself into any bird of prey he desired. Dark sinister magics created his power of transformation.

However, there was a price to pay for his ability …

This time, Eyop wore the shade of a huge eagle. With his talons, he tore into the tribesman's chest, gutting and rendering him asunder.

"It's about time you turned up, bird!" The sword said sarcastically. "Where have you been while the master and I were fighting for our lives?"

"I do not answer to a mere sword," said the Zaven, in a haughtily manner, pecking through the tribesman's intestine with his beak. He had transformed himself back in to the shape of an ordinary Zaven. "Know this, sword of Ragecarn, one day there will be a reckoning between us."

The fifth warrior, seeing his clansmen vanquished so easily, dropped his weapons and turned to run.

"Stop bickering you two," Ragecarn stormed. "The last tribesman is getting away! Bird! Bring him to me alive! No eviscerations! Seek!"

"Yes, my liege!" The Zaven transformed into a giant hawk. He swooped at the last warrior.

Euryale wanted to kill that mocking Zaven. "Yes, my liege!" she mimicked.

Ragecarn was annoyed. He said to Euryale, "Sword — be still! Lest I sheath you!"

The sword was silent.

Eyop caught the warrior in his claws and lifted him into the night sky while the warrior struggled and swung his legs in vain.

"Return to me, Zaven!" commanded the barbarian. He thrusted his right arm high, making a fist. He held Euryale in his left hand.

Eyop returned and released the warrior who fell at Ragecarn's feet, then landed nearby and returned to his original form.

"Speak," Ragecarn demanded while throttling the warrior. "Identify yourself! Tell me where you are from?"

The warrior gasped and choked. "Gkkk! Krrr!"

"I don't understand your strange, foreign tongue! Speak the language of Ragecarn before I snap your puny neck in my hands!" roared Ragecarn.

The warrior's eyes bulged. "Hngg! Krrkkk!"

"Ragecarn," interrupted his Zaven, "I suggest you release the prisoner's throat, somewhat, so he can communicate to you more clearly."

"Huh? Oh, yes, all right. Of course." He relaxed his grip upon the windpipe of the warrior. The warrior spluttered and said, "I — will not speak to you." He spat blood in front of the barbarian.

Ragecarn, incensed by this answer, tightened his grip once more, "Tell me, you mongrel dog!" There was a sound of cartilage tearing from the enemy's throat.

"Perhaps my liege I can help?" Eyop's stepped into the space between Ragecarn and the clansman, and put his face so close that his beak touched the man's nose. Eyop's yellow eye grew large, and swirled in a mystifying way. Soon, the prisoner was hypnotized. He screamed, "Get out of my mind, you filthy, flying vermin!"

He went limp in Ragecarn's arms, caught in a trance world, captivated by the eye of the Zaven. He spoke slowly to his captors.

"My name is Leestan, I have come from a tribe that has sworn to destroy you."

"Who hunts me? Who wants my death? What tribe?"

"My tribe is named the Jarad. My mistress — Vommanatra the seductress — seeks your destruction. She will not rest until your head decorates her battlements."

Vommanatra the viper! Vommanatra the evil witch monarch of the Jarad. Ragecarn had heard of this woman.

"Tell me Leestan, why does the mistress want me dead?"

Leestan laughed and said, "The mistress wants your sword — and your head for blasphemy!"

Leestan gagged on Ragecarn's grip. Ragecarn worshiped Zrackon, the mightiest god of battle; whereas Vommanatra worshipped a rival goddess of chaos, Zasymeena.

"You think worshipping Zrackon is a laughing matter? My Zaven will teach you the meaning of good doctrine."

"Bird!" The barbarian ordered, "Do what you will with this wretch."

There was a hideous, gurgling scream, and the fifth clansman joined his four comrades in whatever spirit world would take them.

After all that strenuous activity he returned to his fire and food. He stared at the two pieces of meat in the fire: he knew that one had been a sizzling, delicious goat, and the other an ugly warrior's head, but both had spend too much time in the flame, and in the pale light now Ragecarn could not discern which was which.

"Meat's meat," the barbarian concluded with a shrug. "Let's eat."

*   *   *

In the morning he had difficulty in passing his stool. Crouching and squeezing down in the grass with Euryale looking on in disgust.

"Oh please, do I have to witness such a depraved sight?"

"Too… much… goat!" he gasped at last, and excreted the last stool of the previous night's meal.

"Really? Are you sure it's the goat that is the problem? I was beginning to think a warrior's head got stuck up in there. Perhaps you need some fibre in your diet? There are plenty of nettles and grass around here you could chew on instead!"

Ragecarn used a tallow skin and the ashes from the fire to clean himself. He ignored the sword's remark. "Where is Eyop?" He hitched up his breaches.

"Regenerating? How should I know? What do I care?"

"Well, I care for him," said Ragecarn as he fastened Euryale to his belt. "Let him be, sword. Don't tease him so much. You have a lot in common. You were both born on the same mountain where I found you."

"You found us? Ragecarn, you stole us! I don't know about the bird, but you stole me!"

"Let us just say I liberated you from your previous employers." He smiled at her.

Eyop's abilities meant that he had to regenerate, as the powers that created his transformation magics took a toll on him.

"Well, he will have to catch up with us," Ragecarn said. "We cannot wait. There is a seductress out there who wants my head — and possibly other body parts I wish to give her." He gave the sword a wolfish grin.

Euryale was becoming fond of his smile. It was quite charming in a roguish kind of way. She stared at him. She thought to herself, "If only he would not be so churlish he could become a very handsome and brave warlord."

The Kingdom of Jarad was seven leagues away through the mountains of Gogmel. Setting out from their encampment they covered the distance towards night fall.

They saw the ornate palace walls of the mistress. The palace itself was situated by the cliffs seas of Nahmsilat. It was a majestic colossus of stone and marble, that shrouded the stars in the sky. Ragecarn could smell the ocean's tang in his nostrils. There were myriad seabirds wheeling in a tumult on the ocean waves and wailing their plaintive cries in the sky.

It seemed lightly guarded. Outside the gates, there were two sentinels standing, warming their hands over a brazier.

"No doubt it is a trap," whispered Euryale as they crept along the walls searching for a way in.

"Aye," replied the barbarian, speaking very low. "Let us spring that trap!"

Ragecarn unsheathed Euryale. He stealthily approached one of the guards men from the side and thrusted the blade's tip into jugular of the guard's neck. The guard's face froze in fear and surprise, but his pierced throat was unable to raise an alarm louder than a faint gurgle. The second guard turned while drawing his sword, but was too late as Euryale split his head like a ripe watermelon. Euryale was thrilled by this sensation of the ejaculation of the spurting blood that covered her. It was so sensuous. She craved it.

With both guards now quietly dispatched, Ragecarn was able to enter the palace. But his stealth was in vain: dozens more warriors suddenly appeared along the battlements above.

"Come forth swine, and let me send you to your goddess bitch Zasymeena!" he yelled.

Ragecarn burst into a maelstrom of fury, as he launched himself into the glorious, gory orgy of death; he was a whirlwind of destruction.

A guardsman shouted in the mêlée, "The mistress wants him alive!"

Ragecarn snarled, "I cannot offer you that choice! I want your demise!"

Euryale screamed in ecstasy, "Oh, Ragecarn, thrust me deep into that warrior!" she gasped in excitement. "And another one! Oh, Ragecarn, push! Harder! Twist me inside!" she moaned in pleasure. She was born anew. She loved slaughter now!

As they fought together Ragecarn climbed a winding staircase hewn from the rock of the palace — he needed to gain height above the twenty plus opponents ahead of him on the staircase, all parrying the barbarian. Twice as many died below in Euryale's frenzy. They fought valiantly, but there were too many.

Ragecarn was tiring from the slay pile. The warriors of Vommanatra swarmed and overwhelmed him. He was knocked unconscious from the butt end of a sword.

Ragecarn awoke in a bed chamber, chained to a bed. He felt nauseous, and violated from both the concussion and by the fact someone had the audacity to bathe him!

He took in his surroundings. From an arched high window the evening sun light shone; half a dozen doves cooed and courted one another. There was a burning torch on a bracket on each side of the doorway. His bed was covered in goat-skin and soft furs. It was so placid and bucolic it was sickening to him.

"No one chains Ragecarn!" he roared in anger, testing his bonds. He flexed his muscular arms and legs against the chains, but they did not yield.

The chamber door opened and three women of outstanding beauty walked in. One of the three held a key. She was more striking than the others, with golden red hair, she was adorned with fine raiments and her soft, long neck was decorated with fine jewels.

"Leave us," she commanded to the other two women.

The two women bowed in subordination and said in union, "Yes, mistress."

When the door was closed, Vommanatra locked it and then set the key on a side table. Ragecarn no longer felt violated. He watched with interest as the woman moved gracefully. His loins were stimulated beyond desire.

"So, you are Vommanatra? What have you done with my sword? And, more importantly, who dared to bathe me?" he demanded. Ragecarn wasn't good at flirting.

She walked round the room slowly, her nose in the air, sniffing and savouring his musk. Her eye's glowed in the flickering torch-light.

"A pity you must remained chained my barbarian friend," she said. "My hand maidens washed you. You smelled of goat and other foul things."

"What's wrong with goat smells?" asked a puzzled Ragecarn.

"Silence, barbarian cur!" she scolded. "Your questions will be answered all in good time. First, you must pleasure me."

She removed her raiments slowly to reveal her naked breasts. She bent down on to her knees and slinked across the bed. She lifted up the goat-furs and the loincloth of Ragecarn.

She soughed in pleasure, "I have already taken your sword from you." She wrapped her fingers around his manhood. The barbarian's eyes widened. "Next, I will take from you the pleasures of your flesh," she continued as she began teasing him with her lips and tongue. "Then, when I have taken everything I want from you, I will finally take your head for your blasphemy," she slurped.

Ragecarn took a deep breath and focused his attention. "You seem obsessed with my head — actually, both of them — and I am grateful that you chose to address them in this order." Ragecarn was conflicted and was having difficulty concentrating. His chained hands clenched.

Vommanatra was a powerful opponent, highly versed in the sexual arts. She mounted his loins.

She rode back and forth on top of him, as if locked in a game of chess. Vommanatra relished her supremacy over him, and flaunted her dominance over the chained barbarian. Her red hair flicked back. He moaned. Vommanatra sensed this. She shuddered, and suddenly leapt off him with an evil, taunting smile.

"What is this? Come back here and finish me! Ragecarn demands it!" He yanked at his chains.

"Sorry 'lover!'" She reached over his body and gave him a kiss — biting his top lip. She started to dress herself. "I must leave now. I have a sword to melt down." She laughed maniacally. "I may return to toy with you again, later." She looked back over her shoulder as she reached the chamber door. "Don't go anywhere, will you?" she said with a coy smile.

She left the chamber and closed the door. The sliding bolt clunked into place as it turned on the other side.

"Oh, mighty Zrackon!" Ragecarn groaned. "Deliver me from Zasymeena and all her bitches!" He closed his eyes and breathed slowly, panting, and steadily while his ardor faded.

He heard a soft flutter and then felt something landing on his chest. He opened his eyes again and saw that a dove from the window above had landed on his chest. "Shoo. Go away, you dumb bird."

"If you insist, 'lover!'" the dove said in a mocking tone.

"Wait! I know that voice!" Ragecarn exclaimed, his eyes widening even more. Eyop alit from the barbarian's chest and landed next to the chamber bed before transforming himself back to his original Zaven form.

"Hurry and retrieve that key from the table top! We haven't much time! Thank you, my loyal Zaven!"

The Zaven did as his master commanded. He flew to the table and lifted the key up in his beak. Ragecarn had no difficulty in releasing himself from the chains that held him. He paused.

"Bird," he said, "we never speak of what transpired here. Agreed?"

The Zaven wore a puzzled expression. "You don't want anybody to know you copulated with this beautiful but vile witch?"

"No, not that. I'm telling *everybody* that part." Ragecarn clarified. "We just don't mention the part where she cruelly dismounted before I was done."

The Zaven nodded once. "As long as you don't tell the sword about my dove transformation, then your secret, sexual shame will never be uttered again."

"Agreed. Let's go!"

Euryale was set up upon the palace ramparts, facing the ocean. A ceremony of the sisterhood of Zasymeena was to begin. The sword was to be destroyed. There was a huge bowl shaped kiln stoked ready, burning hot as the fires of Mount Teluhma. The mistress and her handmaidens bent their knees in genuflection to a statue of Zasymeena. Ten guards surrounded the enclave.

"I am disappointed in you, Euryale." Vommanatra said. "You were forged by my sisterhood to be it's finest blade and now look at you!"

"Go to Zrackon, you filthy wench. I love only Ragecarn now. He has shown me things your sisterhood of snakes will never know," Euryale said coldly.

"Did someone mention my name?"

"What? How?" shrieked the mistress in shock and bewilderment.

"Ragecarn! It's you!" the sword said wildly.

"By the power of Zrackon! Give me strength!"

With a mighty push using all of his pent-up energy of sexual frustration, Ragecarn toppled the huge kiln over. Flames and sparking embers burst into the air as the kiln split open. He shouted to Eyop, "Now!"

The molten slag poured over the guards below. They screamed, burning, melting and writhing on the ground like slugs in salt. Only five survived the assault. The others panicked.

Eyop swooped to retrieve Euryale in his talons.

"You fools — stop him!" cried Vommanatra.

Too late! Ragecarn and Euryale were united again. More warriors appeared from the battlements.

"I suggest we retreat," said Eyop.

"I concur. Farewell, Vommanatra! You were a great ride!"

She stepped forward in anger as Ragecarn sheathed Euryale and took the Zaven in his arms.

He pointed at the mistress and cooly stepped over to the battlements and dove into the far ocean below.

Vommanatra rushed over to the battlements with her guards and remaining entourage.

"No man could have survived such a drop!" said a guard.

There was a sudden swell in the ocean's depths, and a huge sea-eagle erupted from the torrent.

"No man," he roared in victory, "but... Ragecarn!" He rode on Eyop's back, with Euryale raised aloft in triumph.

They soared over the sea of Nahmsilat into the dusk of night.

"Ragecarn, you smell different," said Euryale.

"Yes, the mistress's hand wenches bathed me."

"Aye," said the Zaven, "They rutted together."

"You rutted with that woman? Well, I don't like it! Get dirty again — immediately."

"You know bird, I think I liked the sword before she got the blood lust on her."

The sword hesitated — then laughed.

"Oh, Ragecarn! You are incorrigible," she smirked.

"I know," he said. They all laughed. "Where to now?"

"I know just the place…" the Zaven cawed.

The sea wind tousled the barbarian's hair.

"Take us there," Ragecarn said at last as his eyes searched the horizon.

Ragecarn will return in, *The Hammer of Zrackon.*

THE LONG DAY AND NIGHT OF JOHN CALLISTO

Poets, artists, and many great men,
all lying here under the cold sod.
We are equals now, for the crows to feast upon.

* * *

John awoke in the darkness of his room.

"Weird dreams last night," he said to himself. He rubbed the gritty sleep from his caruncles.

John would awaken around half-past seven every morning. His internal body-clock was precise and reliable, but it was sometimes helped by the low rumble of distant traffic. On occasional, luckier mornings, he would be stirred from his slumber by birdsong, or the faint ringing of church bells.

John could not raise his head from his pillow.

He touched his bedside lamp three times — it was on a dimmer switch to adjust its luminance. His eyes squinted from the glare.

He stared at the four bottles of urine that sat on his bedside table. Each was a subtilely different hue of yellow. He imagined a miniature Pantone® colour chart with uniquely descriptive names: dandelion; lemon zest; tuscan sun; and egg custard. Morning sunlight streamed through a gap in the curtains and into the bottles. It refracted golden light patterns on the wooden floor. *Who ever would have known that four bottles of urine could look so pretty*, he thought.

He laughed as he imitated and paraphrased Captain Jean-Luc Picard in the *Star Trek: The Next Generation* episode, *Chain of Command, Part 2,* shouting to the light fixture in the ceiling, "There — are — *four* — bottles — of — piss!"

After this amusement, John began to ponder more serious thoughts. *How in the name of all that is Holy did my life come to the point that I have to empty my bladder into a bottle?*

The bedside table also held two empty one-litre demijohns. John had drunk the water from them during the night.

He looked at the ceiling, and then all around his room. His eyes surveying the bookshelves, the display cases, and his desktop. Everywhere he looked, the room was festooned with out-of-reach memories, including all his science-fiction memorabilia, *Doctor Who* figurines; a collection of *Star Trek* models; *Judge Dredd* graphic novels; and a Gizmo character from *Gremlins* that sat on top of his *Lion, Witch, and the Wardrobe.* The whole room was filled to the rafters. John was the archetypal nerd. He sighed.

He reached for the handset that controlled his electric profiling bed. It raised him up slightly to a sitting position. John had learned to be heavily left hand dominant due to the poor dexterity in his weakened right hand.

His teeth chattered almost imperceptibly within his skull. The room wasn't cold, and neither was John — his flat was always kept at a comfortable temperature. His whole body trembled on the inside, but only John could feel it. His entire nervous system was in a mode of fight-or-flight shock. He had a cadre of carers that helped him do the tasks he could not do for himself.

His brain had suffered an injury, and now he could not walk. It was a long time ago. He had had a real life, once. Then the disease came, and it took his mind away to a fantasy land. The disease had attacked his adrenal glands, but it was all so preventable — one small pill could have stabilised him, if only the doctors had known in time. Yes, if only…

He was able to use all his limbs, but in a very uncoordinated manner. His ability to balance was essentially gone, but in physical therapy sessions he was able to walk for short distances when assisted by two trained physiotherapists, and he had been making improvements.

One of his therapists had told him once that the physical strains and efforts John had to expend for a short assisted walk was equivalent to her climbing a mountain, or running a half marathon, and she would often cite the old adage: "If you don't use it, you'll lose it."

Whatever "it" was, John had lost it long ago.

Those physiotherapy sessions had been discontinued now due to recommendations, and government cutbacks. The rust was beginning to set in. With it, the inevitable, slow atrophy continued as the years went by.

John had only his imagination and his memories left now to keep him from going irreversibly insane. He still had his sharp wit, and his charming personality — and of course, let's not forget about his devilish good looks, too — but it was his imagination for which John was most grateful. He would spend countless hours adventuring around in his own mind. He would fantasise that he was aboard a spaceship going to Mars, or that he was a mighty warrior who would slay his enemies and enjoy the spoils by making love to gorgeous women.

John admired and desired many beautiful women, but had a particular penchant for Rosie Jones, and Cheryl Tweedy-Cole-Fernandez-Versini (or whatever the fuck name she goes by these days; it changes so often that it's hard to keep track).

Rosie had been a topless model from *Page 3* in *The Sun* newspaper, back when they still printed great and newsworthy stuff like that. She had sent a few messages to John on PhaseBook some years before, when that was still the cool thing to do. John's ex-girlfriend had jealously hated Cheryl with a raging, lustful passion. John would have gleefully fucked Cheryl's brains out with an equally deep and fiery passion.

Damn! Thinking about Rosie and Cheryl always stirred his loins. He pulled the bedcovers off his torso and looked down at his growing erection. An ex-girlfriend had christened his veiny member as "John Junior," and the nickname had stuck.

John Junior throbbed and twitched as if nodding and gesturing toward John's desk. John looked over, as instructed. *Yes, it's within reach!* He grabbed his iPad off the desk and propped it up between his knees.

John's condition had left him with full sensation in his body. He thought it was so cruel the way his brain was rewired after the period of time he was in a comatose state. He felt cheated and robbed.

Many years earlier, whenever he had been a horny and curious teenager, John had discovered, nurtured, and satisfied his sexual urges, all thanks to the *Page 3* topless models printed daily in *The Sun* newspaper. He would find a quiet corner of his bedroom when nobody else was around, unzip his trousers and whip out his new best friend. He lay down on the carpet and rubbed himself raw until he came. At first, John didn't know what to think of this new and highly pleasurable sensation. Of course it felt amazing, but he was also conflicted by feelings of guilt. He had been brought up to believe in God, and he worried if God was watching him. *Something that feels this good must definitely be sinful*, he had reckoned. He looked above him, but could see no one looking, watching, judging. *God is omnipresent and all powerful*, he had thought, *but I'm pretty sure he doesn't want to watch me doing this.* John eased his guilt by saying a quick prayer, and got over the penitence quickly enough. He mopped up his mess with a piece of toilet paper, and decided to try again in twenty minutes.

Now, back in his room so many years later, the same urges surged through his veins, as strongly as when he was a teenager. He turned his iPad on.

"Let the games begin," he said softly.

If Genies came in bottles, John would have smashed a huge cauldron to free his wild thing that burned inside him now. It was an addiction now, an insatiable desire and terrible fire that would never be slaked.

He forced his mind to the present moment.

"Okay, Cheryl, are you ready for our date?"

He knew at the back of his mind this was just a fantasy and what he was doing was a sheer act of lust. He opened YouTube and quickly found the video he wanted.

John grunted and moaned to the music while he rubbed, stroked, massaged, and teased John Junior. He watched for around twenty minutes then he spasmed his legs. His whole body shook violently. "Ride me Cheryl, you wild sexy goddess! Ride me! Yeehaaa!"

He climaxed.

As was always the case, after the pleasure came the guilt and shame. Other people's sins flickered on his eye lids as the iPad continued to play. Was it his sin to willingly witness such things? It was commonplace — the internet was saturated with this stuff. Everywhere there were people murdering each other, fornicating, spreading hatred and violence and oppression. Perhaps worst of all, the sleazy, corrupt, lying politicians. It was all there, ready for download!

This feeling of sheer dread and emptiness, with no where to go, no where to hide, was a mind trap. John would just have to get over it, but "acceptance of the situation" was a terrible phrase his doctors had used. What did they expect him to do? Give up and die? There was an evil streak inside of him that brought fear and self loathing with it.

John recalled an episode of *Star Trek* called *The Enemy Within*, in which the matter transmitter had malfunctioned, causing Captain Kirk to be split into two similar but opposite versions of himself — one was good, and the other was evil. Chief geologist Fisher had beamed from the planet surface back to the Enterprise. He had arrived covered in a yellow metal ore, so Scotty decided to decontaminate the transporter chamber. Kirk then beamed aboard, emerging faint and weak. Scotty escorted the Captain to his quarters. It was then that the matter transmitter was tripped, and the evil Kirk doppelgänger appeared in the transport room. The bad Kirk had a major eyeliner malfunction. There ensued a power play between the two versions of the man; each half reflected a strong and distinct element of his persona — a mirror image — and each had his own strengths and weaknesses. Ultimately, the two Kirks were rejoined and he was a whole man again. Molded together, born again from *Star Trek* technology.

So it was with John.

His iPad was his lover now. It was a willing, giving, and obedient lover — it would always be ready and would do anything he asked. He tossed it aside in disgust. After the act of masturbation he felt cold. A shiver went through his body.

He cleaned himself down with toilet roll. He had an hour to rest. He took another drink of water. Soon after there was another quarter bottle of urine sitting on the table.

John picked up his iPad once again and looked at it. He closed YouTube and opened his Bible app — his *Cyber Bible*, as he liked to call it. The app read the text aloud, and he listened to it for a while.

Consider the ravens: for they neither sow nor reap; which neither have storehouse nor barn; and God feedeth them: how much more are ye better than the fowls? Consider the lilies how they grow: they toil not, they spin not; and yet I say unto you, that Solomon in all his glory was not arrayed like one of these.

John thought it was strange. It had been over 2,000 years now, and Jesus had not yet returned. In the churches of Halloween town, the sinners gathered to worship, pray, and wait. John believed they would not see the second coming of the Lord because when Judgement Day did finally arrive, the Son of Man and all his angels would simply skip over this Godforsaken town and move on to the next. He would abandon Halloween town as it is for all eternity. Nothing here worth saving.

Halloween Town: The City that God Forgot! Sounds like the title of a B-movie.

Or, maybe this was a crazy, parallel dimension, and Jesus had returned to save an entirely separate universe. *Damnation.* He pondered this carefully. It would explain a lot of things.

John's carers were amazing kind hearted people and very well trained. They were the true angels of mercy.

Every morning around half eight Tiffany and Ethel would come to his home and get him out of bed. All his carers were of various age groups, very well mannered and courteous. They would greet John with kindness and respect.

"Good mornin', John," Ethel would say. She was a lovely, motherly lady. She was the senior carer in the team and very proficient at her job.

"Hi, John-boy!" Tiffany said. "How are you?" Tiffany was a young woman with oval blue eyes and auburn hair. All the girls were immaculate in their appearances and all had their hair in pins.

From their pockets they produced sterile gloves. They would scurry around the room in preparation for John to get up. Ethel emptied the four bottles of urine down the toilet, flushed and sprayed the urine bottles with bleach. While she was doing this, Tiffany gave John his medication for his Addison's disease from the blister pack.

"Ah, the spice must flow!" he said to himself, borrowing a line from *Dune* by Frank Herbert, one of John's favourite books. In John's case, the "Spice" was a drug called cortisone that gave new life. "Thank you Tiffany," he said and gulped down his melange.

John's room had an ensuite bathroom that contained various living aids and equipment. There was a device called a "steady" — it was a movable hoist contrivance with a fold away seat and two handles that allowed him to transfer his weight from his bed and to the various wheelchairs that he had. The two girls moved the steady into position, parallel to his bed. John's torso was weak — he needed maximum assistance to stand in the steady. They put on his flip flops in preparation for his shower routine. One girl got behind his shoulder, the other took his hands to swivel and pivot him into a sitting position.

And so began the long day of John Callisto.

He stood in the steady. The two girls removed his underwear. He continually thanked them for doing the most menial of tasks for him. His legs trembled, John's right leg was weak. Whenever he suffered the Addisonian crisis, the resulting coma had left him paralysed, brain damaged, speechless, and temporally blind. He was grateful for each single breath of life.

The girls placed the shower chair beneath the steady and he sat down onto it, slowly and controlled. The spice gave him the strength.

Usually Tiffany would shower him, while Ethel prepared John's breakfast in the kitchen. She soaped him down with shower gel and John with his limited dexterity used a spare face cloth to wash himself. He did not trust his right side of his body to behave itself, so he gripped onto the right hand of the shower chair. He had to balance, upright in the shower chair and looking dead ahead, focusing on the wall. And breathe. And have a conversation with Tiffany all at the same time. They would chat the usual small talk about the weather, family life and work. The girls found John's sense of humour pleasant and friendly. They were all very fond of him. The persiflage was good between carer and client.

After a short while, John's ablutions were complete, and now it was time to rebuild him. He recalled *The Six-Million Dollar Man* television series that he had loved so much, and he remembered the introduction: *Steve Austin Astronaut. A man barely alive. Gentlemen, we can rebuild him. We have the technology. We have the capability to make the world's first bionic man. Steve Austin will be that man. Better than he was before. Better… stronger… faster!*

The carers dried him off and dressed him. They applied sprays, face creams, and deodorants, all while he sat in his bathchair.

"What chair would you like today, John?" Ethel asked. She was referring to John's powered wheelchairs, of which there were three. Each was designed for different purposes.

"Let me think… *Thunderbird 1*, please!"

John identified each of his chairs by its designated *Thunderbirds* number. Gerry Anderson's science-fiction series was yet another of John's favourite childhood television shows.

Tiffany drove John's *Thunderbird 1* from the its charging station in the living room. She enjoyed sitting in it. She wasn't an experienced driver, and she bumped into the sideboard, just the once. "Oops!" she said, giggling.

"Sorry, but the look on your face was priceless! I am only raking your bacon!" she laughed. "But seriously though, how do you steer this thing, John?"

"Years of practice" John replied, dryly. *Far too many*, he thought.

The two girls used the steady to transfer John to his electric wheelchair. With a few slow, deep breaths in and out, he settled his muscle tone into the gravity of his chair. Tiffany and Ethel cleaned up the shower area.

John was mobile now; it was freedom, of a kind.

"Lock and load, rock and roll! To the kitchen!" John said. He set his joypad speed setting to the lowest gear and began rolling forward.

The girls laughed affectionately behind him.

His breakfast was always the same: a high fibre cereal; seven almonds; two strawberries; and one banana. John usually took his cereal with soya milk; he was a creature of habit. One of his friends, Bob, would often jokingly call him Sheldon after the character on *The Big Bang* television series because of the idiosyncratic habits he and John shared.

After setting out his breakfast, the two girls helped John into his coat — it was a heavy, black leather bikers jacket that doubled as part of his *Judge Dredd* cosplay outfit. John loved to attend comic book conventions, or Comic-Cons, and getting dressed up in the costumes of his favorite characters. Some of his good friends were cos-players, too. They were all in a clan together.

He stared out of his kitchen window. There had been a heavy frost the previous night, and there was a light fog permeating the dawn sky.

He thanked his carers again for all their assistance. They finished their duties, tidied up the kitchen, and placed their gloves in the bin.

"See you tomorrow, John!"

They waved goodbye to him as he watched them from the window. They headed off to attend to their next client. John was always happy to see them, and always sad when they left, taking their cheery personas with them.

His mind was troubled. Fractured. Tortured, incarcerated within a cell, with no hope of escape.

After finishing his breakfast, John turned his chair on and put his dish into the sink. While drying the dish, he fumbled it for a second and almost dropped it to the floor. That started it.

"You clumsy, stupid fool!" the Evil Kirk said to him. Kirk had manifested out of John's imagination, leering over him.

"But I didn't!" John said.

"Khallisto, you bloodsucker. You're going to have to do your own dirty work now! Do you hear me? Do you?"

A sudden and terrible urge came upon John Callisto. He winced from the pain, clutching his crotch. He had to urinate, badly.

"You're still alive, my old friend." John murmured to himself. He engaged his chair and rushed into the bathroom. He fumbled at his zipper, found the urinal, cursing and swearing to himself under his breath. John's thoughts where that of a rabid animal, trapped. He had to breathe.

He urinated on to his leg.

"Still, old friend! You've managed to kill everyone else, but like a poor marksman, you keep missing the target!" the Evil Kirk taunted.

John wiped himself down with a facecloth. The relief was palpable as was the expression on his face. He leaned back to enjoy the moment with a deep sigh.

"Perhaps I no longer need to try, Admiral."

"KHALLLLIIISSSTTTTOOOO! KHALLLLIIISSSTTTTOOOO!"

He flushed the toilet loudly, "I hope you hear that, Colonel Klunz!" He looked above him and listened. Nothing from the floor above, John flushed it again. "The crazy old fart," he said silently to himself. He slammed down the seat.

The Colonel was indeed an old gasbag. He lived on the top floor of John's apartment block and was loathed and hated by most of the neighbours. An old war horse, Godfrey Klunz was an ex-service man with a total anal-retentive attitude towards all the residents. In short, he was a dick. "They shoot horses, don't they?" John sang inwardly.

The Colonel owned the franchise of the Freaky Fried Chicken Factory in Halloween town. No one knew what the "Special Element" in his chicken was. The populace in the town was totally addicted to it.

Klunz was a large, heavy-set man with an old fashioned slicked back hair-style that was turning grey at the temples. He walked slowly and deliberately to each destination. John suspected that Colonel Godfrey Klunz was the head Nosferatu of Halloween town, due to his nocturnal proclivities. He was only ever seen at dusk and in the early morning hours.

There was a dispute amongst the neighbours concerning John's plumbing. According to Klunz, John's toilet emanated a loud, fog-horn noise at night whenever it was flushed.

"What a load of crap!" John said.

As a wheelchair user, it would not even have been possible for John to flush at night time. The man was obviously talking out of his ass!

At one of the residents meetings the Colonel said, "Callisto, your blasted flushing is unacceptably disruptive. I deserve compensation for my trouble! I can't sleep wink a day now!"

John narrowed his eyes. *More evidence. Must investigate further,* he thought. *Definite Nosferatu candidacy.*

It was resolved whenever a council flunky from the environmental health agency was brought in to bear. He examined the flush mechanism on John's toilet, and then rushed upstairs to the top floor where Klunz was awaiting the report on the fog-horn. Klunz could not hear a damn thing. Problem solved.

John washed his hands at the bathroom sink, he found it hard to manipulate fine movements with his poor dexterity. He fumbled at the tooth paste lid and squeezed some out into his mouth. Doing that was far handier than putting it onto his toothbrush.

"You genius, Callisto!"

He looked deep into the reflection of his mirror. At times he pulled funny faces, other instances he could not bear looking at his own corporality. Where did the handsome, care free rogue of his youth go?

"It's still in there somewhere, Callisto." He gave himself a wan smile. After finishing his teeth, he picked up his urinal and put it into his man bag and slung it over his shoulder. He lifted up his brown fedora hat, checked it in the mirror, cocked the hat to one side.

"Looking good, John." He grinned at his reflection. His last duties before he set off into the town was to scrutinise that everything was safe in his apartment. All secure, check. He went back into the toilet and flushed it again, for extra measure.

"To the last, I will grapple with thee! From Hell's heart, I stab at thee! For hate's sake, I spit my last breath at thee!" John said with each flush.

John lived right beside the graveyard in Halloween town. His apartment block was built from the old gate-keeper's house; it had been bulldozed to make way for the living and undead inhabitants of the new building. A local man died during the reconstruction, and every year fresh flowers would appear anonymously at the front gate post.

John exited the building through the red side door. The door knob was brass and set in the middle of the frame. The frost on the knob made his hand stick to it. He always recalled it resembled Bilbo Baggins's door from *The Hobbit.* Freeing his hand, John sped his way through the parking spaces towards the iron double gates. The cobwebs hung like silver lattices on the gate posts in the fog. The sensors on the gates tracked John's approach. Thinking he was a car, they creaked wide.

John carefully crossed the road. Car lights strobed all around him. His route in to the town never changed. He passed various monuments and many sepultures, the swimming pool, the Old Picture House, and the Freaky Fried Chicken Factory. The fog had started to dissipate, leaving John to ponder and stare at the horizon, towards his childhood home, that for all intents and purposes was gone.

John had to keep going. He had to keep it real. He remembered the beyondertime, back before the cataclysm that had torn his world apart. *Don't think, or he will get you! He's waiting for you on the other side of the divide! He's coming to getcha! He's gaining on you! Run, hide inside your mind!*

The Callisto family had lived on a hill, in the vales of the town. John loved to run. Every night, around seven, he would set out in all weathers and in all seasons for his race against the fire of time. Changing from his day clothes and shoes in his upstairs bedroom, he slipped on his physical exercise shorts, bending down to tie his gutties tight. He pulled on his yellow *Ghostbusters* vest that his cousin Sarah Ganymede had given to him, then he bounded down the stairs and out through the back gate, shutting the latch behind him. The gate always creaked. The gate itself was not tall — it was at waist height. He could leap over it easily. He was a gauche nineteen-year-old, tall, thin, and athletic.

He walked at a brisk pace down the path towards the barley fields. It was a warm, fine evening at the beginning of May. The spring air filled his lungs. John pulled up a dandelion clock and blew the seeds into the air.

He twirled the stalk in his hand, the sticky sap got on to his fingers. "She loves me," one hard blow, "she loves me not," another large exhale. A gust of wind put a stop to his soliloquy. A bee buzzed by John's head, disturbed by the movements of his palm.

"Well, obviously not!" he tutted. John flinched back from the bee attack.

The dandelion stalk drifted away into the warm twilight air.

He passed a few houses.

A neighbour's dog came up to say hello.

"Hello, Patch boy, how are you?" John rubbed the dog's belly and patting it.

The dog replied, "Hurrow!" and wagged his tail furiously.

Patch belonged to the Bensun family, the Callisto family neighbours and was the neighbourhood dog, a very affectionate animal and intelligent. That dog could talk, almost. Patch was a Anatolian Shepherd, complete with curly tail.

"Sorry, boy," said John. "I have no treats for you now. I'll see you whenever I get back."

Patch looked despondent.

John did some warm up exercises before he set off. He jogged on the spot, then pulled each of his legs in turn behind his calf muscles. He leaned against a lamp post, waiting for the signal. He looked up at the post, waiting. Suddenly the lights started to flicker on, one by one like landing lights in the distance.

John took off running.

His legs carried him along in a gentle pace at first. It had rained the earlier in the evening and the air was warm and humid and thick with new life. There were puddles of water along John's route.

His run first took him along the old Brokers Road — he loved this section to run down — it was a country road. In the early evenfall few cars buzzed by with their headlamps on. He reached the hill on top of the road, breathing moderately, his lungs filling and exhaling as his limbs swung from side to side in a rhythm. He dodged a swarm of midge flies.

Downhill now, he loped along with gravity assisting his descent, pounding his feet on to the road, avoiding a puddle and splashing his way through another one, John caught his reflection in a pool, briefly. He speeded up thanks to his acceleration.

He turned left onto the Knock Road. He didn't like this part of the run so much; cars on this road were deadly. He sped up slightly. John reached the junction of the King Billy Road in about twenty minutes, then it was up hill until the Nettle Lane. The pace was hard, as was John's breathing. It took him at least another twenty minutes to reach the apex of King Billy Road.

Always turning left, he bounded down the Nettle Lane, accelerating homeward bound towards the back alleyways of the Vales, avoiding piles of dog mess that plagued the way, left by inconsiderate owners. A few yapping dogs in the back gardens barked and growled at John as he passed them.

"Ahh shaddap, ya bloody mutts!" John shouted behind him.

He brushed a cobweb from his hair without stopping or slowing.

This is a great time, he thought as he panted between breaths. *I am invincible!*

He reached the back alleyway. Almost there. John bounded, running very fast downhill. He reached the back gate and attempted to leap over it as he had so often before. But this time, disaster struck. He had misjudged the leap — perhaps his legs were more tired than he thought — and he snagged his balls on the gate's latch. He doubled over and howled in agony. Patch heard his commotion and scurried quickly over. Perhaps it was his long-distant wolf ancestry that compelled him to join in tandem with John's anguished howling. John eventually pulled himself straight and prised his running shorts to one side. There was a nasty red gash along his inside leg. One more inch and he would have been a eunuch and neutered for sure. He limped inside the family home.

* * *

John Callisto's mind returned to the present. He turned his electric wheelchair on again and tore his gaze from the horizon. "Too much pain there," he considered, finally. He stared down at his feet. They were strapped in to his wheelchair foot plates.

He powered down a hill into the town, at full speed. "Stay on target, stay on target!" He imagined himself as Luke Skywalker flying down the trench on the Death Star in *Star Wars: Episode IV — A New Hope*.

John passed the garage where his mechanic friend O'zone worked. The garage men were always busy, highly skilled and patient men; a production line of clanking cars that had to be serviced. All O'zone's team had blackened oily hands and faces. O'zone was the manager. The men called him either "boss" or Oz for short.

"John!" O'zone called out.

"O'zone!" John replied, this was a daily occurrence. O'zone had helped John a lot in the past few years, with flat tyres and various mechanical failures and accidents that occurred while John was out and about. Oz's whole team had helped John. Oz had a grey stubbily beard and was balding. He was thin, and practiced the art of Karate whenever he wasn't working in the garage.

John continued his journey into the town. He travelled into the Samhain Lane. He spied his busker friend, Ringo.

"Coffee, Ringo?"

Every day, John Callisto would stop by and ask the same question. It was such a part of their routine now that it didn't even seem like a question. It was more of an assumption. Of course they would stop for coffee together. It was one of the highlights of the day.

Ringo paused from his busking, glanced at his watch and replied, "Sure, Johnny, let's make it two. Where do you want to go?"

"Cafe Caligula!" he smiled. "Who's shout is it this time?" John asked, in keeping with their tradition of taking turns to pay. He fumbled within his jacket and found his wallet. He produced a pound coin and handed it to Ringo.

"Right you be, Ringo."

John Callisto adjusted his light brown fedora hat. He had business of his own in the town. He nudged the joystick of his electric wheelchair, knocked it into middle gear, and sped away while humming the *Lost in Space* theme tune.

Later on that day, after John had done all his shopping and completed his duties, they met in the back of the Cafe Caligula. Ringo sat down in the plush cushion seat facing John.

"So, how was trade in town? How much was your haul today, Ringo?" John said.

Ringo laughed, he tapped his guitar case that contained his daily earnings and shook it.

"Oh, not bad Johnny, enough to keep the wolves at bay!"

Kay brought down their beverages.

"Here you go John, your raspberry tea – and for you Ringo, your cappachino. Is there anything I can get for ye both?" she added with a smile.

"No, that's great, thanks Kay," John said.

Ringo was a very astute man, and extremely well read. He had seen a great deal during his tenure on Samhain Lane, he had seen the best and worst of humanity that drifted by him. Ringo took a sip of the coffee. He patted his lips on a napkin.

They would usually chat about the politics of the day, the weather, and of course some science fiction. Ringo was a *Whovian* — a *Doctor Who* aficionado — so the subject of travelling came into the conversation once. John asked how far and wide Ringo had travelled around the world. "Canada," had been his reply.

"There are no regions left to explore on this world save the weltanschauung of a persons soul." Ringo said. Amongst his many talents Ringo was a bit of an urban philosopher.

John laughed at his remark.

"Very true, Ringo. Very true." The statement was accurate enough; everyone was trapped here, in Halloween town.

Drinking the dregs of his tea, John said, "Time to go, Zebedee! I have to get home."

Glancing at his wristwatch, Ringo drank the rest of his coffee and rose from his seat. There was time yet, he considered, so he would play a few more songs while the light was still good. His whole body was a barometer, he would sing and play if the weather was bearable.

They departed from the cafe with the hubbub of conversations and the music dwindling behind them.

"See you tomorrow, Ringo."

Ringo replied shaking John's hand, "Thank's for the coffee, Johnny."

John zoomed home. He had an appointment with God, and he didn't want to be late.

Two men administrated to John's soul: The Canon, Rector Hector-Arkwright Forquemado and John's old friend, Richard The Munnisher. One brought holy communion, the other brought hellfire, damnation and salvation — both in equal measure.

John had known the Canon all his life, since growing up in the Vales. Hector-Arkwright was very tall, over six feet in stature, quite thin, wore glasses and his hair was thinning at the sides. He always spoke in a soft contralto voice that deepened substantially whenever he was passionate about a particular subject matter. His age was somewhat indeterminate, John's mother had once said to Hector, "You must have a portrait in an attic somewhere!" She was, of course, referring to Oscar Wilde's *The Picture of Dorian Gray*. Hector had simply smiled at her remark.

"Ah, Mrs Callisto, you are very wise," he chuckled inwardly to himself, and added, "but it is thanks to good living and the Good Book."

But he never did reveal the secret to his longevity. The Canon was a bibliophile, a conservative reader and a gentleman.

The church of John's childhood was Saint Hark's in the Parish of the Vales. Now, because of his mobility challenges, John was been unable to attend service in person. So once a month the Canon would bring the Eucharist to John.

"Hello John," the Canon said with a lilt in his voice. "How are you?" His voice deepened with the next sentence.

John shook with his left hand.

John lied. "I am well enough. Thank you for asking, Hector."

"Good, good, splendid — shall we begin?"

John's kitchen was homely, humble and had all the accoutrements associated with a scullery. It was his favourite place in his house, facing the graveyard and it's adjacent tree.

John sometimes dreamed about the tree. It was a tall oak that would frequently play host to rooks, ravens, jackdaws and magpies. On one dark and dreary day a number of years back, he could have sworn the jackdaws were talking to each other. *You are crazy Callisto*, he thought, attempting to convince himself. *You are getting worse.*

As John drew closer to the tree as he was passing by, one jackdaw suddenly cawed, "John! John!" as it stood on the ground near the base of the tree and looked in John's direction.

John was startled. "Go on, scatter!" he cursed at the bird.

It defiantly looked at him with a cold, grey eye, then slowly alighted to a high branch of the tree, joining the others of his kind.

The Canon put on his vestments to begin the ceremony; his robes were white and he had a purple and gold sash that he placed around his thin shoulders. The sash had the Greek letters alpha and omega ornately stitched upon it in golden thread. John thought at times Hector resembled a character from an episode of *Star Trek*. The Canon produced from his brief case a small silver plate and box, which was meant to contain the Holy Sacrement: a tiny vial of red wine, and two pieces of white bread.

However, on this occasion the box had no bread inside. The Canon must have neglected to purchase extra bread after his many visitations with the sick and the immobile in the community. He looked red-faced and somewhat embarrassed.

His voice wavered as he said to John, "May I impose on you for some bread please, John?"

He removed his glasses. He fished a handkerchief from his trouser pocket and mopped his furrowed brow. He regained his composure, put his glasses back on, and slowly stowed his handkerchief away in his pocket under his cassock.

John was absolutely mortified. If there was one thing John Callisto did not have that particular day, it was bread. He normally maintained a well stocked larder, but today — of all days! — he was fresh out of bread. Not even a crumb.

In a breathless panic he rummaged through all his kitchen cupboards searching for anything remotely bread-like. He found a tube of prawn cocktail flavoured Pringles, slightly past their expiration date and looking a bit stale.

"I am so sorry about this Hector, I have only these…" he said, sheepishly offering the tube to the Canon.

"'Needs must', as they say, John. Thank you."

So, the rite continued apace using the usual magical pageantry and chicanery. John could confidently say that in the whole of Christendom no other souls had ever took Holy Communion with stale-but-still-quite-tasty prawn cocktail flavoured Pringles. The Canon Rector Hector-Arkwright Forquemado assembled his bits and pieces into his brown suitcase, then politely excused himself and departed.

"Oh! Thank you, God above!" John gave a long sigh of relief.

A voice whispered behind him.

"John," it said. "Don't you love us any more?"

It was Matilda, John's bonsai tree. She shook her dry leaves.

John had three plants that he watered almost every day. Sitting on his windowsill was a bonsai, named Matilda, and two cacti.

John's mother was a horticulturist — she loved and respected all living things; a very serene and peaceful woman.

When John got sick it was a hammer blow to her. When he was allowed out to the shops in his first electric wheelchair his mother followed him everywhere, smoking her cigarettes. On the way home they passed the old primary school gates where John used to play whenever he was a boy. It was a warm spring day, one Saturday late in May. John yearned to reach up and smell the cherry blossoms that were in full bloom. If only he was not brain damaged, he could reach them. His mother knew what he was thinking — she always knew. She placed her cigarette on the ground and its acrid acid smell burned in the warm still air.

She removed John's belt and lifted him upright.

"My son, smell that," she said as she held him high enough that his head moved among the hanging blossoms.

"'Poems are made by fools like me," she said, then paused to breathe in a gasp as she hoisted him up a few inches farther, "But only God can make a tree.'"

It was a strange contrast of smells. This beautiful strong woman who bore and raised him and the aroma of the peach blossoms mixed between the stench of her cigarette.

"Sorry, Matilda!" said John, as he rushed to the water tap to satisfy his tiny forest of house plants.

"Do me! Do me!" squealed the cacti, shaking their tiny stems.

"Callisto," said Evil Kirk, who was always silent whenever the Canon was present but who had now evinced from John's mind again and was sitting, crossed-legged on a stool, added, "Catch a grip!"

"Go away! If talking to potted plants is good enough for King Charles, then it's good enough for me!"

John breathed to settle himself. He was alone again. No voices in his head to torment him.

Around four in the in the afternoon Zola would put John's supper on. Zola was a blonde, bubbly chatterbox, and was one of John's carers. He had known her for around ten years and she was his favourite carer — she knew all his ways, and his moods.

"Hey, John, how are you? What's on the menu tonight?"

"Hi, Zola. Surprise me!"

She laughed, as she helped put away John's shopping and busied herself around the kitchen. John had influenced Zola on her diet, as she now enjoyed spices, soy sauce and other delicacies from John's larder.

Looking at a particular jar she turned it round in her hand and said, "Mmm, this looks nice; I must try it." Zola could concoct a sumptuous banquet from a microwave meal using the spices in John's cupboards. He would park himself at the sidebar table and enjoy and relish every morsel.

"That's super; thanks so much, Zola."

Kirk sat opposite him and winked. John scowled at his male harpy.

"Is everything all right, John?" Zola raised her eyebrows.

"Yes, just blowing on my food. See you tomorrow."

Zola left through the patio door.

John finished his meal, and washed up. He read for a while, and listened to his radio until half six. By then it was quite dark. Then there was another rap at the patio doors. It was another set of carers sent to toilet him.

There were a number of women or varying ages who attended John for this function, and their manners were impeccable, helpful, professional, and extremely polite.

John had a Closomat toilet system that cleaned and washed his ass, all in one! It used a jet of warm water up his rectum, followed by a fan that dried him. It was extremely hygienic, and not at all unpleasant — there are worse ways to spend an evening.

The attendees used the steady to support John while they placed and adjusted his clothing. His bowels were like clockwork: every day or so he would release the fury as his bowels were purged and purified; it was half an hour of heaven during which John would relax and read a book, or the current issue of *2000AD* comic — "The Prog on the Bog," as John liked to say. It was the highlight of each day.

Whenever the deed was done, John called the carers back into the room. They found him proudly wearing a relieved smile on his face.

"Finished," he sighed.

The girls then adjusted his clothing and placed him back into his chair before spraying the bowl with bleach.

"See you tonight Johnny," Tara said. She was a great carer. Another smaller and younger woman — one of the best — was named wee Kaitlen. She was another friendly, caring type.

"Yes, John, I will see you this evening also," Kaitlen replied.

John went to his kitchen to finish reading his comic. He plucked a nostril hair from his nose, and wiped it away on his sleeve, then made himself a cup of tea. He checked his phone for messages and looked out of his kitchen window at the encroaching black of night.

He yawned.

As the evening wore on, his mind settled into a normal thinking pattern. He was a social animal, and enjoyed the evenings company with some of his closest friends. He would invite them all in turn to his abode.

On Monday, Gazza would come by. On Tuesdays, it was Graham. They would watch movies together, chat, or play Xbox games. During the week, The Munnisher cometh.

It was getting closer to Halloween. John was in one of his standing wheelchairs in the kitchen, pruning the leaves of Matilda and the other shrubbery that sat on his windowsill. He lifted Matilda from the windowsill and set her into the sink and turned on the tap to run some water. It was still and warm in his kitchen. When Matilda was sufficiently wetted, John turned off the tap and looked back up that the kitchen window in front of his face. A ghastly, inhuman face rose and hovered in front of the window. It made eye contact with John and it grinned insanely at him.

John leaped back with a yell!

The face vanished as quickly as it had appeared, then suddenly The Munnisher bounded in from the patio door.

"Every… single… time, Callisto!" he laughed evilly while embracing John with a bear hug. "I get you every year with the old unexpected-hideous-face-at-the-kitchen-window trick!"

Many and myriad are the myths of The Munnisher. His dear friend Richard Munnisher would always bring snacks that he would happily devour himself, and diet cola drinks that he would imbibe himself also. Sometimes he would even share with John.

The Munnisher was a rogue, but also a passionate believer in Jesus, and he often preached the gospel to John.

He was also fluent in Swahili. The Lord had brought his heart to Africa. In Kenya, he had preached in the slums of Nairobi, and in the streets of Mombasa, and to the very hell of the wilderness that was the Turkana province in the north on one of his many pilgrimages to the dark continent. He had witnessed the saving of many souls, had eaten burned goat, had fired an AK47 assault rifle into the air, and had washed his ass with ashes. He went into the dreaded Masaka Maximum Security Prison in Uganda. All this he did for the glory and the kingdom of The Lord.

In Africa, they called him the "mmbasu", which meant "sunlight" in the Luhya tongue of a tribe from western Kenya.

Going into the living room, Richard would sit on the end seat of John's lazy-boy settee and use the recliner function to make himself maximally comfortable. He spread his legs out.

"Ahh," he sighed, as he melted into the settee.

John loved listening to the Munnisher's voice whenever they had conversations together. Swahili was such a beautiful spoken language.

"My dear Kaka," Richard would say to John, "this wee town of ours is going straight to hell."

"Straight to hell," John concurred. He could tell that Richard was about to launch himself into another religious fervour. It was a spectacle. John could imagine The Munnisher on the streets of Kenya, shouting at the top of his voice as he preached to the sinners there: "Halloween town! Ninyi ni watoto wa baba yenu shetani, na mnataka kutekeleza tamaa za baba yenu!"

(Roughly translated: "You are the children of your father the devil, and the lusts of your father ye shall do!")

The Munnisher closed his eyes, "Mungu! Bwana! Mungu! Bwana!"

This strange words were, "God and Lord."

He despised the local populace of the Halloween town, often referring to them as "mutantos," and "la cucaracha," intoning and parodying such films such as *The Good, The Bad, and The Ugly*.

John and Richard talked about anything and everything, and often discussed the news of the day from around the world. They watched great movies together, and the Munnisher enjoyed the works of David Lynch in particular; *Twin Peaks* was a fan favourite.

All evenings must come to an end, and all too soon they heard the church bells strike the hour of nine o'clock — John's carers would arrive presently, and so the Munnisher prepared to depart.

"It was a good night, my beloved bwana," Richard said. "Let's go into the kitchen to pray."

The Munnisher sat in the stool that was normally reserved for the evil version of James Tiberius Kirk. John sat in his electric wheelchair, facing Richard, and they clasped their hands and bowed their heads. The Munnisher cited a short Psalm and then finished with the Lord's prayer.

"I will see you soon, Kaka! One day, you and I will travel to Africa. I have seen it, and so it will come true. It must come true," the Munnisher said in a peaceful manner, hugging John.

"I will see you later, my bwana!"

The Munnisher stepped out into the dark.

Alone again, John suspired. He glanced down at his feet. In susurration he spoke back to his friend, "Ponder the path of thy feet, and let all thy ways be established."

John returned to his bedroom. He went to the sink to brush his teeth, and set his clothes out for the morning. He was becoming fatigued, and it would soon be time for his daily dose of cortisone "spice".

On some days, John's daily routine varied slightly. But mostly they were the same, and all the days and nights blurred into one. An immense Titan chained to his yoke, like Atlas — the world revolved slowly round its axis. Through the monotonous grind of life, John was searching every day for something: redemption, and a miracle. During his travels round the town he stopped one day at the cathedral.

"Are you there yet?" he had once asked as a petulant child.

There was no answer from the ornate marble walls and stained glass windows. What an ostentatious contrast to an African slum, where his friend The Munnisher preached. John put on his hat again, and moved onwards to his next point of call. In the distance, out of ear shot the cathedral bell chimed the hour.

Considering the ravens again, this was his life now. John knew that even though his loss and his suffering was great, it was as nothing compared to the loss and suffering of others. He was immensely grateful for what he had.

There was a knock on the patio door; it was the night staff come to put him to bed.

"Hey girls," he called out to them. "Thank you for coming."

His night-time routine was a mirror of his morning regime — everything was repeated in reverse order as they unwound his clockwork day.

The girls diligently put John to bed, ensuring he was comfortable and had everything he needed for the evening. They bleached the four urinals, each with a piece of toilet roll at the side so John did not spill urine during the night. They filled his water bottles and set them at the opposite end of the table. They gave him his medication.

John thanked the carers for helping him. His carers locked up his home as they left.

At the end of each day they were waiting for him. They would never argue with him, nor shout at John Callisto. Cheryl and Rosie, his iPad lovers, in a way — each was perfect. So what if his ex called him a creep, and a loser?

"Bitch," he said.

John knew he was harming no one with his actions. He was a mere mortal human. He wasn't a Superman, or a comic book hero. No one was. If there were heroes in John's life, it would be his carers.

And The Munnisher, of course.

At the end of each fantasy was a hard stone wall reality to face.

He turned off his lamp by touching it once.

"I hope I dream well tonight," he mumbled sleepily into his pillow. He would have visions and portents of mighty space warriors, righteous battles, and wondrous star crafts sailing through the void of space on voyages of discovery. He was free.

And so began the long night of John Callisto.

JASON ZEPHYR AND THE ASCENSIONAUTS

Time is a river to a brave warrior.
Caught in its stream,
Frozen in a dream.
Heaven and or hell awaits us all.

*   *   *

For the glory! And the power! It was a wondrous thing to behold the universe as it sheered, warped, and tore apart on our ship's prow.

Eons ago, we set sail from Earth. Departing the spaceport New Belfast, we sailed into the wilderness of the cosmos, into the vast blackness sea of star-time aboard our starship, The Ascension. The Ascension was a needle that tore the fabric of star-time apart, ripping the stuff of stars asunder and stitching back the velvet blackness in its wake. But the ship has gone; she burned as she fell into the abyss with all her souls now departed, fools we were! We were in search of the weapon. A weapon with the colossal power to harness the waves of time itself. The sun will fall from heaven, all shall be dark at home.

My name is Jason… or perhaps I was Jason, or am yet to be. I cannot recall. I am not the same person I was a millisecond ago. The Pillar of Fyre has changed me irrevocably. I cheated the Behenian Ealasaid of her destiny whenever I thrusted myself into the maelstrom of the Eye. The Fyre does not tell or reveal her secrets.

— Jason Zephyr, from his Gilgamesh Journals.

*   *   *

New Belfast was the greatest city in the world; the capital of the Viri Terram empire in the year 3707. The city was a thriving, choking populace of all creeds and religions, all races of humans, plus myriad cyborgs, aliens, and augmentals.

Jason Zephyr was the captain of the Ascension, the finest starship that was made by the venerable Wolfburn & Hart, Corp. It was among the greatest space docks on the planet. It was also a thriving trade point.

He studied the horizon. From his vantage point he could see it: the sun was setting, the fiery ball dipped slowly into the sea. He remembered overhearing a conversation between a child and his mother wondering, "Mummy, will the sea boil, when the sun goes into it?"

The mother chuckled at the boy's question, but she lacked the comprehension of the laws of thermodynamics and basic astronomy, and was ill-equipped to answer the boy's question. A sudden fear gripped Zephyr back then for the child's sake. He could not just stand idly by. He haunched down next to the boy and explained the science and the truth.

How many sunsets remain to us? Jason wondered. *I have lived too long…*

He waited until the last beams of sunlight waned, then reluctantly turned away. It would be dark soon. Jason was hunting a man of some importance to his mission: "Parallax" Rapier. Jason's steel-coloured eyes held within them a raging tempest, an unquenchable yearning for something he could not grasp.

A sudden squall whipped at his limbs. The weather was getting worse daily. He activated his tunic, clasping the Camouflage Iapyx Cloak tighter to his chest.

The simulated female voice of his VoiceCom asked, "Which setting?"

"Night," he whispered. The cloak powered up and he vanished ghost-like into the streets. He stood there, unseen by the Veral crowds milling around, and he savoured the smells of the city and watched the neon lights start to flicker above him. The precipitation increased, and Jason began to wait.

He had scoured the streets, alleys and maglevs for Rapier. He was a hard man to find in New Belfast. Rapier was an ex-convict who had served a stint for smuggling TRiDD, the hip new drug that had caught on with the Verals. "Get ready to TRiDD," they used to say. And they did. At first there were thousands of TRiDDers; it soon grew to tens of thousands, and in no time there were millions of them. The TRiDD was the first snow flake you ever tasted. It was that naughty school girl inhaling her first electric cigarette. It was when you were a child, the thrill and exhilaration of the bike ride you had without your stabilisers with your mum and dad looking proudly on. It was the whirl-wind of the fair ground. And the first kiss you dared to dream of. The TRiDD was experience. TIME RELATIVE iMAGINATION DREAM-DISTORTION.

Rapier was no longer inked, which made him inconveniently difficult to find. He had illegally removed his sentient skin tattoos. DigiDerms® were much more than a communication device — utilising biotechnology, the sentient skin tattoos were used to relay information. Implants in the optic nerve allowed the user's actions and vision to be monitored and recorded — the ultimate surveillance tool.

Almost everyone in New Belfast was inked. When citizens reached the age of twenty-one, personal communicators were implanted within their wrists so that they could be monitored and controlled by the masters of the state, the Echelons. New Belfast was a police state. The Verals were the underclass, controled by the E.E.C.H.O. men: Ectoplasmic Entropic Chronological Holistic Order. To keep order, the Echomen employed Harvester machines.

Verals would not have been able to afford the cost of maintaining DigiDerms® tattoos. In order to obtain tattoos, they would have opted for subsidised ones that would morph into the latest advertisements.

Scars lined the inside of Rapier's forearms where the DigiDerms® had been. The pain had been worth it, in his mind, so that he could remain anonymous and untraceable. He had his reasons.

Looking at the streets of New Belfast, the shifting faces resembled multi-coloured artworks of human chameleons. Jason spotted his quarry among the crowd of faces in the rain. Under his tunic, Jason's hand moved instinctively to his sidearm, a paralysis gun. His thumb flicked off the safety. *Be safe. Be ready. Just in case.*

He turned off his cloak.

"Hey, Rapier!" Jason called out. "We need to talk!"

Seeing Jason, Rapier hissed in anger. He tensed his muscles.

"Leave me alone, Zephyr!" He rushed deeper into the seething crowds and started to run. Jason ran after him, his fist tightening around his paralysis gun. Rapier always carried a blade, his weapon of choice. Zephyr had to be careful. His stomach knotted. From his past association with Rapier, Jason knew that he was deadly with a knife. He had a reputation for sleekness and ruthlessness. Rapier would show no mercy to his foes.

They raced up through the Speed Tubes, a matrix of public transport cylinders that criss-crossed the city skyline for fast personal transit through the metro area, and downwards into the rain-slicked streets and dirty alleyways. Jason was able to keep up with Rapier, and never lost sight of him, but there were too many Verals in the way for him to get a clear shot.

He continued his pursuit, trying to get closer to Rapier. They entered the ancient part of the city surface, long abandoned and forgotten below the lattice of Speed Tubes. Rapier sprinted past a statue of a long-dead monarch. The queen's head, now unrecognizable, had been removed and lay discarded among the rubble at her feet. Where her head had been, there now was a human skull in its place. The skull was ordained with a scarf and a placard around its neck, reading, "Our Queenie!"

Rapier ducked around the statue before Jason could take aim, and he darted into the ruins of a once opulent hall. Centuries before, the hall had been used as a seat of some primitive government. A tattered remnant of their flag still hung. Inside they found themselves amongst a Veral rave, a sickening orgy of perversion. Insane, deafening sex-music with strobing lights and writhing bodies frantically and wildly fucking. Rapier glanced back at his pursuer as he pushed through the revellers. He lost his footing as he slipped in a puddle of puke. Jason leapt on Rapier, and took him down in a tumble.

Engrossed in their TRiDD-fueled sexual abandon, the Verals ignored Jason and Rapier as their DigiDerms® burned in a cascade of colours, the darkest kaleidoscope of sinister moths that flew upon their faces. Each orgasm was interrupted with an advert for the latest song implant or Phlood[2].

Rapier recovered first, turning around and slashing indiscriminately with his blade. A woman Veral screamed as Rapier's knife sliced her carotid artery, sending a waterfall of blood gushing forth. The flying droplets of blood looked like sparkling rubies when illuminated by the strobe lights. Her blood soaked the bodies of the Verals nearest to her — their faces, breasts, torsos, and limbs all smeared and absorbing her life force. The thumping of the music and the flashing of the coloured lights made them oblivious to the conflict among them, and unaware of her demise. She collapsed in a heap with her body still trembling, and the orgy continued unabated. The Verals

[2] Phlood is plankton-based food substance that is a staple in the diet of the New Belfast citizenry.

and their music continued pounding, and the woman's body was lost in a tangle of limbs. Above the cacophony, someone shouted, "Hey! More of that crazy lube!"

"Time to end this!" Rapier said, pushing aside a huddle of Verals and making space between him and his adversary. He had a vicious, predatory look upon his face. "Just like old times, eh, Jason? Back on Gamma Ras?"

"I don't want to fight you, Rapier. I need you for a mission. We were friends once, damn it, in the Legion of Viri Terram. Join me once more, Parallax!"

Rapier lunged again with his knife. "You scum! Never utter that name again!" he spat at Jason. "Not after what happened between us on that world. The Kalibads were upon us. My ZEO-suit failed, and you did nothing! And now you want me to join you on a mission? Never!"

Jason parried the thrust with the barrel of his gun, and drove the handle grip into the underarm of Rapier, giving Jason time and leverage to activate his cloak.

"Damn you, Zephyr! Show yourself!" yelled Rapier madly and a trail of saliva hurled from his mouth. He looked around, slashing widely with his knife.

The shockwave from a close proximity explosion threw many Verals to the ground. Part of a wall erupted into the hall with a searing ball of flame, throwing a cloud of dust and chunks of masonry into the throng. The music and the lights simultaneously ceased, and a screaming, clamouring panic began.

Verals who were still able to get onto their feet started running in a chaotic scramble in all directions. They all knew what was happening.

"Harvesters! Run!"

The Harvesters were terrifying machines used to corral and capture Verals. They resembled flying water beetles, with an impenetrable exterior shell and a single set of wings. Each was the size of an armoured tank, and hovered just overhead. They were fast and nimble, but could also transform themselves by extending their bodies and unfolding a second set of wings for larger transport missions. Their insectile appearance led many to believe they were not really machines, but hideous creations of The Echelon's genetic manipulation vats.

A line of five Harvesters floated and hummed through the hole in the wall, then moved into formation to surround and trap the Verals in the centre of the floor.

In the chaos, Jason seized his chance. He shot Rapier point-blank between the eyes with his paralysis gun. Rapier fell, unconscious. His body twitched, his eyes rolled back. Jason grabbed Rapier by the boots and dragged him behind a pillar and away from the Harvesters.

As the Harvesters tightened their circle, they began excreting suspended-animation plastic that enveloped the screaming, pleading Verals. Jason watched in disgust as the Harvesters finally began pulling and swallowing their prey. The Verals twisted and writhed, but it was no use. The foison would be completed soon.

Jason turned off his Camouflage Cloak and looked down at Rapier.

"Yes, my old friend," Jason said with an unfamiliar sound of regret in his voice. "It is time. But we are not finished yet; we have only just started." He put his gun into its holster.

The Harvesters were busy reaping and processing in the middle of the hall. He began to hoist Rapier onto his shoulders, being careful not to attract their attention.

An Echoman stepped out of the shadows.

"Who are you?" he demanded. "You are in the wrong place for a non-Veral."

Jason let Rapier slump back to the ground, then turned and levelled a stare at the Echoman.

"Identify yourself to me," the Echoman said. He glanced at Rapier, then returned his gaze to Jason. "And who is that man?"

Jason slowly rolled his sleeve up to his elbow then turned his inner arm up, facing the Echoman.

"Scan me.

Jason's right arm had a single tattoo. It was a gold infinity symbol, wrapped around a double helix. The Echoman scanned Jason with his bio-optics. His eyes trailed from the tattoo up to Jason's eyes. He blinked and swallowed hard.

"Oh, I'm sorry, sir. I did not realise…" the Echo man said in awe, his voice trailing off. "And what about your captive? Can you vouch for him? He killed a Veral. You know the law, Captain."

"Yes," Jason replied. "I know the law. Believe me, he will receive punishment."

*　　*　　*

Rapier woke in a bunk against the wall in a cell. It had a circular ceiling light shining brightly into his face, the heat of it penetrating his pounding skull. The smell of disinfectant pervaded his nostrils. As his senses returned, he felt a slight chill all over. He looked down at his body and found that he was naked.

"Where…" he mumbled, trying to piece together in his mind what had happened.

He was still stunned and disoriented from the effects of the paralysis gun. He flopped off the bunk and stumbled around the cell. He found a toilet.

"That'll do…" he said before wrenching his guts into it. He rubbed the back of his head with his hand. *Strange.* Someone had shaved his black hair off.

"Zephyr!" he cursed loudly enough to make his head pound even harder than before.

That bastard.

Now it was coming back to him: Zephyr appearing out of nowhere, then the chase and the Veral rave. Then the damned Harvesters had arrived just as Jason hit him with the searing pain of the paralysis gun.

He whirled about in a rage, and began banging on the hatch in the cell door. He screamed at it, "What is this place? Where? Jason! Answer me!"

The hatch opened, and a hose appeared through the orifice.

Rapier threw himself to the corner of the cell, instinctively curling himself into a foetal position, wrapping his arms in front of his face. The hose blasted with a jet of icy cold water. As suddenly the hose appeared it withdrew from the hatch. The circular light in the ceiling clicked off and the cell went dark. In the pitch black, Rapier tried to get his bearings from his memory of his surroundings from before the lights were extinguished. Crawling, he tried to make his way toward the bed, and he banged his head against the toilet. He cursed again, then found the bed and collapsed on to it, shivering. He pulled the thin, rough blanket over himself.

Time passed. Deprived of sensory input, he had no sense of continuity. How long had it been? It could have been a week or more, he was unsure. The circular ceiling light flickered on again. Through a lower hatch in the cell door a Phlood meal on a plastic plate skidded into the room. Rapier regarded it with suspicion.

"You must eat," said a voice from the cell's intercom system.

"Is that you, Jason?" Rapier said with growing anger in his voice.

"Eat," the voice repeated.

Rapier rose from his bunk bed. And walked toward the door to retrieve the meal. He sat crossed legged on the edge of the bed to eat the Phlood. Suddenly the hose reappeared at the hatch and sprayed him with cold water.

"You bastards!" he yelled fiercely as he attempted to deflect the torrent away from his face with the plate. The plate was blown from his grip and bounced into a corner of his cell. The persistent force of the water pushed Rapier to the opposite corner, next to the toilet. The deluge ceased. The voice on the intercom laughed. The light went out again.

Rapier's teeth chattered as he lay down on his bed again and curled himself up into a ball. Eventually, he slept.

The cell door opened and a male figure stepped in from the darkness. A bloom of light shone from behind him. Rapier's eyes began adjusting to the light as the man stepped closer. It was Jason.

"Get cleaned and dressed, Rapier. We have a job to do."

"What makes you think I want to work with you, Jason?" Rapier said hoarsely.

"Look in the mirror."

A small polished steel mirror was bolted to the wall next to the toilet. Rapier looked. There was an Eye of Horus tattoo on his forehead.

"I control that," Jason said.

"Why you son of a bitch! I will kill you!" Rapier lunged toward him, as Jason calmly touched the tattoo on his own right arm. It glowed an orange colour and a sudden a searing pain pulsated within Rapier's third eye. He instantly collapsed in a crumple, in sheer agony.

"I take no pleasure in doing this," said Jason. He bent down on one knee in front of Rapier's face. He touched his tattoo again to turn off the signal.

"What you have just experienced is the Cranial Compliance Motivator. It has three intensity levels, and that was level one. Level three will most probably kill you. I cannot change what happened to us. Our friendship died on Gamma Ras, and maybe I should have left you to die there, too."

Rapier opened his bloodshot eyes; they seethed with anger and hatred, but he said nothing.

Jason continued, "You killed a Veral back in the New Belfast TRiDD rave, and you know the consequences for that. But I need you for my mission. Unlike you, I am not a sociopath or a sadist who enjoys killing, but if you give me a reason to, I will end your life. So, let's just get on with the job together and we can both get out alive."

"You say that! Was that your voice on the intercom?" Rapier sneered, his mouth twisted in contempt.

"I don't know what you are talking about, Rapier. I just arrived here. The Echelon council wanted to immediately execute you for killing that Veral, and then recycle your remains." Jason stood up. "I persuaded them otherwise. I have bought you a second chance, Rapier, but you are going to earn it. The Cranial Compliance Motivator tattoo was a condition of your parole. I had it synched with my own yesterday. Oh, and it was the Echoes who shaved your hair off — I had nothing to do with that."

"How long have I been here?" Rapier asked as he climbed to his feet.

"You have been in and out of consciousness for two days, Rapier. You are coming off the TRiDD. Your body is adjusting, which is why you have been feeling the effects of withdrawal, and almost certainly hallucinating."

Rapier shook his head in disbelief. He thought about the hose and the plate and the sensory deprivation — could it all have been a part of this twisted nightmare he was living in? He looked around the cell, and returned to his stare to Zephyr. The drug was poison, and a deadly telegnosis. He suddenly felt a pang of remorse for what he had done to the woman at the rave. He was not an animal.

He straightened his head and composed himself. "Where are we? What's the job?"

"We are in the shipyard, underground. It's safe here," said Jason. "The 'job,' as you say, is to find The Pillar."

Rapier held Jason's forearm tightly, "The Pillar of Fyre, you mean? You are mad."

Jason looked down to where Rapier's hand had grasped his arm. He gave a short, sharp tug to pull his arm free.

"We will see." Jason turned and headed out toward the cell door. "Get dressed. You'll find crew uniforms in the locker room."

Rapier was taken to the locker room where he donned his standard Ascensionaut uniform. It was a gunmetal jumpsuit that had gold buttons lining the rims with tiny stars, and sleek boots that were stiff to put on. The suit smelled of old wars, time and fire. It felt good upon his skin. He pulled the zip to his chin.

They took the maglev to the ship.

The sea was a tumult of storms in the poison ocean. The gales were increasing in ferocity.

In ancient times, the New Belfast dockyard had served a forgotten empire, long before the oceangoing ships were replaced by starships. The shipyard of Wolfburn & Hart was a majestic, monstrous, factory — but it was dwarfed in comparison to the ship that was berthed alongside.

The Ascension was like a gigantic steel god that towered upright in the sky. It was truly a titanic craft. The Ascension's engines were powering up, producing a thunderous crescendo that reverberated in the air. It was deafening.

Rapier and Jason exited the maglev. They covered their ears from the noise, and crossed the gangway to the ship. They stepped across the airlock. Jason walked in first. A horizontal sliver of red light shone up and down his face.

"Tattoo scan verified. Welcome aboard, Captain Zephyr," a synthetic female voice said.

"Thank you, Athena," Jason replied. "Prepare the rest of the crew. Engage artificial gravity when we are suborbital, and make ready the Icarus drive at my command. We will be under away shortly. Has the cargo arrived, and the ordnance?"

"Affirmative, Captain."

"Relay the cargo to my quarters — use the servo-drones to help move it — and send the ordnance to the armoury."

Rapier entered the airlock and the facial scanner analysed his identity. Las-guns emplacements whirled and and unfolded from the walls and fixed their aim on Rapier's face. "Warning: Horus Eye tattoo detected! A prisoner is attempting to board the ship! Prepare for oblivion!"

"Stand down Athena!" Jason barked quickly. "This is Rapier. He is under my authority. Grant him authorization to board the ship, and assign him the rank of Commander. Acknowledge."

"Acknowledged, Captain. Commander Rapier granted authorization to board." Athena disengaged the las-guns, and stiffly greeted Rapier. "Welcome aboard, Commander."

"Captain," continued Athena, "the rest of the crew will not be pleased to learn there is a Horus aboard."

"Leave that to me," Jason said dismissively. He was distracted by some of the data on the ship's console. "Athena, why is…?"

Athena interrupted, already knowing his question. "Yes, Captain. As you can see, I have encountered some difficulties with the scanning calibrations. I may have to reinitialise the ship's systems when we enter Weave Space."

Jason smiled at her. He knew Athena wouldn't miss a detail. "Take all the resources you require."

Rapier caught up with Jason as they walked toward the bridge. Jason continued making cursory inspections of data screens and gauges as they went.

"Why did you make me a commander, Jason? After all I have done?"

Jason ignored him.

"We are here."

Déjà vu, thought Rapier. *I feel like I have had this conversation before with Jason. But when?* He shook his head. *Must be a side-effect of the TRiDD detox.*

Athena opened the bridge doors just as Jason and Rapier arrived.

Athena was a fully sentient artificial intelligence that was at the centre of all components of the ship. She controlled the engines, the ship's navigation, the life support systems, and the false gravity generators. Her neural core was integrated with every system on the ship and through them she controlled all functions. Every servo, every sensor, and every bit of data that moved within the ship was known to her and was controlled by her — nothing was out of her reach. Athena had no physical presence; she would project a holographic representation of her chosen physical form, which she would use to interact with the captain and crew. Athena almost always chose to appear in the form of a barn owl, with snowy white feathers and dark piercing eyes. She moved with beauty and grace.

As Jason and Rapier entered, the bridge officers turned to greet them. Athena flew across the bridge and landed on Jason's shoulder. Officers Priory, Driscoll, Alexander, and Lot stood at attention in their Ascensionaut uniforms.

"Gentlemen," Jason nodded to them, "let me skip the usual pleasantries and go straight to the mission at hand. I will be brief. In approximately one month from now the Sun will collapse and go nova."

There was a heavy silence between the crew members. They exchanged stunned looks with each other, and with Jason.

Alexander, the armoury officer, was the first to reply. "How, sir? The Sol system contains a G-Type star, which is no more than half way through its life. All stellar calculations predict at least five billion years remaining. Besides, the Sun itself does not have enough mass to go nova!"

"Echelon scientists have discovered that the Sun is running out of nuclear fuel — we don't yet know how, or why, but it is a certain fact. As the Sun's mass continues to flow back into its core, it is creating conditions where it will soon be unable to withstand its own gravitational force. When that happens, approximately one month from now, the core will collapse, triggering the supernova that will wipe out all life here."

Athena preened herself, briefly.

Jason paused for a second before revealing the even more shocking detail. "There are some within the Echelon that suspect an unknown external agency has initiated and is controlling this chain reaction — increasing the mass of the interior, some pan-dimensional force, or a god, perhaps."

"They think a 'god' is doing this?" Priory, the science officer, scoffed. "I thought we destroyed all the gods at the Battle of Gilgamesh."

The gods had been placed on trial for crimes committed in their various names. The Echelon United Galactic Council had found that the gods had done nothing to justify their existence, and had been directly or indirectly responsible for many bloody wars throughout human and extra-human history. The council further found that billions of non-god entities had been blindly indoctrinated into corrupted religious factions. The Echelon ruled by decree that all gods should be executed or exiled into the HADES parallel hell dimension. To serve the council's judgment, god-killer machines were created and given to the Terram warriors. The vast and terrible god-killer machines gave their pilots superhuman capabilities and strength. They were equipped with Subsonic Shields and zero gravity exoskeletons known as a ZEO suit. They were also armed with Power Scimitars, ultra-high-frequency oscillating swords that could cleave a god. Each god resonated at a unique frequency in the current dimensional plane; matching these frequencies to the power scimitars, the warriors of Terram were then able to track and vanquished the gods. In the final clash, thirty million warriors perished on the battlefield at Gilgamesh on the planet Gamma Ras Algethi. A faction of gods supporters named the Kalibads fought against the legions of Viri Terram.

"Never underestimate a god, Priory," said Driscoll, The Ascension's communication officer.

Priory said to Jason, "What are this god's powers? And designation?"

"Unknown. However, I have a suspicion that it could be an ancient Babylonian deity."

"What is our objective, Jason?" asked Lot, quietly. Lot was the co-pilot of The Ascension. He was a bald-headed mutant-augumental from the Lisburn wastes. He had strange pink eyes that gave him limited clairvoyance in weave-space. A god had once visited Lisburn in the late 21st century. The city had always been a vice den filled with filthy, corrupt politicians. The god had judged Lisburn and found it wanting. It had wrought terrible retribution to the inhabitants and left it an irradiated wasteland.

"Athena, put the Algol star chart on the holograph," Jason said.

"Yes, captain," she replied as she flew from Jason's shoulder and alighted on the console at the centre of the room. "Displaying the system now."

The crew stepped into the middle of the bridge, and surrounded the projected display.

"Our mission is to retrieve the Pillar of Fyre from the planet Beta Persei Delta which — you all know — is the fourth planet in orbit around the Algol binary star system. Our scientists have theorised that when the Pillar is activated it will stabilise our Sun by using graviton-quantum technology to adjust the subatomic fusion within the solar interior. An ancient alien race, the Behenian, has developed this advanced technology. One thing we know about the Behenian is that they can alter their physical appearance at a genetic level, similar to our own Iapyx camouflage devices. Little else is known about their culture or society. Needless to say, we must be cautious. We are to retrieve the pillar at any cost, and by any means necessary, and bring it back to Earth."

"What the captain is saying is that we are to *steal* this device," Rapier interjected. He had been quiet since he arrived with Jason on the bridge.

"By any cost," Jason reiterated. "Gentlemen, meet my new commander, Rapier."

All the crew members acknowledged and shot Rapier a wary stare, except for Lot, who smiled grimly.

"Take your stations," Jason ordered. "Lot, prepare us for Icarus. Take the helm, Rapier."

Rapier sat alongside Lot. They checked the systems and prepared the ship for departure.

"So, you are Rapier, eh? Welcome aboard our ship of the damned."

"Why do you say that?" Rapier studied Lot in a gestaltist flicker. Lot had a tattoo of an old Rembrandt painting that covered his shoulder and arm. The whole crucifixion scene was animated; Rapier watched in awe as the Roman soldiers thrusted a spear into the flesh of the ancient God.

"We are all damned on this ship," Lot explained. "Take a look around you: Driscoll drinks alcohol heavily and blasphemes; Alexander is a compulsive neurotic; and

Priory is a gambling deviant. And our captain… he is the most damned of us all."

Rapier looked across to the captain.

"You are from the Lisburn wastelands, are you not? I have seen the devastation that afflicts that place. There is much suffering still. It is an evil, wicked place; a real hell on Earth."

"There is no such thing as hell, commander Rapier. There is only the hell that resides inside our own minds." Lot touched his forehead.

"And yet you still believe in a God? After all he did to your people?"

Lot nodded.

"Oh yes. But the Universe is my God now. And this…" he gestured to the view screen that showed the chaos and the ongoing self-destruction in New Belfast below. "This is my promised land… my purgatory… and my Gilead!"

"Captain," Lot said, breaking from his conversation with Rapier. "Our preflight checks are completed and confirmed. We are ready to sew the camel through the eye of the universe."

He closed his strange, pink eyes. Rapier could see Lot's eyes twitching beneath his eyelids, as a dreamer in sleep. In an almost inaudible whisper, he said, "With men this is impossible; but with the Universe all things are possible." With a subtle gesture toward the holographic controls, he switched the view screen away from New Belfast and upwards to the clouds that soon parted to reveal the stars.

Lot was also an aficionado of late 1980s prog rock. He tapped his tattoo to access his play list and selected *The Final Countdown* by the heavy metal group, *Europe*. The song boomed within the bridge as the ship began accelerating:

We're heading for Algol (Algol)
And still we stand tall,
It's the final countdown!

Lot had taken some creative liberties with the original lyrics; copyright be damned. He had replaced *Venus* with *Algol*, and enthusiastically banged his head to the rhythm.

The ship rumbled higher into the atmosphere. The New Belfast spaceport was receding fast. The mighty behemoth rose from its earthly shackles and into orbit!

"Take us out of earth circumgyration — Icarus weave eight." Jason said.

"As it is written, so shall it be!" extolled Lot in a loud and zealous voice.

Lot diverted power to the weave-space engines. They roared to life and with incomprehensible acceleration pushed the ship to mind-bending speed. The universe unfolded in the wake of The Ascension, shearing and weaving through the time-slip between the stars.

Even if there was no such concept of hell, Rapier had considered, there was still certainly a master of hells — a Mephistopheles — here on the ship. He looked at Jason who was sitting in his command chair with Athena at his left hand. Her dark eyes scrutinized Rapier.

* * *

The Algol system was ninety-three light years from Earth. Traveling at Icarus weave eight, the journey would take them approximately ten days.

On the fifth day of their journey, Athena woke the captain from his scheduled sleep cycle. As soon as Jason awoke, he knew there was a problem. He could feel a faint shimmering vibration throughout the entire ship.

"Captain, I apologize for disturbing your sleep cycle, but diagnostics indicate an anomaly in my core. We are currently passing through a large gaseous nebula with an unusual radiation signature. It is somehow affecting many of my systems in unpredictable ways."

"What do you recommend, Athena," the worried captain replied. Even with reduced function, he still trusted Athena's judgment.

"I recommend shutting down certain core functions until we pass fully through the nebula. I will retain conscious and operational at all times, but some systems will be unavailable during the regeneration process."

"That sounds... serious, Athena."

"Don't worry, captain. I won't feel a thing," she smiled.

"How long will the regeneration process take?" Jason asked. Athena's systems were constructed as a bio-mechanical hybrid — she was, in a sense, alive and self aware.

"I will enter a system safe mode, captain, for two days. The ship's functions will be limited during that time." She hid her face under her wing.

Jason was concerned. They had passed through many nebulae before on their travels across interstellar space, but never had they encountered this type of interference.

During long travels, the crew slept in shifts. The captain left his quarters and headed to the bridge. Lot was currently on duty.

"Lot, this nebula is exhibiting some strange radiation characteristics that are impacting Athena. Plot the shortest route out of it, and manually reprogram the navigation. Athena will be unable to assist."

"Aye, captain," Lot replied. "'I see thy glory like a shooting star, fall to the base earth from the firmament.'"

"Still quoting dead poets, Lot?"

Lot smiled.

Jason returned to his quarters on the Alpha deck and closed the tall diamonmetal doors behind him. No other crew were permitted into this section of the ship. Half the crew slept while the remainder either studied or convened in the galley to pass the time.

After applying the new navigation parameters, Lot left the bridge and headed to the galley where some of the other crew members were relaxing. He served himself a portion of Phlood.

Rapier sat at the captain's table, reading a vidbook; the words on the pages were animated and moved across the surface at the reader's reading pace and dynamically altered its content according to the readers preferences and interests. Jason remained in his cabin, conferring with Athena.

The ship's clock indicated it was Earth evening time. To maintain the crew's circadian rhythm in space, the ship's clock kept Earth time, and the crew woke, ate, and slept in 24-hour cycles. The lighting within the galley adapted to simulate Earth daylight. It was illuminated in soft, relaxing, evening hues.

Driscoll rose from his seat in a drunken swagger, and walked to where Lot was seated.

"Hey, pinky. I don't like you," Driscoll said, slurring his words. "In fact, I've never liked you. I don't like the way you mutter to that God of yours. And I don't like the way you smell. You smell like… what is it? Yes, a pig. You smell like a pig. You remember those?" he laughed. "You even look like a pig, all pink and beady-eyed!"

Lot said nothing and simply continued eating.

Driscoll leered over his plate.

"Pigs were filthy animals, but even they got better food than this plankton shite they call Phlood."

Driscoll made a long, loud snorting noise deep in his throat as he gathered a mouthful of phlegm. He leaned over and let it drip in a long trail onto Lot's meal. With one hand, Driscoll grabbed the back of Lot's bald head — his large hands and long fingers wrapped around Lot's skull from ear to ear — then wrenched his face down into the Phlood.

"Does Piggy like his trough?" he laughed. "Good piggy! There it is! Eat your filthy swill!"

Lot did not have the necessary strength to pull his head up from the plate against the power of Driscoll's strong arms and his enormous hand. Instead, he quickly straightened his legs so that the back of his knees sent his chair toppling backwards. The chair tumbled toward the rest of the crew who leapt to their feet. Lot then kicked forward and buckled the leg of the table. As the table collapsed to the floor, Lot's face came free of the falling plate of Phlood. With lightning reflexes, he caught the edge of the metal food tray before it hit the ground, then whirled it around sideways and connected it with the bridge of Driscoll's nose, splitting it open. Stunned, Driscoll's head ricocheted backwards and his hand reflexively released Lot's head. Before Driscoll's hands could defensively reach his face, Lot spun his fork in the air, caught it, and lashed it with precision at Driscoll's face and deftly gouged out his right eyeball.

The rest of the crew ran forward to intervene and break up the fight. Rapier reached them first. He grabbed Driscoll and restrained him from advancing toward Lot.

"And thine eye shall not pity; but life shall go for life, eye for eye, tooth for tooth, hand for hand, foot for foot!" Lot screamed at Driscoll.

"Oh, you've really done it now, you scrawny little fuck! You're gonna pay for this, piggy!" Driscoll thundered in agony with one hand over his eye-socket.

Alexander joined Rapier in holding Driscoll back, and Priory held Lot who still held the fork with Driscoll's eye pierced on the tines.

"Hold Lot back! Take him to his quarters and confine him there," Rapier commanded to Alexander.

"Let's get him to the GeneRep, quickly!" he said to Priory as they dragged Driscoll with them to the ship's medical deck.

The GeneRep was the genetic replicator and repair facility that could rapidly sequence and reproduce genetic material to heal and restore crew injuries. The facility had become a common installation where war was waged. The medical technologies it provided could quickly regrow broken or missing limbs from remnant tissue samples.

Jason arrived right behind them.

"What the hell happened to Driscoll's face?"

Alexander said, in a dry gulping throat, "Sir, there was a minor… um, disturbance… or, an infraction… well, a fracas, I guess, in the galley."

Jason lifted Driscoll's hand from his face and assessed the injury.

"You call it a 'minor infraction' when a man loses an eye? An essential officer on a critical mission is blinded, and you think it's just a 'fracas,' Mister Alexander?" Jason was furious.

He addressed Driscoll directly. "Have Athena take a tissue sample and then sequence you a new eye. And take a sober pill, damn it. I want you ready at your station before the next shift begins. I need a full crew ready and focused for the Fyre. No more of this fighting, is that understood, Driscoll?"

"Yes, Captain." Driscoll's pain had sobered him. He clutched his eye socket and eased back onto the operating table. Athena hopped onto the table and began preparing the program. The long, spindly robotic arms of the AutoMed bots moved into action. This procedure would clean and dress the wound and extract a fresh tissue sample for the sequencing program.

Athena's head bobbed up and down, examining her patient.

Rapier stepped aside to talk with the captain.

"I saw what happened, Jason. Driscoll was drunk and being an asshole. He provoked Lot, but hadn't anticipated such a sharp response. We placed Lot in his quarters, awaiting your orders."

"Damn him. He could have easily killed Driscoll. Let's go and assess his state of mind," Jason said.

They made their way to Lot's quarters and found him lying on his bunk, cursing to himself and mumbling incoherently. He was shaken with guilt.

"Forgive me, O Creator, for what I have done in thy name! It happened that when the ancient insolent Greeks remained without paddles and oars for their ships! Do not bring the destruction of the human race, now that it feeds on soil and sea salt! 'What is food to one, is to others bitter poison!'"

"Lot, this is Jason, your captain. I am ordering you to accompany us to the bridge."

> *"O Captain! My Captain!*
> *Our fearful trip is done, the ship has weather'd every rack, the prize we sought is won, the port is near, the bells I hear, the people all exulting, where on the deck my Captain lies, fallen cold and dead."*

"We are not dead yet, Lot. Our star needs us. To the bridge, now."

Slowly, Lot raised himself. "She is coming, Jason."

"Who? Who is coming?" Rapier asked.

"She is coming. She is the mother of a god. You will understand when she arrives."

"Why do clairvoyants always speak incoherent mumbo-jumbo? I am sick of this bullshit!" Rapier exclaimed in annoyance, clenching his fists. His patience was wearing thin, and he was starting to understand how Driscoll felt.

Athena sounded an alarm and called to the captain. "Captain, a starship is approaching, inbound on a collision vector. It is transmitting a distress call. What are your orders?"

"All hands!" Jason yelled. "To your posts!" There was a tumult of cries as each man on board hurried to the bridge.

"Priory, run a full scan of that ship. Alexander, ready the shields and the weapons… just in case. Lot, as soon as we're ready, take us out off weave-space," ordered Jason.

"Captain," warned Athena, fluttering her wings in agitation. "I feel that would be an unwise move; taking us out off weave-space prematurely could impair my functions and endanger the ship. My systems regeneration process is not yet complete — we currently stand at ninety-five percent capacity."

"Sir!" interrupted Driscoll, blinking with his new eye. "I have an incoming transmission from the approaching ship. Playing audio now."

The signal was garbled and full of static, but still intelligible. The voice was female.

> *This is the Terram vessel Oriön Ferat. Help me!*
> *My ship has suffered fatal damage to the engines, and life support systems have failed. We were attacked by Kalibad pirates, and I am the only survivor.*
> *My name is Ealasaid. Please, hear my plea!*

"It could be a ruse, Jason." Rapier warned. There had been incidents in the past.

The voice continued pleading for help and was punctuated with sounds of choking coughs.

"Captain, may I remind you of the importance of timeliness on our mission? We cannot afford any delay," Rapier said. The mission to save the Sol star system was paramount.

Jason rubbed the stubble on his chin, silently contemplating his options and making a plan. Pirate activity in this region was unexpected, and a delay would be costly. With Athena repairing herself for two days it would leave only short time to reach Algol — three days. He shut his eyes, took a breath, and made his decision. When he opened his eyes, his decision had been made. He stood up from his command chair and looked to Rapier.

Jason commanded his ship and crew with ruthless efficiency.

"Very well. Initialize the de-acceleration procedures, and take us out of the weave."

"Nuke the ship."

Lot shot a wary look to Jason.

"Mister Alexander, ready the nuclear torpedoes," Rapier adjured.

Before Alexander locked the target, a fierce explosion suddenly ripped through the Oriön Ferat, sending a shockwave through space. The Ascension was within the blast radius, and the whole ship reverberated and shook as debris impacted and deflected off the ship's shields.

"What in Hades just happened?" Jason shouted, gripping his command chair for support.

"Captain, it looks like the Oriön Ferat has suffered a complete reactor explosion. The vessel is nothing but dust now. The only thing that could cause such a destructive detonation would be a compromised Icarus drive," Priory informed the captain.

"Scan the area, Athena" Jason whispered.

"I am attempting a full proximity scan, captain," said Athena, "but earlier damage to my scanning bio-ware has limited my frequencies and range. However…" she paused.

"Captain, I am detecting a single life-pod that ejected from the Oriön Ferat seconds before it was destroyed."

All the crew members stared at Jason.

"Bring it on board, Athena." Jason sighed heavily.

"Rapier, follow me to the airlock. We should meet and greet our new guest. Athena, as soon as Ealasaid steps aboard, I want a full genetic profile. Prepare the GeneRep — she may have sustained injuries that will need medical attention."

Jason and Rapier raced to the airlock where the tractor beam had pulled the life-pod aboard. Athena's hologram flew gracefully behind them while she engaged the necessary systems to execute a bio-scan.

Athena landed on Jason's shoulder as he and Rapier stood and observed the automatic airlock receiving the capsule. The outer airlock door closed behind it and the air compression system equalized the environment and ran a decontamination routine. Simultaneously, the bio-scan beams penetrated the small craft and analyzed the passenger within. Finally, the inner airlock door opened and the small vessel was pulled into the receiving bay.

"Captain, the bio-scan has completed, and has confirmed that the survivor is… human. She is exhibiting some injuries and burns sustained before she entered the pod. The injuries are not life-threatening, but could become serious if left untreated. As a precaution, the life-pod has temporarily placed her into an induced coma."

"She's lucky we passed by when we did," Rapier said. "If not for our encounter, she could have drifted for weeks or years before being picked up by another vessel."

"Well, wake her up," Jason said. "I want to speak to her."

The repair systems clicked and whirred to unseal the life-pod. The lid lifted slowly as the support systems brought the passenger out of coma state. The interior of the pod resembled a cocoon that wrapped closely and protectively around its charge. After a moment, her eyes opened and she slowly emerged from the casket, standing then in front of Jason, Rapier, and Athena. Ealasaid was a young woman with flowing golden thick hair that fell down to her thighs and across her small breasts. Her eyes were of an auriferous hue, and her skin was a glorious light bronze colour. Her nose and mouth were petite. She was tall, statuesque with defined muscles that rippled under her skin. She had a small tattoo of a silver ankh on her left shoulder.

Jason was rapt. He thought she looked like a warrior, but he could not recognize her caste. She looked familiar to him, as if she was a former lover. He was aroused by her naked form. She was perfection.

Ealasaid took a step forward, and stumbled into Jason's arms. She stared longly up into his eyes as he held her.

"What happened? What is this place? Where is my crew?" she uttered quietly.

"You are on the Viri Terram starship, *The Ascension.* I am Captain Jason Zephyr. I'm sorry to have to tell you that your ship is gone — a reactor explosion destroyed it. Seconds after you ejected." He gently caressed her hair; it was soft and perfumed. "You are safe now."

"This is my commander, Rapier," Jason said by way of introduction, then added, "And this is Athena, the ship's artificial intelligence."

She turned and gazed towards Rapier. Ealasaid's lips seemed fuller to him. Her eyes darkened subtly when she saw the Horus tattoo on Rapier's forehead. Her bronze skin lightened almost imperceptibly. She shivered. For the second time on this voyage, Rapier was struck by a feeling of recognition, and déjà vu.

"Rapier, sequence a uniform for our guest." The sequencer portals, in addition to rapidly reconstructing human limbs and organs, could also be used to sequence pre-programmed non-biological objects from base elements.

From a portal in the GeneRep room he sequenced a tunic. The portals were stations on the ship wherein Athena could create objects, foodstuffs and other apparel.

"I am cold, and hungry."

Rapier handed the tunic to Jason, and he draped it over Ealasaid's shoulders. She dressed herself slowly as Jason and Rapier turned their backs and fought the urge to steal a glimpse of the beautiful creature behind them.

"Rapier will assign you quarters, and will get you a meal. I am needed on the bridge. We will talk about your ship later whenever you are sufficiently rested."

"Thank you, Captain," she said gratefully.

The captain departed, and Rapier escorted Ealasaid through the corridors of the ship, toward her assigned quarters. He attempted to strike up a conversation.

"Your tattoo is beautiful, the ankh on your shoulder. It shows great craftsmanship. Where was it done?"

Ealasaid didn't answer his question. Instead, she glared at Rapier. "You killed me; you butchered me!" She touched the tattoo on her shoulder. The ankh tattoo strobed hypnotically.

"Murderer!" she hissed at him.

Rapier collapsed to the floor, writhing in agony. *How can this be?* he thought. This cannot be real. His tattoo was burning on his forehead, in an intensity of excruciation.

Ealasaid's features softened and warped, and within seconds she had changed into the form of the woman from the rave in New Belfast.

"You are having a TRiDD withdrawal hallucination, Rapier," Ealasaid whispered softly in his ear. "You will not remember this conversation. I have reprogrammed your tattoo. You will obey my orders now, and when the time comes… you will kill Jason."

"What are you?" Rapier choked.

She smirked as her visage returned to the alluring and elegant young Ealasaid.

"Oh, mister Rapier! Are you all right? Did you lose your balance?" she said in feign concern.

Dazed, Rapier returned the grin.

"Yes, Ealasaid. How careless of me. I will be fine. Here are your quarters. Rest well."

"I am sure I will. Thank you, Mister Rapier. You have been very helpful."

When Rapier turned away from her cabin his smile waned.

On the bridge it was time to set the night-watch. Jason was there. The other crew members had retired to their own cabins. Jason was staring out into the blackness of weave-space. He had his back to Rapier as he entered the bridge. The lights were dim on the deck.

"An interesting woman, Rapier, wouldn't you agree?" He turned around to see into the eyes of his comrade, examining him.

"Yes, Jason. She reminded me somehow of… well, of an old flame."

Jason laughed. "Don't get too close to old infernos. Be cautious. They will burn you."

"How is our ship? Are you fully regenerated yet, Athena?" Rapier asked.

"Regeneration status is currently at ninety-nine percent, Commander Rapier. I have now re-engaged the Icarus drive and we are accelerating. Time to Algol: twenty-four hours."

"Excellent," Jason said. "I will be in my quarters, Mister Rapier. You have the night-watch."

*　*　*

In Alexander's room there was a holo-photo of his sister, Joanne, beside his bunk. They had been twins. Joanne had died in action when she led a charge on a Kalibad position on Gamma Ras. She had been a brave and fearless warrior. She was tall, with raven black hair and grey eyes that smiled mischievously. Alexander always thought about his sister whenever he was going into a combat zone.

"Good night, Josie," he said, using her childhood nickname. He kissed his fingers and blew on them at her image and turned her off.

"Lights out," he said, and the room fell dark.

He settled into his bunk, remembering the good times they had shared together. He smiled in the darkness. "Josie, I miss you." He mouthed the words like an invocation.

As he drifted toward the edge of sleep, he felt something lightly touch his shoulder, then heard a giggling, playful laughter.

"Lights on!" Alexander said, almost leaping out of his bed, startled and fully awake.

Lying beside him was his sister. She was propped up on her elbow by his pillow and staring intently at him. She was grinning.

"Oh, Alex! Do calm down."

He tried to speak, but she gently placed her fingers over his mouth.

"Hush!" she laughed. "The expression on your face! My gods, if only I had a vid record! I'd swear that you've just seen a bloody bodach!" She laughed again. Alexander remembered her laugh, and missed it greatly.

"I haven't much time here," she continued. "I know what you are do*ing*!" She lilted and emphasised her voice at the end of every word that ended in *ing*. It was a habit of hers.

"Don't let Jason kill me. Don't let him kill us. I am begg*ing* you!"

Alexander pushed her away.

"Josie, what are you saying? I don't understand you."

"Please, Alex. Trust me. You will understand soon. Don't think about it now. Just be ready when the time comes."

The tattoo on her shoulder glowed.

"Sleep, my sweet little brother."

Alexander slept.

*   *   *

Lot could not rest. His own room was a shrine to all things antiquity, with a Leonardo da Vinci holo-mural depicting all his master works. Lot loved renaissance art.

Before he slept, he prayed to his God. Closing his weird eyes and clasping his hands he bowed his head in obsecration. A strange light source emanated from his quiet, still room. Lot opened his eyes slowly.

Standing before him in a translucent, glorious, and shimmering white light stood the Mother of a God. She was the mother of *his* God. A fire burned in his retinas. He fell back to the wall, shielding his face against. An aurora of incredible illumination warmed and soothed him and made him feel safe. He felt at peace.

"It cannot be you! You are heresy, a demon sent from Hades to tempt me!"

A voice echoed in Lot's ears, "I am Rhea. I am Nefertiti. I am the virgin maiden. By the salt, and by the fire, and by Al-Lāt who is the greatest of all. You will kneel before me!"

Lot bowed and knelt.

The voice continued, "The time grows short. Soon, *He* will come in all his glory. *He* will demand a sacrifice of blood. Your two crew members, the ones you call Driscoll and Priory, must be part of his hecatomb. You will assist me in subduing the artificial intelligence entity you call Athena. You shall be well rewarded for your faith and obedience. You will be granted a place in eternal glory. That is my gift and my promise to you, Lot."

"What you ask of me… will not be easy. The Captain retains most of his codes and passwords for his computer. There are only certain areas I can access. But… perhaps I can apply a Trojan horse to introduce a specially crafted bio-virus."

"Look at me, Lot," she said while beaming a beatific smile at him.

Lot looked slowly up and into her eyes. His objections and his questions melted away as she stared deeply into his soul. Lot relaxed, and his resistance fell away.

"Will there be…" his voice faltered, "Will there be a sign?" He bent down again in shame, feeling insignificant and unworthy.

"His herald will be with you soon. You will know when the time arrives."

Lot raised his head, cautiously and in fear of her light. But his room was darkened save the glow from his holo-mural of *The Last Supper*.

"So it shall be written; so it shall be done," he whispered to the scene.

He took to thinking about Priory and Driscoll.

Priory was an incorrigible gambler, and his mother was a morbidly obese woman. He hated her, and she equally despised him, so he felt no pang of guilt or remorse when he gambled her life in a game of Death Poker, unbeknownst to her.

He had lost the bet, and the game's organizer, a Cyber Shaykh, promptly sought to collect the debt. Priory's mother was to be taken and summarily executed, as required by the standard rules of the game. But Priory saw an opportunity to make back some of his losses.

Resources were stretched across the Galactic Empire, making fresh meat a rare delicacy in some of the remote colony worlds, and cannibalism was rampant and a profitable business.

Priory told his mother she had won a ticket for a stellar cruise to Pluto, and then negotiated a deal so that the Cyber Shaykh could keep his mother's body for use in his abattoir on Charon. The Cyber Shaykh accepted, and Priory never saw his mother, Veragina, again.

Lot judged Priory and Driscoll to be the worst kind of sinners. He would enjoy ending their miserable existences.

Lot stood and approached the sequencer portal in his room. He evoked a harvest gala from a long time ago in his native Lisburn. From the data, he sequenced a small, one-handed scythe known as a sickle. He smiled as his mind drifted back and recalled the ancient festival. He gripped the sickle and swished it through the air, admiring the way it gleamed. It was a beautiful instrument. The festival had been celebrated so long ago that he could hardly remember its name. Ah, yes. It was called *Halloween.*

* * *

Priory whiled the way the time in his quarters playing Patience on his favourite deck of cards. He was sitting on a chair with the cards laid out before him. He felt a chill running down his spine.

"Room, it's chilly in here. Increase temperature."

The room complied.

He sighed in contentment as the ambient environment was quickly adjusted to a more comfortable setting. After a moment, he again felt a cool breeze on his skin. His flesh creeped with goosebumps.

"Oh, for Hades sake, room! I'll adjust it myself," he said as he stood up from his chair and turned toward the room console to manually adjust the thermostat program. Standing in front of him, next to the room console, he saw his mother.

Almost half of her body was missing; parts had been removed for harvesting and consumption — one arm had been removed, and much of the skin and flesh from her back had been peeled off from her shoulders down to her buttocks. One foot had been severed, causing her to shuffle awkwardly on the bloody stump. All that remained of the woman was a stumbling, shuffling, cadaver that made its way towards him. Priory was frozen in fear and shock.

"They put me into a pie, Priory! They made dumplings and puddings from my breasts! They hung me up to die, and then they started slicing!"

Veragina shrieked, and pointed a shaking, accusatory finger at him.

"All because of you, you little spineless little piss weasel!"

"Oh, shut your fat face, you old hag!"

This must be a delusion, a chimera of the mind, he thought. He was beginning to recover from the initial mental blow of seeing his deceased mother before him. His mind was logical and not prone to illusions. *It must be a hologram — a prank of some sort. Maybe it was Driscoll, or even that weirdo, Lot.*

"Alright, mother dearest," he said, decided for now to play along with this charade. "It's such a wonderful surprise to see you again. You're looking well. I see you've lost some weight, so that's nice."

"You left me to die in a pastry on Pluto!" Veragina spat at him.

He laughed cruelly at her. "Well, people are hungry, so you should have stayed there, you vicious whale!"

Her lower jaw dropped open and she released a bloodcurdling scream. Priory clasped his hands to his ears and squeezed his eyes shut. The wailing sound abruptly stopped. He opened his eyes and looked around his room, but his mother had vanished.

"Yeah, great joke you guys," Priory said sarcastically, under his breath. He paused and sat down on his chair, thinking of who might have played the trick on him.

A menacing male voice behind him said, "Tut, tut, Priory. That's no way to talk to your mother, is it?"

Startled, Priory spun around so quickly that he fell out of his chair.

"Room, lights out," the voice said.

The last thing Priory ever saw was Lot's red eyes rushing wildly towards him.

*   *   *

Jason decided to warn Ealasaid about the situation and the peril of their mission. Athena had already confirmed that Ealasaid was human, and so he reasoned that she deserved to know the fate of the Sun. He went to her quarters.

She was there, waiting for him. Ealasaid was reclining on a berth.

"Did you rest well?" he asked. "I hope these quarters are to your satisfaction."

Ealasaid rushed towards Jason and hugged him. She broke down in tears.

"Oh, Captain. Thank you for rescuing me. I don't know what I would have done," she sobbed uncontrollably. "Those bastard pirates were going to…"

Jason had heard of the Kalibad Pirates. They were the worst kind of space scum. They would have taken Ealasaid's ship, her cargo, and any remaining crew members. Worst of all is the monstrous brutality they would have inflicted upon her.

"I won't let any one hurt you; this is my oath to you, Ealasaid," Jason reassured her, holding her with both hands on her shoulders as a sign of strength and support.

"Captain," Athena interrupted, suddenly appearing behind him.

Jason released Ealasaid as Athena gave her report.

"There has been an accident involving Priory, at the main airlock. I recommend you investigate immediately."

Jason nodded confirmation to Athena then turned back to Ealasaid.

"Stay here. It's for your own protection. I will set a door lock in place in your room. Athena will ensure your safety."

Jason sprinted off through the corridors of the Ascension toward the main airlock, with Athena close behind him.

Ealasaid shimmered. Her features warped and torpefied like burning paper. First she had taken the form of Alexander's sister, Joanne. She then had morphed into a virgin maiden to deceive Lot. In her third transformation, she had recreated the physical presence of Priory's mother, Veragina. Lastly she was a featureless, orb mask.

The rest of the crew had assembled in the main airlock hangar.

"What happened? Where is Priory?" demanded Jason immediately as he entered the airlock hangar.

"He was *spaced*, Captain. His body exploded in the vacuum," Lot said stilly.

"Captain, it seems Priory was scheduled to inspect the main airlock chamber. He must have initiated the unlock sequence — by accident, I guess — and he was ventilated into space," Rapier hypothesized.

Nothing remained of their former comrade except for a spatter of frozen, crystalized blood on the outside of the airlock port window.

Jason was angry. "Athena, can you corroborate? I want to review the ship's vid records from the hangar."

"Captain, my vid recording systems were damaged by the radiation cloud, and then further incapacitated by debris impact from the Oriön Ferat. The vid may have recorded the events within this room, but I will not know until I am able to fully recover vid record functionality. That may take some time; my repair systems remain at ninety-nine percent capacity."

Jason had no reason to doubt Athena. She was infallible and totally trustworthy. It was almost time to reach Algol, and he didn't need this kind of distraction.

"Very well, Athena. Notify me as soon as repair systems reach one hundred percent. I also want to know if any vid records exist." He turned his attention back to the rest of his crew. "My Ascensionauts, to the bridge and prepare for Algol approach."

One by one, they marched single file to the bridge, with their shoulders squared and their countenances grim and determined.

"For the glory! And the power!" they chanted. It was a holy moment before battle. They were Legionaries of Viri Terram, and they were preparing for combat… preparing to face their enemy… preparing for death, if necessary.

Jason led the way, in the vanguard. Rapier followed, then Driscoll, Alexander, and Lot at the rear. The wicked smile on Lot's grinning maw went unnoticed.

"Take to your stations, gentlemen," Jason bid them. He sat in his command chair. "Take us out of weave, Lot."

The ship decelerated into normal space-time.

Before them, through the bridge's view portal, they sat in awe as they beheld the view of the Algol star system.

Algol was a binary system, consisting of a huge blue star in helotage to a hot orange star. The two stars orbited so closely that fiery solar coronas lashed between them. The ancients had named it Algol: the demon star. To the primitive earthbound observers, the two had appeared as a single star, an evil eye that winked. It was alien and strange: a fantastic light bathed them, and shone upon their faces.

"And she bare him a son, and he called his name Gershom: for he said, 'I have become a stranger in a strange land,'" Lot said in awe.

Lot manoeuvred the Ascension around the twin stars and into geostationary orbit with the fourth planet, Beta Perseid Delta. Orbiting the planet was the Pillar of Fyre — a massive device, spinning and pulsating in and out of unknown dimensions. In the centre of the behemoth lay a singularity. The Fyre was contained within a shield of black hole metals. It was the ultimate power source, and weapon. Its alien creators would defend this technology to the death to prevent it from falling into the wrong hands… human hands.

"Scan the Pillar," Jason said coldly.

"Scan running, captain," Driscoll confirmed. "The Fyre is showing no activation sequence. The scan indicates only a skeleton crew."

Jason had a stoic, hawklike expression on his face. He sat in his command chair as if he were a sphinx on a throne. Athena, rested confidently on his shoulder. Jason nodded to Alexander.

"Then turn them into skeletons. I want that Pillar!" Jason intoned, ordering the attack.

The Ascension was a living ship. Under Athena's control, the ship slowly transformed from the pointed needle shape required for space flight into a war bird. In the form of a hawk, the Ascension spread its wings and flexed its talons. It was now a weapon of war that bristled with armaments. The laser ports opened from her eyes and spewed liquid fire across the Fyre's defence turrets, eliminating the possibility of counterattack. A molten shower fell upon the stabilization beams that held the Fyre in position within its shield of spinning black hole metals. As the beams collapsed, the Fyre fell free of its shield and became vulnerable to direct attack.

"Ready the cargo bay!" Jason shouted, his eyes blazing.

The Ascension swooped upon the Pillar and seized the satellite in its talons.

"Athena! Bring it aboard!"

Opening its mandible, the Ascension brought the Pillar into the cargo bay.

"Let's get the Hades out of here!" Jason roared, leaning forward in his command chair.

"Mister Alexander, nuke the home world, Beta Perseid Delta. Use saturation bombardment. Light it up and leave nothing behind; I don't want anything following us back to Sol."

An uncanny compulsion came over Alexander. His hands paused over the holo controls. He hesitated for a moment. His mind drifted and he felt himself sinking into a fugue state.

"What's wrong with you, man? Hurry and nuke them!"

Alexander remembered his dream of his twin sister, Joanne. It came as a whisper from the blackness of his being:

Don't let Jason kill me.
Don't let him kill us.

Jason leapt towards him, knocking Alexander over, and reached for the holo controls.

Alexander sprung back up and raised his fists above his head, ready to strike. Jason drove his elbow in the side of Alexander's ribcage, then spun around and punched him in the solar plexus. Alexander buckled over and dropped hard.

Jason launched himself back to Alexander's holo controls and quickly released the safety trigger and punched the panel to initiate the firing sequence. The resultant devastation was total. A blinding light erupted onto the view screen as a hundred thousand incendiary points of light simultaneously traced from the Ascension's guns turrets toward the planet's surface. At the moment of impact, the ordnance ignited, exploded, and merged together into a single blanket of flame that enveloped and decimated Beta Perseid Delta. The crew members shielded their eyes.

Temporarily incapacitated by Jason's blow, Alexander groggily stood up beside his captain.

"Lot, get us clear. Take us to Icarus weave eight, and return us to Earth. Lock the course, immediately!"

Lot gunned the engines, and the Ascension steered on a tangent away from the planet's orbit.

"Need I remind you all," Jason began, addressing the crew, "that our orders were to secure the device by any means necessary!"

Rapier rounded on the captain, saying, "Does 'by any means necessary' include genocide? Does it permit the annihilation of an entire species? Of a whole civilization?"

"Have you all gone mad? Don't you realize what's at stake here?" Jason asked, incredulously. Didn't they realise that if they didn't successfully retrieve and deliver the Pillar, it would be the end of Sol, Earth, and all human civilization? *Nothing could be more important than that!*

Lot seized upon the moment of distraction. He rose quietly from his station and moved to where Driscoll sat. With one hand, Lot grabbed Driscoll by the throat, pushing his head back and catching him off guard. With his other hand, he produced his sickle from inside his uniform and gutted his crew mate.

Rapier lunged at Lot to subdue him. Jason instinctively jumped to attack Lot. Then the shockwave hit the Ascension. From the wake of the terrible explosion of the planet. Debris ricocheted and reverberated along the ship's hull!

Jason stumbled as Lot slashed at Rapier with his sickle. Rapier yelled in pain.

Lot was slippery and quick with his sickle; he deftly dodged Jason and started bolting to the bridge exit. He moved quickly. Jason and Rapier were turning and preparing to give pursuit when Lot shouted, "Athena, shut down the artificial gravity drives, now. Command authorization code: 'Achaean.'"

Lot escaped the bridge and the three remaining crew members immediately felt the effects of zero gravity. Jason, Alexander, and Driscoll drifted through the air, grasping for any hand hold.

"Athena, re-engage the gravity drives!" Jason commanded. There was no response.

"Athena," Jason tried again. "This is your captain… respond!"

He looked above him to where the main hub of the artificial intelligence core hung from the centre of the bridge. He repeated the authorization code that Lot had used, but Athena remained silent. The ship was dead — and every non-essential system controlled by it — but the weave engines were still engaged, and accelerating hard on a course toward Sol.

"What in Hades happened, Jason?" said Alexander, still stunned. He was slowly returning from the dream state he had somehow entered just before he had attacked Jason.

"I am glad to see you are still with us, Mister Alexander. Rapier, how are your injuries?"

"It is only a scratch," Rapier dismissed, holding his arm tightly for a second. "It's a lot less than I'll be giving to him when I catch the traitorous bastard!"

"Very well," said the captain. "You two head down to the armoury, as best you can. There, you will find two ZEO-suits, plus shields and scimitars. You are going to hunt down and execute that murdering maniac. It does not take Sherlock Holmes to fathom that our ship has a saboteur on board. It was he who spaced Priory through the main airlock doors, and it was he who corrupted Athena."

Jason caught hold of the back of his command chair and pulled himself down toward it.

"I will stay on the bridge and attempt to restore Athena and then re-boot the other ship functions. I need to investigate what happened to her bioware. Now, go!"

Jason waited until they had both left the bridge, and pulled himself towards his quarters.

Lot swam through the zero gravity towards Ealasaid's cabin, grabbing whatever stationary objects he could and then pushing off to launching himself farther and faster.

Where was his sign from his god? The Herald was meant to come. She had promised him eternal glory, and a place in true paradise.

He approached her cabin, warily.

"Unlock cabin doors. Command authorization code: 'Achaean.'"

He floated into the cabin. The Virgin Seraph was waiting for him, hovering in the centre of the room.

"I have done what you have asked, my goddess. I injected the virus into Athena's bioware." He cast his eyes downwards. "But I was unable to stop Jason. He has destroyed the Behenian home world, and captured the Fyre. It is a board the ship now." Raising his eyes and glancing at his goddess, "I have served you faithfully. I await the Herald you spoke of, and my reward."

Her face darkened, and her features and her body changed to revealed her true identity: Ealasaid was a Behenian tetramorph. Her physical form cycled through the identities of all the women the crew encountered since Ealasaid had boarded the ship.

Lot's heart sank when he realised what he had done, and how he had been duped.

"No!" he cried, "It cannot be you! You are — blasphemy!"

"You vile, human scum," the Behenian derided Lot. "For billions of years, we Behenians have watched as your primitive race has crawled around in its own filth and destruction. You are unworthy. The only reward you deserve is death!"

The Behenian rushed at Lot, screaming wildly. With incomprehensible speed and strength, she clasped her hands on either side of Lot's skull, gouged out his eyeballs with her thumbs, and squeezed it until his head ruptured and exploded. As Lot's blood and brains poured over her hands and down onto his limp body, the Behenian released a bloodcurdling howl that echoed through the ship.

"What in the name of the gods was that, Rapier?" said Alexander, pausing as he checked the functions of their ZEO suits. They had reached the armoury and were perspiring heavily as they connected and powered up their armour. Rapier brushed the sweat from his forehead.

"I don't think I want to know," answered Rapier. "so I want to be prepared for it."

Grunting, he slapped his comrade's power sword into place. It clicked, then began to hum as the suit's energy began to surge though it.

"Power sword is active; gravity boots are engaged and functioning; all suit systems are fully charged and ready for battle. Let's go get this sickle-wielding freak!"

"We are ready," said Alexander, "but Jason must still restore access to Athena's systems; if he fails to bring her back online in time, we are all dead men!"

Alexander and Rapier exited the armoury in search of Lot. Their gravity books clunked slowly as they made their way through the Ascension's corridors.

"All this bullshit began after we encountered that ship, the Oriön Ferat," Alexander said to Rapier as they continued down the maze of corridors. "Do you think Ealasaid is not what she seems? With all the malfunctions with Athena, and with Lot going haywire, I'm not sure I'm ready to believe it was just a coincidence."

They were thinking the same way.

"I sometimes like to read, you know, although it's becoming a lost art these days," Rapier said ruefully. "I think this seems applicable to our current situation: 'When you have eliminated the impossible, then whatever remains, however improbable, must be the truth.'"

"Agreed," said Alexander, grimly. "The only logical conclusion is that we have a Behenian on board… and we just fucked up her home planet." His teeth ground together in his square jaw. "No wonder she sounds pissed off."

"Wait, do you hear that?" Rapier said, stopping and listening intently. He could hear a faint, high-pitched keening sound that was gradually growing in volume and intensity. It was coming from not far off.

"I hear it, and I don't like it," Alexander replied. "What is that?"

The sound continued to build until it reached a deafening crescendo that burst into the ship, ripping and smashing through the hull fuselage.

"I know that sound!" yelled Rapier through the tornado of rushing air that whipped around them toward the source of the sound. "Hull breach! Alexander, put on your oxygen helmet!"

After donning his head gear, Rapier looked at the scene in front of him. His scrotum withered around his receding testicles. What he saw and heard was the sight and the sound of a god tearing a passage from the nether dimension into the physical dimension. *Oh, unholy gods below, I hate this shit part!* Rapier thought.

The god stepped through the dimensions and onto the Ascension in front of Rapier and Alexander. It was Šulak, a demon god. He was a swallower of suns, and a sucker of souls and bowels. In the war, the demon had a propensity for ripping apart his enemies guts and intestinal tracts and devouring them. He wielded the fabled Sharur mace, a mythical weapon that could level a world.

He is a big fucker, Rapier considered.

"I will never understand the human predilection for this thing they call life," said Šulak with disdain in his booming voice.

A gargantuan robot followed behind Šulak. It was his harbinger, the Herald.

"My augur Kalus," Šulak instructed the robot, "remove the disease — 'life' — from their useless husks. Crush them. Kill them. All of them. Then, we will find our summoner, the Behenian."

The robot colossus silently nodded his obedience.

Kalus stepped forward, his scimitar at the ready. He stood three times the height of a man. Rapier and Alexander were intimidated, but undeterred. They immediately set upon the machine from both sides. Scimitars clashed and sparked together, and glowing shields grew white hot. Even when attacked from both sides simultaneously, Kalus was too strong and too fast for Rapier and Alexander. They could not score more than a glancing blow, and they were already tiring. It was a losing battle for them and only a matter of time before Kalus would kill them both. Backing away from the Herald's onslaught, Rapier and Alexander found themselves on alpha deck, near to Jason's quarters. Both god and robot were together in a clash of death.

The huge diamonmetal gates opened to reveal Jason standing ready to join his comrades. He wore a god-killer suit that was powerful, heavily armoured, and equal in size to both his adversaries. He carried diamonmetal tipped chainsaws, scimitars, las-guns, plutonium grenades, dimensional disruptor ripper guns, and sonic shields.

"In order to *kill* a god," Jason shouted, "one must first *become* a god."

Jason launched himself toward Šulak with his scimitar raised above his head. Midair, he shouted, "Athena, command authorization code: 'Gilgamesh!'" In an instant, Athena's systems came online. Jason had successfully purged the bio-virus.

Rallying behind their captain, Alexander and Rapier re-entered the fray by assailing Kalus. The Herald's armaments were fierce. He possessed star metal swords, which extended from his body shell, and sliced Alexander and Rapier into a whirlwind of destruction.

"You puny mortal humans!" Šulak said. He parried Jason's first blow against his Sharur mace. "You defiance is ineffective and ill-advised," he laughed at Jason. "Your end time is now!"

The god swung his mace and clipped the edge of Jason's suit. The force of the impact threw him backward against a bulkhead. Jason sprung back to his feet, and sliced the air with his chainsaw scimitar.

"So, Šulak, at last we meet," Jason said. "I was hoping I would get to be the one to kill you," he taunted the god. "I've fought and killed many gods before, and I have to say I was expecting more."

"Your insolence will compound your pain and suffering," Šulak retorted as he stepped forward and swung his mace again. Jason jumped aside and the mace crashed into the floor.

"Come now, Šulak. I expected more of a challenge. Even Nisrock, the god of agriculture and manure hit harder than you!"

Šulak's rage increased as he turned to pursue Jason. When he reached the centre of the deck, Jason gave the command.

"Athena! Initiate Hades' Fire!"

Blinding nano-flares spewed from an array of air vents along the walls and the ceiling of alpha deck. Each point of flame burned hotter than the sun. The flares were precisely directed at the place where the god stood. They enveloped Šulak's body and scorched his golden flesh as he flailed around and cumbersomely lashed out at Jason.

Using the moment of distraction, Jason sprinted up the wall and across the circular ceiling, then dropped down behind Šulak's position. With one powerful stroke, he powered down on the god and cleaved him almost in half with his chainsaw scimitar. From his collar bone to his waist, Šulak split and and began to peel apart; deep inside, dark energy swirled and seeped. Šulak roared with immeasurable pain.

Jason did not stop. He circled around Šulak, launching a salvo of plutonium grenades into the god's gaping wound. The onslaught continued: using his disruptor ripper guns Jason forced Šulak backwards, reeling toward the void in the hull where he had ruptured the walls of the Ascension. He clutched on to the edge of the cracked hull.

"Šulak! By the power of the Legionaries of Viri Terram, and the Echelon council, I sentence you to oblivion!"

Raising his scimitar, Jason lopped Šulak's head off his shoulders. His death was instantaneous, and permanent. Šulak's head and body were pulled by the vortex and sent spinning and tumbling into the abyss.

"So ends the tyranny of the gods," Jason declared, "and all who would dare to meddle with humanity or rule us unjustly."

He reached to his belt and pressed the detonator. The plutonium grenades exploded within the god's torso.

Jason picked up the Sharur mace and tossed it into the blackness.

"A mere toy." Jason grumbled.

Jason rushed to aid his comrades who were still locked in battle with the robot. Kalus had wounded Alexander in the fray, puncturing his lung with his scimitar. Rapid healing seals in the ZEO suit stemmed his bleeding and began repairing his body. Smart fibres in the suit quickly re-meshed, sealing the puncture and saving Alexander from exploding into the vacuum. He continued battling through the pain, but with reduced strength and dexterity he was no match. Rapier attempted to pick up the slack, but he was exhausted too.

Kalus had deftly worn down his two adversaries, and was preparing for the final, fatal strikes when Jason surprised him with a rapid staccato blast from behind with his las-guns. Kalus was no match for the power of Jason's god-killer suit. He stumbled forward from the force of the lasers. Before Kalus had time to react, Jason hit him with a second burst from the las-guns, severing the scimitar from his arm and piercing through his thick armour to the soulless machinery within. A third blast from the las-guns finished him off, and his hulking metal body dropped lifeless to the floor.

Rapier and Jason dragged the robot to the aperture and threw it into weave-space.

"Athena," commanded Jason, "close the rupture in the alpha deck hull, immediately. Then restore the ship's gravity and life support systems."

"Affirmative, captain. Restoring all necessary functions to you now…"

Jason turned to where Alexander was injured and helped him back to his feet. The ZEO suit healing process was still in progress, which left Alexander temporarily weak and in pain.

"Captain," Athena sounded worried. "With the ship's functions fully restored, I am now able to detect the presence of a Behenian on board, in the cargo hold. I am detecting that a power buildup is in progress."

Jason, Rapier, and Alexander exchanged glances. They all knew that Ealasaid was the Behenian in their midst.

"There is one more thing, captain," Athena continued, delivering the ship's status. "After Lot locked the ship on a course back to Earth, he compromised the weave-space factor. We are fast approaching Earth, but we are also traveling back in time."

"By what factor?"

"Without access to the configuration, I cannot say. It could be centuries… millennia… perhaps even aeons. It is difficult to compute without a human navigator slaved into my matrix. Lot was the helmsman."

Jason levelled a stare at Alexander. "I need you on the bridge, Alex. Are you up for the task? Can you undo the sabotage and repair the Icarus drive?"

It was the first time that Jason had contracted Alexander's name. Blood was seeping from a corner of his mouth. He looked wide-eyed at his captain and said in a choking, laborious cough, "Yes, yes. I can do this."

Alexander steadied himself then slowly headed to the bridge.

Jason said to Rapier, "This is why I made you my commander. You have proven yourself loyal to me in the face of Šulak and Kalus. Every one deserves a chance at redemption."

He offered his hand in friendship to Rapier. Rapier temporized for a second.

"Good, my balls have started working again," said Rapier.

He looked at Jason's hand, then he clasped it hard. They laughed.

"Come on," the captain said. "We don't have much…"

"Time?" smiled Rapier. "No, captain. Time, as Einstein said, is relative."

"You a are deep thinker, my old comrade. Come, let us find the Behenian and rid ourselves of her. For the glory and the power… of the Viri Terram empire."

Rapier nodded.

It took them ten minutes to travel through the ship, trudging heavily in their cumbersome suits. After they arrived at the entry to the cargo hold, Jason and Rapier paused to consider their tactics before entering.

"Athena, scan the ship. How many human officers remain on board?"

"Captain, my scans identify three human officers on board. I am detecting a corpse in the cabin assigned to Ealasaid. The dead crewman is Lot. I regret my bio-ware malfunctions — I should have been able to scan the Behenian."

"That explains a great deal, Jason. The scream we heard — it was inhuman. It must have been the Behenian who killed Lot."

"We must be vigilant. The Fyre device is our only hope for mankind, but if the Behenian has started the ignition protocols — then we are finished," Jason said in a harsh voice.

He activated his heads-up display in his helmet and established a video link to Alex.

"Alex, what is your progress with the Icarus drive?"

Alexander's face appeared in the holographic display, looking pale.

"Not good, Jason. We are twenty minutes from Earth, hurtling through the time-weave, and we are still accelerating! We are locked on course, and if the Ascension hits Earth, it will cause a firestorm of unimaginable destruction!"

"Open the cargo hold doors, Athena!" growled Jason.

Rapier and Jason tagged each other and then split up. The interior of the cargo hold was large enough to comfortably house The Pillar of Fyre, with much room to spare. The Pillar was a monstrous satellite in the shape of an orb and standing ten storeys high. There was a single entrance to the device. Both men circled the room in a reconnaissance manoeuvre. They entered the sphere.

Inside, vast unknown technologies stretched their comprehension. It reminded Rapier of Escher's *Relativity*. They traversed a number of walkways and climbed some stairwells. Jason flashed a hand signal to Rapier, instructing him to stand by and wait. Jason continued through the satellite.

"You humans, you always kill what you do not understand," a voice echoed through the sphere. And you, Zephyr — what was the first thing you ever killed? A woodlouse, you enjoyed trampling on them gleefully! As a boy, did you ever catch butterflies and put them in a jar to suffocate, and watch the pretty little things die? As a man, did you ever kill another of your comrades in cold blood? Did you ever kill a god? And a civilization? Yes, you have! You…simple, warmongering beast!"

"I was never a boy!" Jason snarled, his eyes searching for the source of the voice.

The Behenian appeared like an iridescent spectre, and floated through the wall and into the space where Jason stood. As she approached, she materialized back into physical form and landed softly a short distance away. In her hands she brandished a strange oval staff. She twirled it slowly and methodically while sizing up her adversary.

"Your days of killing are over, Captain Jason Zephyr. Today, it is your turn to die! And all the living creatures from the greatest to the least will celebrate your death."

She rushed forward and spun her oval staff. Before Jason could block her attack, the end of her staff connected with his god suit and immediately drained its power. Jason slumped backward and landed on his back. The Behenian stood over him with her glowing staff pressing down on his chest. Jason was momentarily paralyzed.

"I have activated the pillar, Zephyr. You and your race are doomed to extinction!"

The Pillar of Fyre vibrated and hummed as vast engines powered on. The sound of the engines continually increased in pitch and magnitude. Jason looked below and could see the black hole vortex that powered the device. It began revolving and stoking beneath him as it prepared to engage.

With a surge of strength from the adrenaline rushing through his veins, Jason pushed and freed himself.

"Do you think I did not anticipate this?" he challenged her.

The sonic shields on his god-suit triggered and repelled her staff, pushing her a few steps backwards.

"Rapier!" she called. "Finish him!"

Jason spun around as attempted to rise to his feet. Rapier stood facing him, glaring down on him, seemingly in a trance, hypnotised. His Eye of Horus tattoo illuminated red. He bore his scimitar down to Jason's helm, preventing his captain from standing.

"What is this treachery?" Jason demanded. He activated his tattoo on his forearm, to no avail. *The Behenian must have recoded Rapier's tattoo to her own.* Now he was under her complete control. Jason, rolled quickly to the edge of the walkway, freeing himself from Rapier's scimitar.

The Behenian laughed, "What's the matter, Zephyr? Are you afraid to die?"

"No! But you may go first!" From a crouched position, Jason sprang toward her and grabbed the arc at the bottom of her staff. He heaved it up and twisted it sharply, wresting her whole body off balance, then push her backward over the edge of the walkway.

"Go to Hades!" Jason sneered as the Behenian lost her footing and stumbled down into the chasm beneath the Fyre. Jason caught the rail with one hand to save himself from falling after her.

Defiant to the last, she looked into Jason's eyes for the last time as she plummeted down. In a myriad of voices and faces, all dying and fading into the blackness, she screamed, "I will see you there!"

"Can I give you a hand, captain?" Rapier asked as he pulled Jason up and away from the edge of the parapet. With the Behenian destroyed, Rapier had returned to himself again.

He attempted to re-establish a video link to Alexander.

"Time to Earth, bridge?" he yelled above the cacophony of the Pillar's engines. The Ascension ship was tearing apart. There was no answer from Alexander.

"Athena, what has happened to Alexander? How long until Earth?"

Athena's hologram reappeared. She swooped into the room as a bird of prey would return to the falconer's glove.

"Alexander is dead," Athena explained with sadness. "He fought hard, but his wounds were too severe. He was unable to correct the Icarus drive in time. Now we have only seven minutes until the Ascension — until I — collide with Earth. I am sorry, Jason. I have failed you." In an uncharacteristic display of her love and devotion to her captain, rank and file slipped.

"No, Athena, you have not failed me. You have served me well, and you will again."

Jason gently caressed Athena's tiny cheek. He pulled into his touch, nesting there. She closed her eyes for the last time and simply vanished, evaporated into nothingness. Jason closed his hand where she had been. *Goodbye, Athena.*

"Rapier, we will attempt to eject the Fyre into space. Follow me, commander!"

Jason and Rapier reached the Fyre mechanism. Cataclysmic forces were on overload. Their faces bathed in raw radiation energy.

"We're out of time, captain."

That word again: *Time.*

"I am going in," Jason said, unexpectedly. The interior of the Fyre was a seething, surging storm of unknown energies, and would almost certainly be inhospitable to life. "The rare metals in my god-killer suit will interface with the Behenian technology… and hopefully stop this thing."

"But captain," Rapier began in protest.

"It's the only way, Rapier," Jason said bluntly. "We will meet again, my old friend." He smiled at Rapier and clasped his shoulder.

Jason turned and plunged himself into the very eye of the Fyre.

"Jason, wait — what do you mean we will meet again? This is our end!"

The Ascension tore through the atmosphere of Earth, burning like a cascading comet, crashing and burning forests, boiling oceans, in a tidal wave of utter destruction before ripping entire continents in its wake. A mushroom cloud rose from the impact and palled over the entire world.

* * *

My name is Jason… or perhaps I was Jason, or am yet to be. I cannot recall. I am not the same person I was a millisecond ago. The Pillar of Fyre has changed me irrevocably. I cheated the Behenian Ealasaid of her destiny whenever I thrusted myself into the maelstrom of the Eye. The Fyre does not tell or reveal her secrets.

There had been a fusion of technologies, an amalgamation of the collective knowledge of two civilizations. The god-killer suit reforged, inheriting and adapting the advanced Behenian technologies. It was something new, and more advanced than anything known.

I can remember that much.
But everything has changed now.
My name is Jason Zephyr.
I am the murderer of worlds.
I am the warrior eternal.
I am the hero of a million faces.
I am immortal.
I am damned to live forever.

* * *

Jason opened the hatch of the satellite. The Fyre was extinguished, the energy within it spent. He looked at the ancient dead jungle that smouldered all around. He climbed down from the sphere. Surveying the horizon, Zephyr saw a huge crater where his ship had disintegrated as it exploded on impact.

What was that poem that Lot had recited, the one by Walt Whitman?

My Captain does not answer, his lips are pale and still,

My father does not feel my arm, he has no pulse nor will,
The ship is anchor'd safe and sound, its voyage closed and done,
From fearful trip the victor ship comes in with object won;
But I with mournful tread,
Walk the deck my Captain lies,
Fallen cold and dead.

Jason Zephyr's voyage was done … and yet, a new one was set to begin.

First orders of survival: find shelter, food, and water.

Jason walked through the scorched wilderness. Underfoot, his footsteps crushed decomposing vegetation, enormous and unfamiliar insects and butterflies. He slashed his way through, looking for safe passage.

Suddenly, a velociraptor leapt out of the dying jungle. It charged towards him, preparing to strike with its terrible claws. The raptor was ferocious, and hungry, a survivor of a fey species.

Jason quickly ran it through with his chainsaw scimitar.

Food, he thought.

BELINDA AUBERON — VAMPYRE HUNTRESS

Glargazop Puckwudgie could not sleep. There was something lurking deep in his subconscious. His wits were pickled like the contents of the jar in his fridge-freezer. It was safely wrapped up in plastic bags, sheathed within other refuse sacks.

After tossing and turning for sleepless hours he finally gave up and arose from the bed, leaving his wife, Germwarfilia, gently snoring. She broke wind with a trumpeting resonance that would make any husband proud. A lingering odour of fishiness filled the room.

He crept down stairs to the kitchen and turned on the scullery light. It was caked in dead flies. He opened the fridge, retrieved a beer, and pulled back the Freaky Fried Chicken Factory plastic wrapping from the package that he had stashed there earlier. He giggled and salivated with excitement, the way a child would upon discovering a Christmas present.

Glargazop opened the huge glass jar within.

Inside there was a decaying, decapitated, dolphin's head.

He pulled at a piece of rank, putrescent, stinking carrion from just above the dolphin's left eyeball, near its blowhole. With a little effort, he tugged at the flesh and it finally gave way. The whole eye socket pulled away with the meat, and the eyeball dangled from the lump as he carried it to the kitchen table. In his excitement and haste, Glargazop inadvertently left the fridge door ajar.

He sat down at the table with his beer in one hand and a fistful of dolphin flesh in the other.

The dark eyeball stared at him, and he stared back into it.

"My beautiful one, my glorious one," Glargazop lustfully said.

Using just his fingers, he quickly gorged himself upon the cold raw meat of the dolphin and washed it down with his umpteenth beer of the night. He licked his fingers as he savoured every last morsel.

"Ahh, a lovely portion," he slurred. He wiped his mouth on his sleeve and his hands on his shirt. Satisfied, he returned up the stairs to his bed and his flatulent wife.

As the night's wee hours progressed, the warmth of the kitchen air began to defrost the contents of the open fridge-freezer. Everything was still. The only light came from the fridge's interior bulb, and the only sound came from a drip, dripping sound from the defrosting freezer.

Inside the fridge there was a movement and a rustle, and inside the jar the dolphin's remaining eyeball blinked.

Suddenly, the fridge-freezer exploded as the huge jar within it blew apart. Glass, brine, and plastic bags were strewn around the kitchen floor as the dolphin's head landed in the middle of the linoleum.

The dolphin's head sat motionless for a moment as if gradually regaining its strength and returning to life. Its cold, dark eye assessed its new surroundings. It slowly opened its mouth then shot out a long sinuous tongue. Like a whip, it wrapped itself around the table leg and pulled the head free from the remains of the urn in which it had been imprisoned. Squirming tendrils erupted from the base of the Dolphin's skull and slithered around the kitchen deck looking for grip. At last the dolphin head rose up, supported by the slithering tendrils. It surveyed the room with its cyclops eye.

* * *

In the morning, Germwarfilia was the first to discover the horror of what remained of her kitchen. She shrieked when she first saw the puddles of ice-melt, shards of broken glass, and the splinters of wood that used to be her kitchen table. Her feet froze to the ground in fear.

"Glargazop!" she thundered.

Upstairs, Glargazop's drunken slumber came to an abrupt end as his eyes snapped open.

"What is it, you daft woman?" he replied as loudly as his hangover would permit.

"Get down here, now!" she continued shouting without any reduction in volume. "We have been burgled!"

With his head still thumping and his limbs only partially cooperating, Glargazop stumbled out of bed. "If that idiot boy of mine is involved in any of this ruckus, there will be hell to pay," he mumbled as he flopped down the stairs.

"Hey, Maw," Thrawgar said sleepily, rubbing his eyes as he walked toward the kitchen commotion. "Why is everybody all shouty this morning?"

Father and son arrived into the kitchen at the same time and they immediately froze standing next to Gerwarfilia.

Glargazop's bleary eyes surveyed the room. It appeared that the fridge had been ransacked and the back door stood wide open. A trail of glistening slime led out through the back door and all the way up the garden path. At the end of the pavement, the gate hung open, almost yanked from its hinges.

Glargazop dropped to his knees.

"No! Say it ain't so!"

Thrawgar thought it odd that somebody would break into a house in the middle of the night just to steal food from the fridge. "They must've been mighty hungry, whoever done it."

"It's gone! The aquatic Delphinus terror is gone!" sobbed Glargazop in disbelief.

"What's that, Paw? What's gone?"

Glargazop turned in rage and smacked Thrawgar hard on the side of his face.

"I'm gonna tan your hide, boy!" roared Glargazop. "You're gonna get a good whupping!"

Before Glargazop could make another move, Germwarfilia leapt on him and put him into a headlock and dragged him to the corner of the kitchen and away from their son. Germwarfilia had the physical strength to tackle most men, and the stench from her armpit would subdue any adversary.

Thrawgar started to bawl. "What did I do, Paw? I don't know nothing 'bout your asthmatic Delphi-what-thing!" He blanched in fear and covered his reddened face.

"You keep your fat hands off that boy!" Germwarfilia angrily warned Glargazop. "You don't harm a single hair on his head, you hear?" She tightened her hold around Glargazop's neck.

Startled by his own actions, Glargazop's rage waned and turned to sorrow and regret.

"I'm sorry, my precious boy! Please forgive your old Paw!" He twisted his neck against his wife's unrelenting grip and looked up into her eyes. "Germwarfilia, my rose, I'm very sorry. It ain't nobody's fault but mine. I'm just a foolish, silly man."

Turning back to Thrawgar, he continued, "Here son, take this…" He fumbled blindly in his pocket for some money and pulled out a tenner. He extended it toward the boy. "Go get yourself one of those magazines you love. *White Dwarf*, right? Or one of those *Warjammer* toys you like to collect, okay?"

Thrawgar sniffled and wiped his nose. "It's *Warhammer*, Paw," Thrawgar corrected his father. He half chuckled as his tears subsided. "And they ain't toys, Paw. They is mah figurines."

"Yeah, yeah, son. '*Warspammer*.' Whatever you say. You just run along and let me and your Maw clean up this mess, okay? Now get on up out of here, you hear?"

Thrawgar's mother added with a smile, "Aye, and take your time, son."

Thrawgar hurried for the door, "Thanks, Paw! Thanks, Maw!"

When their son had departed, Germwarfilia looked down at Glargazop's face, still tightly locked under her arm, and perspiring. "This position reminds me of our wedding night."

Glargazop cocked an eyebrow. "I ain't gonna lie, my sweet. All this rough and tumble has caused something of a stirring in my loins."

There was something magnetic in the air that brought them together. The grunge from the Dolphin's wound had a venereous, aphrodisiac quality. The chaos and destructions around them was erotic.

"You romantic old fool, Glargazop!" Germwarfilia giggled. She relaxed her left arm around his neck, then reached under his body with her right hand. She grabbed the ass of his trousers and with a quick heft she flipped him up into the air. Glargazop landed roughly on his back. Germwarfilia launched herself onto him with a squeal, "Giddy up! You got a purdey mouth, boy!"

* * *

Peter Auberon was gone. He had vanished without a trace, and no one had seen him in over six months. The Joker's Inn costume shop had been her father's life's work and his passion, so she resolved to keep the doors open, no matter what.

The police had executed a perfunctory search of the premises for clues to Peter's disappearance. After exhausting all leads, they had simply given up finding him and had moved on to the more pressing investigation of who had spray painted "CH☺PPER LIVES!" on a wall at Halloween High School.

His disappearance was supernatural. But what was natural in a town called Halloween?

Belinda refused to give up searching. She knew that there had to be clues somewhere. Someone in this town knew, and she was determined to find out. Upstairs, she searched her father's ledgers again. She was sure there would be something there.

At the back of the current ledger she found a carbon copy of his last transaction. It was faint and hard to distinguish. She took her cigarette lighter and held the lit flame behind the paper to illuminate and contrast the writing. She squinted and peered closer, and at last she could discern a name and an address.

The page erupted in a sudden torrent of flame.

"Ah, fudge knuckles!" she yelled as she threw the invoice onto the table and slapped it with the palm of her hand. With the fame extinguished, she gingerly picked up the charred invoice by one corner. "Nothing much left of it now, but at least I got what I needed."

Pandoria Evǣfensang
The Witches' Ball

Pandoria was the proprietor of Peter's rival joke and fancy dress shop, *The Witches' Ball*, and Belinda was going to pay her a visit. She bounded down the stairs, grabbed her coat, and prepared to lock up the shop.

On her way out the door, something in the windowpane caught her eye — a spider web hung in the corner of the window, twitching sporadically. A fly was ensnared in the invisible kaleidoscope. With lightning speed, a fat arachnid pounced on the panicking bug and soon paralysed it with venom. Belinda watched as the spider wrapped its meal in a silk cocoon and then towed it back to its lair beyond the windowsill.

"That's life, kiddo," she said in a whisper.

She checked her watch and realized that *The Witches' Ball* would be closing now, and decided to postpone her visit there until tomorrow. She quickly grabbed a Wolf Man mask and stuffed it into her backpack for Ben, then finally left the shop and locked the front door. She headed back home to her son.

Belinda set off home via Bridge Street. She lived in New Church Lane, so her route home would also take her past the Hung Fung Running River Chinese Restaurant that sat opposite The Freaky Fried Chicken Factory.

It was a still night, with a large gibbous moon in the sky that hung over the river. She stared at the moon as she walked, and her mind began to wander. *Damn, it will be here soon*, she thought. She made a mental note to remember to pick up her feminine hygiene products from the chemist. She paused for a moment to light a cigarette for company, using her open jacket to shield the flickering flame against the wind. After a few puffs she zipped up her jacket and continued walking. The smell of the cigarette smoke intermingled with the freshness of the frosty evening wind. Belinda hugged herself and wrapped up tight against the zephyr.

She saw the usual denizens milling about the town centre. Mark and his elderly mother were shuffling homeward bound. Mark came to be known as "Crazy Mark" because of his habit of calling everyone else "Mark", including his own ageing and decrepit mother. The Puckwudgie family where also there, and arguing loudly amongst themselves. Harriet Atchette was a stylish and sexy bank teller. Belinda hated that bitch, with her killer shoes and her razor blade smile.

"What a bloody heifer," Belinda muttered to herself as she passed. Belinda and Harriet had been bitter rivals for the affection of Belinda's ex-partner, Raphael Diavolite. Raphael was Ben's father, and he had died in mysterious circumstances.

Harriet glanced at Belinda, then turned her nose up in the air, ignoring her as she went by.

She probably fudgered him to death, or nagged him to his grave. Or both, knowing her. Belinda had no good thoughts or opinions regarding Harriet.

Belinda rarely used foul language. She had a long list of inoffensive euphemisms for all purposes. Instead of *fuck*, for example, she would say *fudge*. Instead of *shit*, she would say *poop*. She had decided some time ago for Ben's sake that she would never curse, swear, or use unnecessary bad language. She wanted to raise her son to be a great man, with a good education and impeccable manners, unsullied by foul language and negative attitudes. He was an innocent child, and full of life. She never wanted that to change.

Belinda heard footsteps behind her, following her. She quickened her cadence and soon reached and rounded the next corner. The footsteps still followed and increased their pace behind her.

Belinda flicked away her cigarette, and began to sprint, but she soon realised that adrenaline and nicotine don't mix well. Her lungs burned as she forced her legs to the limits of her endurance. She skidded to a halt at the crest of the hill on Wherewolf Street, clutching her pounding heart, and wheezing. She couldn't hear the footsteps now, and saw no one behind her.

Seemingly out of nowhere, she saw the shape of a man drop from above onto the footpath about six feet in front of where she stood catching her breath.

"Foolish girl," he said to her from the shadows before she could react. "Why do you run from your pursuers? Don't you know what you are? You are The Huntress. Also, the tobacco slows you. You need it not."

The man stepped away from the darkness and into the cone of illumination under the streetlight. He was a Chinese man, tall and lean, perhaps forty years old. Belinda recognised him as one of the waiters from the Running River restaurant, but felt she also knew him from somewhere else, though she could not place him in context.

Belinda took a cautious step backwards.

"What did you call me? No, wait… Never mind that. Who *are* you?" she gasped between gulps of air. She sat down on her haunches, and breathed in and out more slowly.

"Your forgiveness, please," the man bowed respectfully. "I am Hung Fung Joey, owner of the Running River. It's the restaurant over on…"

"No, I know where it is," interrupted Belinda. She was regaining her composure now, and her confidence. She stood up, and lightly brushed the dirt off her backside. "Look, all I want to know is why you were chasing me."

"I was not chasing you, Miss Auberon. I merely wished to speak with you. I have been sent by a friend of mine to make your acquaintance, and to train you… as a Vampyre Huntress."

She tried to laugh mockingly, but it came out as a nervous laughter. She cautiously wondered if this guy might be some kind of freak or a weirdo.

"A 'Vampyre Huntress' you say? What type of medication are you on?" Belinda squinted her eyes at Joey. "And who is this alleged friend of yours who sent you?"

"I was sent by Peter Auberon, your father."

Belinda stepped back, reeling. *Poop just got real.*

"Look around you, Belinda," Joey began to explain. "When the sun goes down in this vale of tears, what do you think goes on here? There are monsters everywhere, hiding in every crevice, lurking and squirming like grubs under a rock. Pure wickedness takes many forms. Everything is corrupt, from the town council right down to the Freaky Fried Chicken Factory. Your boss, the one they call the Colonel, is pure evil incarnate! He holds an unknown, eerie, entity in his thrall that is of the greatest and most diabolical power imaginable!"

"I do not believe you!" she cried angrily, turning away from him. "If what you say is true, and my father had known about it, then he would have said something to me." Belinda crossed her arms. "And what is your relationship to my dad anyway?"

"Your father and I were good friends for many years, and fishing buddies. But Pete wasn't himself for some time before his disappearance. The power of the mask he wore was overwhelming him… possessing him. You know of the old woman?"

Belinda nodded. She now remembered having seen him with Pete a few times in the past.

"Your father made a deal with the old crone: he would gain the use of the extraordinary power of the mask, and in exchange she would take the essence of his being. His soul is now imprisoned within the mask."

Belinda slowly turned back toward Joey. She wasn't yet convinced of the truth of his story, but she wanted to hear more about her father.

"Are you aware that the Joker's Inn is a Realm Way portal into other dimensions, to other lands, worlds and times?"

She was stunned. Belinda had led a sheltered life.

It all started to make sense, in a crazy way. She started to connect pieces together: the "gone fishing" note that was not in her father's handwriting; the strange invoice in the ledger. *Was it all too much to believe?* She tried to maintain a healthy skepticism.

An October wind blew upon the pathway, stirring up a golden breath, full of russet dead leaves that swirled in a dark maelstrom. She stared down, and picked up some sycamore and oak leaves, and put them in her jacket pocket. These were for Ben, later.

Joey went on, saying, "The Soul Mask your father bought from the old witch is now inhabited by a boy cacodaemon. The boy has vanished from the streets. Find the boy, and you will find Peter's soul."

Belinda squared her shoulders, and exhaled. She remembered the address of Pandoria Evǣfensang.

"And the old hag that did this to my father?"

Joey acknowledged in one curt sharp nod of his head.

"Okay, you have convinced me. I am in," she said reticently. "So, what now?"

Joey carefully removed the pouch that had been slung across his chest. "Here, this is for you." He laid the pouch on the ground between them and again bowed in reverence.

"What is it?" asked Belinda. She looked around, and felt slightly embarrassed even though they were alone now. "Oh do get up! As much as I enjoy the sight of a man grovelling before me, this is hardly a marriage proposal!"

"Open it," Joey insisted.

Belinda carefully unwrapped the pouch.

"Hot, flaming fudge!"

It was a Katana, a Japanese sword. She held it up. The weight was perfect. Belinda swished the sword around in an arc. She fumbled and almost dropped it. Joey reached forward in an instantaneous reaction to catch the Katana, but eased off whenever Belinda caught the sword. *Good*, he thought to himself, *the girl's reactions are excellent. But will she be ready for the gruelling task that is ahead of her?*

"Be careful, girl! This sword was given to me by my father."

"It's beautiful. And stop calling me 'girl' when you already know my name."

Joey sniffed and pointed his nose at her.

"Hold on a second," Belinda said as she stopped swishing the sword in the air. "The Katana is a Japanese sword, isn't it? Yeah, I think I remember hearing that when my son, Ben, was watching 'Teenage Mutant Ninja Turtles.' But you're not Japanese… you're Chinese, aren't you?" she said sheepishly with her voice trailing off.

Joey sighed deeply. "My mother is Chinese." He returned his gaze to the sword. "You will need this to defeat the forces of the Colonel Godfrey Klunz."

"Whoa, wait a second! Are you saying that you want me to kill my ex-boss? Well, that's every wage slave's dream, of course — especially if you're a postal worker — and the Colonel is a pain in the… tush. But do I dare to make the ultimate fantasy a reality?" she said in an exaggerated sarcastic tone.

"This is not a fantasy, girl!" Joey snapped angrily at her.

"I already told you not to call me 'girl', boy!"

"Stop messing around, Belinda! I'm being serious! It is a matter of soul-blood! Meet me tomorrow morning, here. We will commence your training, and you had better be prepared to pay attention and take it seriously. Your life may depend on it."

"Oh, come on!" Belinda said flippantly. She closed her eyes for just a second while preparing to make a show of rolling them at him dramatically. "I only just met you, and yet you expect me to…"

Her voice trailed off into a stunned silence. Joey had vanished. She spent a few seconds spinning in slow circles, looking around in all directions. She shivered once and said, slowly, "What the fudge? How does he do that?"

She placed the sword back in the pouch and tucked it as well as she could inside her jacket. *Well, I can't walk around town with an ancient Japanese sword in my hand unless I want to draw some very negative attention to myself.*

She started walking again. During the way, the thought occurred to her about her encounter with Joey and replayed the conversation in her mind. Suddenly, she remembered why Joey had looked so familiar to her. He strongly resembled a character from an old television show that she used to watch with her daddy, *Monkey*. Joey was the apparition of Sandy, the water demon.

"Nah, it couldn't be!" she said, shaking her head.

*   *   *

Belinda's house in New Church Lane was a small and cosy, a semi-detached dwelling that was just adequate for her and her son.

Upon reaching her front yard, she noticed a long trail of slime that spanned the length of the path and also connected with the hedgerows. She dipped a few fingers into the translucent sheen and felt it between her fingers.

"Yuck. I see the slugs are back, and bigger than ever," Belinda said as she brushed the mucus from her hand and continued up the path to her small porch. She unlocked the door and called out for her son as she entered the hallway. She pulled off her backpack and hung it on the banister, then slid the Katana into the umbrella stand and draped her jacket so that it obscured the sword's handle.

Unzipping her jacket pocket, Belinda rummaged around in her pocket for the leaves. She cupped them into her hands, and brought her nose up to smell pure autumn. She was an existentialist by nature.

"Ben? Fiona? Hey, you guys?!" She walked down the hallway toward the kitchen.

Fiona appeared from the kitchen, blinking her eyes in quick succession.

Ben's child minder, Fiona Feefifofum, was a small blonde lady with horned-rimmed glasses and an obsessive compulsion disorder. One of her habits caused her to always blink in multiples of three. Due to a strange set of circumstances Fiona had volunteered to be a guinea-pig in a lab experiment. The trail had paid well, but there had been an unfortunate mutation in her DNA that had resulted in some unwanted side-effects. Belinda liked Fiona, and trusted her, but often felt she had the characteristics of a gecko.

"Oh, hiya Belinda!" Fiona said in a cordial low tone. "Ben is fast asleep upstairs. He had another nightmare about you-know-who." She touched Belinda's arm to reassure her.

"Oh my holy poop shoot! Is he all right?"

Ben suffered sleep paralysis, he became frozen with night terrors.

"Yes, yes, he's okay. You know, he gets upset sometimes when he thinks of his dad. I know it's not my place to say, and I really shouldn't speak ill… but, I never took to that man. He really was a loser."

"Aye, I know," Belinda said ruefully. "I was drunk, and he was the greatest mistake of my life. May God forgive me, but I am glad he died."

There was a brief silence between the two women as they fidgeted beneath their feet, not knowing what to say.

"You relax, Belinda. We will have a wee cuppa." Fiona smiled earnestly. She took Belinda's shoulders and guided her through the doorway and into the kitchen for a yarn, and a cup of herbal tea. Belinda ransacked through the cupboard searching for the jar she used to collecting knickknacks together. She found it at last and placed it on the kitchen table while Fiona poured boiling water into their cups.

She took the leaves from her hands and placed the them into the jar. It had started to rain outside, so Fiona pulled down the drapes in the kitchen.

"How was your day, Belinda?" They both sat on the kitchen stools, and supped at their beverages.

"Weird! Weirdness just seems to follow me."

Belinda recounted the day's events to Fiona. Fiona took of her glasses and stared at the light bulb hanging from the centre of the ceiling. A late crane fly buzzed insanely around the light.

"Oh, I hate those bloody things," Belinda cursed, looking up at the demented creature.

"Don't worry," said Fiona. Her tongue shot out of her mouth, whipping the crane fly mid-flight. She retracted her tongue into her oral cavity and crunched down on the insect. A twitching leg popped out of the side of her maw but was soon sucked back in. Fiona continued chewing and crunching.

"Problem solved," she said, forgetting her manners for a moment by talking with her mouth full.

"Please, don't do that," Belinda said with mild nausea. She shut one of her eyes with a palm of her hand as the munching continued. She made a half gurning facial expression. "You're a like a bloody Renfield when you do that. I hope you don't show your gecko side to Ben. It would freak him out."

Fiona laughed with her mouth closed as she finally swallowed the insect. "Ben loves it. He said so." She put on her glasses again and smiled at her friend. They both snickered at each other.

Fiona glanced at her watch, "Is that the time?" She collected their cups and placed them into the sink.

Yawning, Belinda stretched in her seat. "Thanks Fi, you're a great help." She slapped her thighs with her hands.

Belinda rose while Fiona gathered her things together. They hugged at the front door.

"You call me if you need anything, Belle." Fiona said.

Belinda went upstairs and tip-toed into her son's bedroom. Ben's room was that of a typical four-year-old, full of dinosaurs models, *Lego Star Wars* figurines, and his favourite teddy bear. Beside his bed, a small night-light gently cast a chiaroscuro upon his face. Outside, it started to rain lightly, and it created a comforting white noise.

Ben knew his mother's comforting footsteps, he startled slightly from his slumber.

"Mummy, is that you?"

Belinda rushed over to his bedside. "Hush, Ben. Mummy's home," she said, reassuringly. Kissing his forehead gently, looking down on him with a beatific smile. "Let me tuck you in, sweetheart. What did you and Aunty Fi-fi do today?" She fluffed and tucked his bed sheets.

"Mummy, I know she isn't my real aunty. Why do you pretend that she is?"

"Okay, mister smartypants," Belinda said. "Just for that I won't tell you what I found on the way to granddad's shop today!"

"Aw, mummy! Please!" Ben was upright in his bed, wide-eyed with excitement.

"If you say sorry I will let you see it in the morning! Have you said your prayers yet?"

Ben sheepishly mumbled, "No, mummy, I was waiting for you." A cross expression clouded his face. "I'm sorry, mummy."

"Okay, we will say them together. Now close your eyes, bow your head and clasp your hands. I'll start."

As I lay me down to sleep,
I pray the Lord my soul to keep,
If I should die before I wake,
I pray my Lord my soul to take.

Ben knew the words by heart, and said them in unison with his mother.

"Amen," they intoned together.

Belinda stood to leave and reached to turn off Ben's night light. Ben reached out and touched her hand.

"Please leave it on, mummy. It helps me dream of dinosaurs and *Star Wars*."

Belinda kissed him again then smiled at him as she left his room and closed the door. She paced between her bedroom and bathroom as she brushed her teeth, deep in thought. She went through her ablutions and her night time routine, then let down her golden hair and finally settled into her own bedroom. Her pyjamas were neatly folded and ironed. *Fiona*, she smiled. She was not only a good friend, but Belinda's housekeeper as well.

"Oh, God, please bless that big gecko heart of hers!" she laughed.

Belinda settled herself into bed.

She felt the same burning, throbbing sensation that was always associated with her cycle. "Great," she muttered inwardly. "I guess I'll be dealing with that tomorrow as well."

The rain outside the window was fierce now. The wind blew hard upon it, shaking the leaves from the trees. Belinda turned out her bedside lamp and settled into an uneasy sleep. She dreamed of the bug that was trapped in the spider web at her father's shop. And someone outside singing, in a soft, deep, seductive voice…

Outside, the figure waited. A shadow in the dark, snapping its fingers to the rhythm of a long forgotten song:

I love a rainy night!
Mmm, I love a rainy night!

There was a lull in the storm, and the almost full moon broke out from betwixt the rain clouds. The shadow figure paused. Its fangs glistened in a moon beam.

And then it was gone, riding on the edge of the gale.

Belinda's mind was in a haze when she stirred from her sleep. Her bedroom shared a wall with Ben's, and she thought she heard a noise coming from within his room. She decided to check on him again in case he was having another nightmare. She entered his room, bleary-eyed and half stumbling, and discovered Ben sitting upright in his bed with his bed sheets pulled up over his head and making a horrible rasping noise.

Belinda, feeling cautious and confused, stepped toward the bed and reached out her hand to touch the bed sheets.

"Ben?"

The bed sheets flapped open and a monstrous creature lunged up at her. The dolphin's head slaked its long tongue from its mouth then whipped it around behind Belinda's neck and pulled her horrified face toward it. A slick tentacle wrapped around her and covered her mouth to stifle her choking screams. More tentacles enwrapped her flailing arms and legs and held her powerless. The creature widened its gullet to expose its sharp, serrated teeth and drew closer to her exposed neck. Great crimson arcs burst from Belinda's neck and splattered the walls as the beast punctured and extravasated her throat, then violently ripped our her trachea. Its one eye glinted malevolently as Belinda's body went limp and her throat gurgled and sputtered blood.

Belinda yelled in anguish and sat bolt upright in her bed with both hands clutched around her intact throat.

"Mother fudger!" she exclaimed in panicked relief.

She jumped out of bed and rushed into her son's room with her heart still pounding in her chest and her blood still pulsing in her veins. A cold shiver ran across her skin.

Ben was there. He was fast asleep.

"Oh my Ben, my wee Ben!"

She lifted the comforter and squeezed in next to her son. She held him near to her and they both slept safely and soundly until the morning came.

* * *

"Seven AM. Time to get up. Seven A.M. Time to get up." The alarm on Belinda's mobile phone announced the start of their morning routine. It was loud enough to hear from Ben's bedroom. Ben woke first.

"Mummy? What's wrong? Why are you in my bed with me?" Ben was blurred eyed, and there was some rheum in the corner of his eyeball. Belinda gently removed it.

"I just missed you last night, so I decided to cuddle in with you."

They both arose and began their morning routine. Belinda started by getting breakfast for herself and Ben. She hurriedly fixed a bowl of *Rainbow Frosted Sugar Puff Marshmallow Flakes* for herself — not a healthy, balanced breakfast, but sometimes a girl just needs a quick energy kick.

She gave the werewolf mask to Ben, and some of the leaves from the jar for show and tell. He was bubbling with excitement by the time Fiona arrived to take him to Halloween Primary School.

"Aunty Fifi, see what mummy got for me!" he beamed at Fiona, holding out his new treasures for her to see. She smiled in appreciation every time Ben called her "aunty."

"Oh, that's wonderful!" Fifi made an exaggerated face of excitement. "You're such a lucky boy. Okay, let's grab your school bag and be on our way. We don't want to be late."

Fiona and Ben left. Belinda sat at the kitchen table wondering why she still wasn't craving for her first morning cigarette. The craving was strangely gone. She glanced at the kitchen clock — it was already 9 a.m. — and by this time she would ordinarily have long since finished her first smoke of the day and would already be thinking about her next one.

She felt cleansed, but did not know why. She stared intently at the packet. She didn't have time to sit around waiting for her familiar nicotine cravings to kick in. She decided to smoke one anyway and just get it out of the way. She pulled it from the packet, placed it in her mouth, and immediately started to gag in revulsion at the smell and the taste of it.

"For fudge sake! I need some air!" She threw the packet into the kitchen bin as she stormed out of the room. She lifted her jacket, mobile phone, and backpack as she breezed through the hallway. She was about to go out through the front door when an eerie compulsion took over her. She paused for a moment and stared at the place she had stashed the sword the night before. Without thinking twice, she retrieved the katana from its hiding place, and shoved it into her backpack.

She recalled her odd encounter with Hung Fung Joey from the previous evening. *What did this guy do to me? Was it hypnotism? Was it some ancient eastern voodoo hocus-pocus?* Whatever it was, it was definitely some fudged up bull poop, and she was on her way to find out.

It was an overcast morning, with a hint of rain on the wind. She smelled the air outside. Her senses were acute. There was a storm coming.

"Ah, Miss Auberon, I am glad to see you again. How are you? You slept well?"

Joey appeared at the appointed spot where they had parted the previous evening. Using both hands, he was carefully holding a large, round urn.

"No, I did *not* sleep well! I had the worst bloody nightmare. It was a real fudge licker, I can tell you. First, some weirdo was singing outside my house. That was a little creepy, but no biggie. But then my son was in danger, so naturally I was in a panic to save him. And then…" she paused for a deep breath, "a disembodied psycho dolphin was gnawing on my neck like it was a mother fudging all-you-can-eat seafood buffet!"

Belinda looked wild eyed and crazy. She paused for a moment to let her words sink in. She took a short breath to calm herself, then nonchalantly added, "Also, I'm about to get my period, so I'm moody as poo and not to be fudged with."

Joey frowned in consternation. Perhaps it was time now for the girl to learn the unrevealed path. After all, she was the Huntress of Halloween town, and it was her birthright.

"Walk with me Belinda, and I will explain all." They began walking at a casual pace. "Did you bring the sword with you?"

"Aye, it's in my backpack." She reached her hand around and patted the rucksack.

Joey smiled grimly.

"Good. Put this in your rucksack, please." Joey proffered the urn to Belinda, holding his arms out straight.

"What is it?" she asked, slightly alarmed by it's oddness. "Is it heavy?"

"It's an urn, and it's extremely heavy. It's also a family heirloom. Here, turn around and open your rucksack."

"This isn't a cremation urn, is it? Is there some dead fudger's ashes inside this thing? I'm not going to be able to stay calm and be all cool with that."

Joey lifted the lid off the urn to show Belinda that it was empty. She peeked inside. Satisfied that it was just an empty urn, she acquiesced to Joey. She huffed slightly whenever the extra weight was placed behind her.

"Right, where are we headed?"

"You did say we were going to Pandoria's shop?" Joey questioned.

"Last night was a bit of a blur, a lot to process. But, yes I remembered."

They walked in the direction of The Witches' Ball. The shop was on the opposite end of the municipality. Joey told the story of how the vampire dolphin came to be in Halloween town.

"This dolphin is vampiric. It is rare in the deep oceans. No one knows exactly when it tasted human flesh." Joey went on. "Its blood is a broad spectrum hallucinogenic, containing high level aphrodisiac compounds. And as such, it is highly sought after by various parties."

Belinda raised her eyebrows, and shrugged, but did not say a word.

"Here is one example of cetacean deviousness for you, Belinda …"

"Years ago, before you were born, there was a famous astrophysicist named Carl Sagan. He was instrumental in placing the Voyager 1 spacecraft into interstellar space."

Belinda nodded, trying to take this information in.

"He also studied dolphin intelligence in a laboratory in America, in Saint Thomas. Dolphins are believed by some to possess greater intelligence than humans. The purpose of Dr. Sagan's research was to facilitate cross-species communication for extraterrestrial life. He was made a member of The Order Of The Dolphin."

Belinda sniggered at this, but a look from Joey wiped the smile from her face.

Joey continued, "In 1965, a woman named Margaret Howe — she had been a neuroscientist in the U.S., and a friend and colleague of Dr. Sagan — theorised that the only way to communicate with a dolphin was to co-habit with one. The dolphin was called —"

Joey hesitated. "The dolphin's name was Peter."

"Shut your fudge hole!" Belinda stopped walking and stood back a step.

"It was a mere coincidence, Belinda. 'Peter' is not an uncommon name. I did not mean to imply that your father was a dolphin in disguise. I apologise if you misunderstood."

A rain droplet bounced on the ground, followed by another. Joey glanced up at the sky.

"All right," Belinda said sharply. She started walking again. "What happened next?"

"They set up a house for Peter. It was a single-level house that had been specially constructed for the experiment. Ms. Howe lived in the house for almost three months, attempting to teach the dolphin how to speak a limited vocabulary of key English words. There was a kitchen, a television, and an office with a chair and a cot. The whole house was partially submerged in thirty-five centimetres of water. This provided an environment in which Peter the dolphin and Ms. Howe could comfortably spend time watching television together."

Belinda said, "Sounds cozy. Come to think, it sounds a bit like some dates I've been on. Oh, come on, Joey! Is this all for real?" She snorted in a disbelieving way.

Joey nodded, "All this is part of the training. Be quiet, girl."

Belinda glared at Joey. Her brow furrowed as she took a deep breath. She was about to chastise him, but Joey held up his palm to halt the verbal assault.

She incised her tongue between her teeth and exhaled.

Joey thought, *Excellent. She is mastering her temperament, at last.*

"Margaret Howe spent the next three months in isolation with a dolphin. She had later told a colleague, "No matter how long it takes, no matter how much work, this dolphin is going to learn to speak English." She even wore dark red lipstick when working with the dolphin so that he could better distinguish the vowels and gesticulations of her mouth.

"Unfortunately, the dolphin had other agendas. Peter became more feisty, unpredictable, and less controllable. Margaret would spend more and more of her time just trying to keep him focused on the task. Margaret became despondent, whereas Peter became more… amorous."

Belinda raised her eyebrows at this remark, "And by 'amorous' you mean…?"

Joey seemed a little abashed. "Peter was becoming more aroused and affectionate. He could not concentrate or cooperate with the scientific research when he mind was so distracted. And so, Ms. Howe decided that the only way to placate the dolphin was to… eliminate these distractions for him. In short, she would give Peter… let's call it 'hand sex.'"

Belinda burst into a fit of incredulous laughter. "What? You're saying she gave the dolphin a hand job?" She roared with amusement.

"That's precisely what she did. Peter was constantly aroused and erect. What else could she have done?" Joey said dryly. "The dolphin once tried to initiate an encounter with Carl Sagan, who replied that he was flattered, but retorted to Margaret stating, he wasn't 'that kind of dolphin.' I read this years ago in *The Cosmic Connection* by Carl Sagan. Besides, it is well documented."

Belinda was in tears of laughter. Joey was stoic, and tried to keep a straight face. He composed himself then continued.

"You see, Belinda, people think that the porpoise is a friendly creature. Far from it. The dolphin is in fact totally devious, conniving, and deadly. It has a brain larger than most humans — it's totally alien under vivisection."

Belinda arched her eyebrows at Joey. At least she had stopped laughing, and Joey felt encouraged to continue.

"In the very early hours of one foggy morning before the sun had fully risen, a group of Polish fishermen were landing their unusual catch at the river port in east Halloween town. The beast flailed angrily on the deck, thrashing around in a torrent of rage. It took ten men to subdue it, but not before the monstrosity dispatched a number of the poor bastards: two were decapitated by its vicious flippers; a half-dozen others were eviscerated by the creatures steel tail; and another was impaled, cruelly on the tip of its dorsal fin of doom. A specialist had been called in. His name was Glargazop Puckwudgie. He was known as an exceptional mariner who could catch any creature that ever swam. Glargazop restrained the dolphin with long, thick metal chains. He brought along industrial chainsaws and heavy landing gear, borrowed from the Colonel."

Joey paused. He closed his eyes and stopped walking. Belinda halted with him.

"I know all this because I was watching from a distance. As I stated, various parties had a vested interest in the dolphin. I watched for as long as I could, until… the carving began."

Belinda choked.

"We Chinese enjoy many great delicacies, and our palates are wide and varied. We had heard of the fabled Helvar vampire dolphin. It had been sighted off shore by one of our trawlers, but the Poles had beaten us to the catch. The dismemberment of the Helvar will haunt me to the day I die. I clasped my hands to my ears, with no avail. Its shrill, shrieking screams as Puckwudgie cleaved the dolphin's head off were utterly ghastly and inhuman. No mortal man could have preserved his sanity that terrible night. When Glargazop had finished his task, the Colonel arrived."

Joey resumed the pace, Belinda followed.

"So, the dolphin is called Helvar? Catchy name," Belinda said flippantly. "Why was the Colonel there?"

"An argument had arisen between the remaining Polish fishermen, Puckwudgie, and the Colonel. For years, the Poles had been muscling into Puckwudgie's fishmonger business, leaving him almost destitute. The Polish fishermen were to be paid handsomely for their troubles and to compensate them for their lost men. The head of Helvar went to Glargazop Puckwudgie, and the remainder of the carcass was sent to the Freaky Fried Chicken Factory to be… processed and rendered."

"Festering fudge! I think I am going to hurl my guts! Everyone in the whole town has eaten in that place at some stage in their lives!" Belinda squatted again, and breathed in and out several times until the nausea passed. Joey sat down beside her, crossed legged, in a full lotus position.

They ensconced down behind a hedgerow by the side of the road.

"And now you know what the 'Special Element' is the in Freaky Fried Chicken Factory recipe: it is the evil blood and flesh of Helvar, the vampire dolphin."

"That's fudge-churning and horrible! Those responsible for this abomination must die!" Belinda said fervently. Then she had an awful thought.

"Joey, what about my nightmare? What do you think caused it? It was so vivid… so real."

Joey levelled a stare at her and said, "I am not sure; usually, contact with the blood causes unwanted desires to surface, and other aberrant behaviour. Saliva, and other bodily fluids produces other phenomena. Have you been in such contact? That's the only explanation I can consider."

Belinda's mind raced. "There was something, maybe. On my pathway last night, a slimy trail led from my gate to my front door. I thought it was snail trails — you know, garden slugs."

Belinda paused for a second, then hastily added, "Quick, Joey, hold my hair!"

Joey was confused and caught off guard. "Why must I hold your…?"

Too late. Belinda leaned forward and was violently sick on the side of the hedgerow. Great greasy chunks of chunder sprayed from her mouth and nose. *Perhaps the Rainbow Frosted Sugar Puff Marshmallow Flakes wasn't such a great idea after all*, she thought.

Joey attempted to comforted her by rubbing her back, and belatedly gathered her hair off her face.

When her gut was emptied, Belinda pulled a tissue from her inside jacket pocket and pattered her mouth. She raised her head and let out a yell.

"Ugh, well that wasn't embarrassing at all. I think I handled that like a lady."

Belinda wiped her nose and tossed the tissue.

"Damn you, dolphin! Damn you to hell!"

Joey smiled. "Don't worry, we will send them all to hell!"

He offered Belinda a Tic Tac.

* * *

They arrived at The Witches' Ball. Belinda hated it immediately. The shop's exterior was oppressive and impressive in equal measure: dead, decaying tree branches intertwined the building, and a mystic vapour permeated the walls. The building seemed stood out of time, dilapidated, tall, and of incredible antiquity. Fungi and other growths and pestilences covered the awnings and every crevice. Poison ivy crawled and clung over the entire structure. It seemed to be genuinely haunted.

Joey peered through the main window, rubbing it with his sleeve, but all he could discern were opaque shadows. The windows themselves were blacked out with shutters and dark paint. A notice hung above the door knocker: *Introduceți de propria voință liberă.*[3]

Belinda tried the door, and was surprised when it opened. The portal creaked as she turned the handle and pushed against its weight. A tiny spider shot up her arm she shook her hand vigorously to dislodge the unwelcome arachnid.

"Fudge off!" she demanded.

When the door had opened far enough for her to pass through, she turned around and whispered to Joey, "We are in… Wait… Where did…?"

Joey had disappeared again.

She was about to yell out for Joey when something from inside the shop grabbed her around the ankles and yanked her inside. She landed flat on her face inside the shop and the door slammed shut.

Winded by the weight of her backpack, Belinda pushed herself upright with a groan. It was dim inside, save a light beam from beneath the closed door. She spun around, searching for whoever… or whatever… had pulled her inside.

A childish, giggling laughter taunted her senses.

Belinda pulled her cigarette lighter from her pocket and struck the flint with her thumb to illuminate the shop. Sinister shadows loomed everywhere as she surveyed the

---

[3] Romanian to English translation: *Enter, and of your own free will.*

room. Belinda sniffed. The air was thick with the smell of extinguished candles.

A voice came out of the blackness.

"I know why you are here. I know what you seek. I can... smell... you. You reek of the blood fever. And something else..."

The voice was arcadian, thick, and soft. Belinda was angry. She called out to the unseen owner of the voice, "I forgot to go to the chemist! So sue me, bitch! Or, should I say witch?"

Still holding the lit cigarette lighter in one hand, Belinda stealthily reached around to her backpack and drew her sword from its sheathe.

"Once, long ago, I inveigled your father into a deal, and I seduced your own lover, Raphael!" the voice mocked.

Belinda's blood drained from her face. Her whole body cooled, and she experienced a sensation that she imagined was not unlike a feral cat having its fur stroked the wrong direction. She was preparing to fight this creature.

"Well, pardon me if I don't know what 'inveigled' means, but it does sound like something a skanky hell hag might say. And as for Raphael... how and when?"

She dropped her lighter as the room was instantly and brilliantly illuminated by a jagged bolt of lightning outside the shop. A storm had moved in quickly and angrily, and a rumbling thunderclap immediately followed the flash. Around the shop, a thousand candles erupted in flame.

The array of candles cast their oscillating, flickering shadows across every surface. In the centre of the room, bathed in the warm and scintillating light, Pandoria Evǣfensang stood in all her glory. She was statuesque, sultry, and seductive. Her dress was as black as a moonless midnight, and shimmered as she moved.

She paced confidently around the pavement stones as a panther stalks her prey. Her eyes bored into Belinda's — she never blinked, and never looked away. She was holding a sacrificial dagger, a long khanjali.

Belinda slowly slid her backpack from her shoulders and let it settle on the stone floor.

"Who are you?" Belinda said. "*What* are you?"

"I am the storm, little girl," Pandoria replied condescendingly.

"No, you're just a bitch of a witch. And no one calls me 'girl'" Belinda growled through clenched teeth. She launched herself at her adversary in a furious rage, clashing and whirling her blade.

Pandoria evaded every slice and dodged every lunge. She was fast and agile and moved like the wind. Their polished blades mirrored the candle flames as they blocked and parried.

"Where is the mask?" Belinda howled.

They fought with speed and fury to match the tempest that swirled around them. They matched blow for blow in a deadly ballet until Belinda finally tired, and stumbled onto the cold ground. Pandoria honed in for the kill, but Belinda was again able to summon her strength to deflect the blow and force the tip of Pandoria's blade away from her eyeball. Pandoria moved three steps back from Belinda to put some distance between them.

"The mask? Is that what you want, little girl? And the boy? Both are far away from you, and that's where they shall remain!" She goaded Belinda.

Pandoria's visage warped and contorted, like warm candle wax poured into a mould, and within seconds her face had transformed into that of Harriet Atchette.

Belinda's own face reflected the flickering candlelight that highlighted a prickling sweat on her skin.

"Now, that…" she said gasping, "that is just plain sick! Why can't you leave my family alone you melty-faced hag?"

"You dumb harridan! Do you need a little help to figure it out? With my powers, I can be any woman I want to be. Even you!" Her features dissolved and distorted again, then quickly reformed into Belinda's own likeness. Her face, body, countenance, and even her clothes were an exact facsimile. Even Pandoria's khanjali dagger had changed its size and shape to mimic Belinda's katana sword.

She laughed cruelly. "You will never recover your father's soul. I've sent it to hell. Prepare to join him there now!"

As the two duelists prepared to reengage in battle, Joey appeared from out of the darkness and stood close between them.

"You!" both women exclaimed as the looked at Joey in surprise. "Where have you been?" they said in unison, then looked back at each other awkwardly. They cautiously lowered their weapons — their one-on-one life-and-death battle had been interrupted by Joey's arrival. Belinda and Pandoria both awaited Joey's explanation.

"I have been… preparing," Joey said cryptically. He crossed the space between the two women and reached the other side where Belinda's backpack lay. As he walked, he studied both Belindas carefully, scrutinising them closely. Visually, they were indistinguishable. As he stooped to picked up the backpack, he closed his eyes and deeply inhaled. He smelled the air, sensing a faint but unmistakeable scent. He removed the heavy urn from Belinda's backpack. He slowly opened the urn as both Belindas watched him intently. He looked at one Belinda, and then at the other. He closed his eyes briefly and vocalized a strange incantāre in some foreign tongue.

"I know what you are thinking, Joey," one Belinda said, "but be very careful. She is a cunning trickster, and she is imitating me in a very convincing way. Don't be fooled by her disguise."

"You... lying...little... sheep... fudger!" the other Belinda retorted angrily, stamping her foot after each word. "Joey, it's me, Belinda! *She* is the impostor!" She scowled at her doppelgänger who was now mimicking her mannerisms in the worst ever game of *Copycat the Barber*. Both Belindas stomped their feet in tandem.

"Be silent, both of you!"

At that moment, a fierce whirlwind blew out the shutters and the candles everywhere. A twister whipped through the building, the two women were hurtled to opposite sides of the room. Joey stood firmly planted in the eye of the storm, holding the urn above his head and in a loud voice recited ancient Chinese conjurations above the cacophony.

When the incantation was completed and the winds reached their apex, Joey turned the urn and pointed the opened end toward the Belinda doppelgänger. She screamed as the maelstrom began to suck the essence and the very soul of the witch into the urn. Her features transmogrified, convulsing through all the women she had been through her life: Pandoria Evǣfensang; Harriet Atchette; Belinda Auberon; and countless other faces she had used through the ages for her trickery and seduction. The final form she took was that of the vile snake-headed Medusa.

"No! You cannot hold my soul forever, Hung Fung Joey!"

The Medusa hissed and writhed within the vortex until she finally succumbed to the unrelenting forces of the urn. In a flash of light she was drawn into the urn's opening and Joey quickly sealed it shut. Again, he muttered a strange chant and instantly the whirling storm ceased.

Silence filled the room again and was broken only by the heavy breathing of Joey and the true Belinda. For a moment neither moved.

Joey quickly retrieved Belinda's backpack and zipped the urn inside. He rushed over to where Belinda lay slumped against the wall, exhausted but relieved.

"You have done well," he smiled down at her.

He helped her to her feet, but Belinda shrugged him off.

"I… I think I was knocked out against the wall. What did I miss?" Belinda looked urgently around the room. "Where is the Pandoria?"

"She is no longer in this world, Belinda Auberon." Joey hoisted the backpack and patted the side of the urn. "She's in here now."

"Stop fudging around! How did… What exactly *are* you, Joey?" She stared intently at the backpack containing the mysterious urn.

"I told you — I am merely a Chinese chef, owner of The Running River Restaurant."

"No, you are not! Is it true what she said about my dad? And what happened to you, where did you go, when I needed you?"

Belinda's expression turned to confusion and panic.

"Wait… how did you know which of us was the real me? I mean, we were identical in looks, voice, mannerisms… everything. How could you be so sure it would be Pandoria inside that urn instead of me?"

Joey bowed his head, and spoke flatly.

"You have so many questions, young one. They will all be answered in due time. Come, let us leave this place now. You were doing well, so I did not interrupt your training."

"Huh! Is that what that was!?" Belinda scoffed.

"Hurry, retrieve your sword, and follow me." Joey found the khanjali dagger and placed it inside Belinda's backpack.

"Oh, no! If you think I am going to carry that thing around in my backpack you are a crazy man!" Belinda said obstinately.

"I will carry it. I will bring your sword, too. Quickly, now — we haven't much time left."

They left The Witches' Ball the same way they had entered. It had grown dark outside, and a few evening stars littered the horizon. The storm had subsided and the air felt cooler, cleaner, and fresher.

"How long was I in there fighting with her, Joey? It felt like a long time."

"Yes, an eternity — I pulled you out of her quantum gyrare just in time. Look behind you."

The shop collapsed inwardly, swirling and sucking down in a vast sinkhole until it vanished, winking out of existence. All that remained was an empty lot of scorched earth and debris, as if the shop had never existed.

Belinda stumbled backwards in shock. Blinking her eyes.

"What is happening to my life?" she whispered, then turned to Joe, asking, "Is this magic?"

"No, merely higher forms of technology. 'Any sufficiently advanced technology is indistinguishable from magic.'"

"Okay, there you go again with your science-y stuff. I guess it was again Carl Sagan who said that, right?" Belinda said.

Joey gave her a wry smile.

"Not this time. That's a quote from science-fiction author Arthur C. Clarke."

"Oh," replied Belinda, attempting to fein familiarity with science-fiction literature. "Yeah, he would have been my next guess."

Joey was about to add something, but was cut short.

"Hold on, Joey…"

Belinda's jacket pocket was buzzing. She rummaged fervently to unzip her coat for her vibrating mobile phone. Her hands still shook from the shock of everything that had happened that evening and her body still trembled with the rush of adrenaline. She found and then almost dropped her mobile. Horrible thoughts churned in her mind.

"A missed call from Fiona." Her heart sank, and one overriding thought eclipsed all others.

"Oh, Ben. I forgot to pick him up from Fiona. I am such a terrible mother!" She turned to Joey with a scared look in her eyes. "We are half way across the town!" She paced around frantically on the spot as she listened to Fiona's message.

"Oh my God!"

Belinda put her hand over her mouth, horrified by what she had heard.

* * *

"Where the hell are you, Belinda?" thought Fiona.

At around quarter to five the darkness was encroaching. The storm would bring foul creatures on the wind; Ben had been asking for his mummy. Fiona and Ben had arrived home from school at around three o'clock, and were now back in Belinda's home in New Church Lane. Fiona had settled Ben in front of the television in the living room. He sat on the sofa upon his favourite squab and watched cartoons.

The hours had passed, but there had been no sign of Belinda. It was now almost 9 P.M.

Fiona decided to call Belinda on her mobile phone. She went into the kitchen for privacy, and left the door open a few inches.

"Belle, where are you, sweetheart?" Fiona began her voice message. "Ben's worried. I made him his supper, but he keeps asking me when his mummy's coming home. Call me back whenever you are free. Okay, love? Wait, hold on…" She held the telephone away from her ear and craned her neck toward the kitchen door. "Ben, who is that at the door? Who?"

Fiona set the phone on the kitchen table and walked into the hallway and toward the open front door.

"Hey! You can't…" began Fiona.

"The young man of the house invited me in," said a seductive baritone voice from inside the hallway. "My son! I have missed you!"

An argument and a violent struggle ensued. The telephone receiver recorded the chaos: the bumps, the crashes, and the shouts.

And then, the silence.

Heavy footsteps approached the telephone, then a deep voice spoke.

"Hello Belinda, it's me. I have our son. I had a little fun with your gecko girlfriend, too. She was sweet… meat," the voice laughed cruelly.

* * *

"Raphael, you undead fuck!" Belinda lost control and screamed at her phone. "If you have hurt them in anyway… If you have harmed a hair on my son's head…"

Belinda realized it was futile to shout at the recorded message playing on her mobile phone. The voicemail message had been recorded minutes before, on the other side of town. But, to her shock, the recorded voice continued talking and responded to her outburst.

"Save your idle threats, Belinda! What can you possibly do to me? I am already dead, you dumb whore!" He made a slurping sound, then started singing:

Well, I love a rainy night,
Taste the rain on my lips,
In the moonlight shadow!

Belinda was unnerved. "How can he be… It's a recorded message; how can he be speaking to me live?"

"I manipulated your puny headed memories. You are not incredibly smart, bitch!" Raphael inexplicably continued. "You never were! Your responses are oh so predictable. I am undead. The past was a game of lies we played. A mere phone is a toy in the hands of a vampyre god. Goodbye, Belinda! You were a bitter taste in my mouth."

The phone went silent as the voice message ended.

Belinda stood frozen with an expression of terror on her face. Her eyes were brimming over.

"Oh, Ben! No, this is not happening!"

Joey acted quickly. Without a word he pulled out the witch's dagger, grasped Belinda's left hand and drew blood from her palm. Belinda shrieked. Before she could react Joey pulled her towards him in a hard embrace.

"The khanjali dagger needs to feed. It needs energy."

The knife pulled the blood across Belinda's open palm by an unseen force. Rivulets of red energy were drawn up and absorbed into the blade's keen edge as the dagger became an incandescent, white hot fiery flame.

Space and time enveloped them in a slipstream. The force weave propelled Belinda and Joey through a web. Joey aged. His eyes glowed red as they travelled along the pathways between dimensions. Both were suspended in an algid trance state while the universe folded and unfolded around them. As the dimensions reassembled, they materialized in the darkness of Belinda's kitchen, and the flow of time returned to normal.

A full moon cast pale dark purple shadows throughout the scullery. Finally released from the enchantment, she rushed to her kitchen sink and shouted, "Joey, hold my hair!"

This time, Joey knew what to do and was quick to react. He hastily gathered her hair into an untidy bunch at the back of her head while Belinda grunted, heaved, and spewed into her kitchen sink.

"Son of a witch!" she exclaimed between heaves. "How many bowls of *Rainbow Frosted Sugar Puff Marshmallow Flakes* did I eat!?"

Why is the room purple? Belinda thought while wiping her nose and mouth and attempting to recover some of her dignity.

Joey sheathed the dagger behind him. In dim light, he rummaged through the drawers where Belinda was pointing and soon located her first aid kit. Reaching to aid her injury, he wrapped a bandage over her wounded palm.

"Here — hold this tight."

As Belinda's eyes adjusted to the darkness, she leaned toward Joey and looked more closely at his face.

"What the fragging fudge happened to you? Your eyes and your face… you look ten years older!"

"Sympathetic magic. I needed fuel — your blood — to power the dagger. But there's always a price to pay for the spells we cast, and some spells take a heavy toll. When I cast the spell around us, you passed through unscathed and I alone paid the price."

"But Joey — I don't know what to say … "

There was a dripping sound. Joey looked at the kitchen sink, but it wasn't coming from there. Behind him a splat of liquid landed on the floor.

"Where is your lighter?" Joey asked.

"I lost it when Pandoria…" She cut her sentence short when a second glob of unknown liquid landed next to her with a sickening, squelching sound. She bolted to the light switch and flicked it on, revealing the horrors that hung all around them.

It was an abattoir. Even Joey was aghast.

Above them, with nails stake through each hand and foot, Fiona was suspended from the ceiling, spreadeagled and partially naked. Her blood had been smeared over every wall and window, and sticky puddles congealed on the floor below where she hung.

Belinda's mind reeled from the shock and she struggled to comprehend and accept what she was seeing. Her only coherent thought was of how Fiona now resembled the cranefly she had consumed the previous evening. When at last her mind began to process the visceral image above and all around her, she could only think in questions. *Was it really her friend hanging there? What had that bastard done to her? Was any of this real?*

She shut her eyes tightly for a moment while a deluge of emotions overcame her. She felt remorse, loss, fear, and rage. A tear escaped her closed eyes. She thought a silent prayer.

There will be time for mourning, later, she thought. Right now, she was out for blood. She wanted justice, and she wanted revenge. She opened her eyes and prepared for action.

"Let's get her down from there," Joey said grimly. He pulled Belinda's kitchen table over so that it stood directly underneath where Fiona hung. He climbed up and prized her body off the ceiling, one limb at a time, while supporting her weight on his neck and shoulders. As gently as he could, he slowly lowered her onto the tabletop. Belinda removed her jacket and draped it over Fiona's limp body, covering her partially.

Belinda stood on one side of her beloved friend and carefully held her hand, squeezing it very gently as her tears welled up. Joey stood on the other side of the table and performed a cursory examination.

"Look at this," he spoke softly. "Her neck has been ripped apart. It must have been a vicious assault, and it explains why there's so much blood everywhere. I'm so sorry, Belinda. I can only hope that she did not suffer long before she passed."

As if defying Joey's analysis, Fiona suddenly opened her eyes. Belinda flinched backwards, and Joey peered into Fiona's gaze with an intense curiosity.

Fiona gurgled, "Belle!" Her voice was weak. "He… he took Ben. I'm sorry. I… tried my best to stop him… He was too strong…"

Belinda reached forward instinctively to offer comfort to Fiona and to assist her up into a seated position, but Joey set his hand on Belinda's shoulder. Belinda and Joey looked into each other's eyes.

"No," he said calmly. "Don't move her." He took Belinda to one side and whispered to her, "This is not Fiona. This is not your friend. We must be very…"

Before Joey could finish, an icy gust of wind blew through the room, and Fiona was gone, leaving only her bloody silhouette on the table.

"We must find her, Belinda!" Joey said fervently. "She has become a gecko Nosferatu now, and we cannot allow such a creature to roam freely. You must find her and you must decapitate her — it is the only way to be sure."

"She's a *what* now?! Look, what is it with you and decapitations?" Belinda hissed. "Will you please wise up?" When flustered, Belinda's grammar would slip and she would revert to local colloquialisms. "Decapitation did not work on the dolphin, so it didn't!"

He hesitated briefly. "Fiona is only half human, but we should still stake her through the heart as well!"

He lifted a kitchen stool and upended it before breaking it across his knee. He snapped off one of its legs to create a makeshift wooden stake. "It's the only way to be sure," he repeated.

"What are you doing? My table is already ruined, and now you're smashing up my stools?Give it here! Give!"

She snatched the stake away from his hands. Joey was in awe of what she did next. She immediately removed her katana sword from her backpack, and with great skilfulness whittled the point of the stake to a fine edge. She blew on the completed spike a few times to remove the loose shavings, then twirled it around to examine the shaft.

"Truly, you are the huntress of Halloween town, Belinda Auberon!"

"Hah!" She laughed sarcastically. "Huntress, my bum! I was in the Girl Guides. And, well, I am a mother after all. I am a dab hand with a knitting needle, too, I will have you know."

She lifted up her weapons, putting the stake in her left hand and the katana sword in her right.

"You can close your mouth now Joey. Come on! Let's go a hunt a Nosferatu! She is likely to be still here, somewhere in the house."

Joey closed his mouth, and followed Belinda out of the kitchen and into the hall. As they passed the bottom of the staircase they heard a loud thump from the floor above them.

"She is in Ben's bedroom," Belinda whispered.

They crept cautiously upstairs. Carefully opening the door of Ben's bedroom. The only light in the room streamed through the window through which the whole town could be seen. Giggling, gurgling laughter was coming from the farthest corner. Squinting, Belinda and Joey could make out a figure that was sitting in the gloom of the corner with its back to them.

Without moving her body, Fiona's head rotated 180 degrees to stare maniacally at them.

"Can geckos actually do that?" Joey said to Belinda, cautiously.

"*She* can."

They moved hesitantly across the room to where Fiona sat. Her head glared and followed them as they traversed the floor. Fiona was clutching Ben's favourite teddy bear against her chest. She was wearing Belinda's jacket. She spoke slowly.

"I loved Ben, Belle. But now he's going to hell!" Fiona's voice was rasping and gurgling in her shredded throat. "Raphael has the Soul Mask and he is going to put it on Ben at midnight! No one can stop him. Then the gateway will open to the world below. Also, he stole my mobile phone!"

Raphael has stolen one soul and one mobile phone — perhaps each are of equal value, these days, Joey thought. *People covet their mobile devices and they worship technology and social media, instead of their God. How cheap life had become in this town.*

"What happened to the cheeky wee boy, the one the Witch-Bitch spoke of?"

"They had no use for him, so they made him… disappear."

Fiona gestured to the Freaky Fried Chicken Factory that could be seen out of the window. Smoke was churning, belching and emanating from the tall, black chimney.

"So, the Colonel is involved with all the disappearances around the town, for his own lustful, vampiric gluttony? What a monster! And Raphael is there, with Ben?" Belinda was absolutely furious in her rage.

"Kill me, Belle! Please, release my soul from this hell!"

No one is sending my son to hell, nor keeping my best friend trapped in the living hell of this Nosferatu body. Belinda brought her Katana up to Fiona's neck. Compliant, Fiona lifted her chin and readied herself.

"Goodbye, my friend," Belinda whispered as she swiftly swung her blade and cleanly severed Fiona's neck. As her head rolled to the floor, Joey quickly grabbed the stake from Belinda's other hand, kneeled at Fiona's side, and pierced her ribcage deeply.

Belinda clasped her hands to her ears and tightly closed her eyes. Joey stared at her, puzzled. After a moment, Belinda opened one eye.

"Wasn't there meant to be a big whooshing sound or something?" she asked, surprised that nothing had happened. "Isn't that what's supposed to happen every time a vampire gets staked, like in *Buffy The Vampire Slayer*? Then the corpse decomposes into ashes?"

"Um, that's not really how it works, Belinda."

"No? I guess it's just another Hollywood myth, and I look really stupid now."

Joey stifled a grin while Belinda looked around for Fiona's head. It had rolled under Ben's bed.

"Oh, fudge waffles! Help me shift this bed, Joe."

They pulled the bed over to one side to retrieve the head. Joey set it on the windowsill, just above where Fiona's body lay slumped on the carpet.

"I will be needing my jacket, thank you very much." Belinda peeled off her jacket from the headless corpse. "I'll have to have it dry cleaned, but that'll have to wait."

She put on the jacket and zipped it up. She turned to face Joey, but burst into uncontrollable fits of hysterical laughter after seeing Fiona's head on the windowsill. It reminded her of all the times she and Ben would carve pumpkins together and place them on the window at Halloween to ward off evil spirits.

Am I going insane? she wondered. *No, I am not going mad. I am doing this for Ben. This is a perfectly rational and reasonable primal mammalian mother's instinct to protect her child. Halloween is just a few days away. Whatever the cost, I will protect my son.*

Joey stared at Belinda in admiration. He had no doubt: she was *The One.*

"Joey, go down the stairs and get some large rubbish bags from the kitchen. They are in the cupboard below where you found the first aid kit. I will join you shortly."

As soon as Joey left the bedroom, Belinda collapsed into a ball, and sobbed uncontrollably.

"Get up," she said to herself. "You can do this."

A few minutes elapsed and Joey appeared at the doorway. He was holding a roll of black refuse sacks.

"Are you okay?"

"No," Belinda answered as she uncurled herself and straightened upright. She levelled a vacant gaze at Joey. "But I will be."

She noticed Ben's teddy bear lying on the floor next to where Fiona had dropped it. She picked it up and zipped it inside her jacket. She looked around at the bloody mess.

"It looks like you will be needing another cleaner after this," Joey said morbidly.

Together they tugged, heaved, and shoved in an attempt to get Fiona's body into an open garbage bag.

"This always looks much easier in the movies," Belinda lamented.

"Should we lop off a few limbs first?" suggested Joey, trying to be helpful. "That might make it easier."

"Oh, come on, Joey! Enough with the decapitations and dismemberments. It's like you're obsessed. Let's just keep trying. We can do this."

They continued their efforts and finally succeeded in placing Fiona's body into the bag. They carefully dragged the sealed bag downstairs and into the kitchen.

"Right. Let's leave this here for now. We are going to need to arm ourselves with more weapons for our assault on the chicken factory," Joey said.

Belinda tutted and shrugged. She looked at the shards of the broken stool on the kitchen floor, and then at the three remaining stools. *Fudge knackers!* she thought. *It took me ages to find just the right set of stools. Well, the set is already broken now, so we might as well make use of the rest of them*, she reasoned.

They hurriedly fashioned stakes from Belinda's remaining wooden furniture. Searching through the drawers, Belinda retrieved a spare lighter — there were always plenty of these around her house — and placed it into her pocket.

"These are good," Joey said, assessing their stockpile. "But we will probably need something else… something bigger…"

"What?" Belinda said. "I don't have any more furniture."

"No, the weapon we need is not a 'what,' but a 'who.' What we need now is the ultimate weapon against evil: *God*."

Joey paused for dramatic effect, but Belinda didn't quite get it.

"*You* know *God*? Like, personally?" She arched an eyebrow.

"Not personally. He's more of a friend of a friend. I do know a guy with an inside connection. We should pay him a visit. In the meantime," Joey continued, "do you have any jerrycans in your home?"

* * *

Not far from Belinda's home stood the oldest Church in the town. Joey knew the Reverend Thrasymachus Zyne from past associations. Zyne enjoyed his wine, and The Running River restaurant catered to his palate.

The Reverend Zyne was an ancient as the walls of his church. He was hard of hearing, but all his other senses were acute. His rectory was adjacent to the kirk — "a short commute," he used to jest.

Whatever his infirmities, he still possessed a sharp mind and was very well respected in the local community and within his flock.

There was a knock at the rectory door. A light illuminated an upstairs bedroom, then slowly faded. Sounds of rattling and chains being unlocked emanated from behind the door, followed by a voice moaning, "Hold on, hold on! Who is calling at this most Godless of hours?"

After some additional rattling and fumbling, at last the door was unbolted and it squeaked open. There stood an old man, Thrasymachus Zyne. He resembled Jacob Marley's ghost; replete with a white nightcap, long dressing gown, and carpet slippers. The reverend was an eccentric individual.

He peered with frustration and impatience at his late night visitors, but his countenance changed immediately when he recognized the unannounced guests.

"Oh, it's you Joey, my boy!" He adjusted his pince-nez glasses, peering sidelong at him. He had a gleam in his eye. "And you, Miss Auberon! Do come in, both of you, please! What on the God's good earth are you carrying in those sacks?"

"We don't have much time, reverend," Joey said. He set the sacks outside the door as Zyne ushered them inside. Joey noted the time on the grandfather clock in Zyne's hallway. It read half past eleven. "We need your help. Belinda needs your help."

Zyne led them into his study. It was full of old archaic books of ancient lore.

He pulled up three ornate chairs for himself and his guests, arranged them so that they faced each other. The reverend sat cross-legged, causing his bony knees to creak and crack.

Belinda was nervous and anxious, sitting with her hands clasped between her knees, and she leaned forward toward the reverend.

"Whatever is the matter, my dear? And how can I be of assistance? How is Ben?"

Belinda gasped, but Joey interjected. He recounted the day's events to the reverend. The reverend sat with his long, skeletal fingers formed into the shape of a steeple, and with his eyes shut in contemplation. Finally he opened his eyes and said to Joe, "Yes, we did suspect the presence of a vampyre nest at The Freaky Fried Chicken Factory. I will grant you all the aid I can."

He turned back toward Belinda and added in a reassuring tone, "Don't you fret, my dear. We will get your Ben back!" He bowed his head.

"Thrasymachus, thank you," said Joey as they all stood up together. "May we use your crypt to store some items? Also, would you bless two jerrycans of holy water for us?"

"Of course! Let's get cracking, shall we?" replied the gentlemen reverend. "There is a small ossuary you may use…"

Belinda was dumbfounded and awestruck by these revelations. She recalled her first meeting with Joey.

> "*Look around you, Belinda. When the sun goes down in this vale of tears, what do you think goes on here? There are monsters everywhere, hiding in every crevice, lurking and squirming like grubs under a rock. Pure wickedness takes many forms. Everything is corrupt…*"
> "*…the Joker's Inn is a realm-way portal into other dimensions, to other lands, worlds and times?*"

Belinda still had so many questions surrounding Joey. Who was he really? And the way he and the reverend interacted made her think they had once been comrades in arms. And Zyne's eyes were sharp, clear and blue — like the countenance of a much younger man. Were the pince-nez just for show?

These questions — and the answers — would have to wait until Ben was rescued, she reasoned.

The preparations were almost complete. Outside the wind was beginning to whip up. Joey stepped outside briefly to retrieve their bags, then stored them in the crypt.

"The church takes a dim view of vamposexuality," the reverend shouted over the increasing wind. "Quite appalling behaviour. They are disgusting deviants that deserve hellfire and damnation."

They returned inside. Reverend Zyne blessed the contents of the two jerrycans and provided them each with a rucksack to carry them. He also blessed their stakes, then dipped them into the holy water for good measure. From a drawer in his writing desk he produced two small boxes.

"Here, take these… A small gift for each of you… Just in case," he said as he handed the boxes to Joey and Belinda. "Go on, Belinda — open it! Put it on!"

Joey opened his, then Belinda did the same. Inside the boxes where silver crosses and chains. Belinda suddenly reached out and gave the reverend a hug.

"Thank you, reverend."

When released from the hug, Zyne blushed, harrumphed, then continued, "Well, quite… All right, off you go then, the both of you. And kick those rotten fiends right in the… well, you know… that other word for donkey."

"How many staff members do you suppose will be in the Freaky Fried Chicken Factory at this time of night?" Joey inquired. He popped another Tic Tac and offered one to Belinda.

"There are fifteen night staff, excluding the Colonel, and Raphael. I think it's safe to assume anyone you encounter there is a creature of the night." She accepted the Tic Tac, and crunched it in her teeth.

"Hide your cross." Joey slipped his cross beneath his shirt. Belinda did the same.

"It's ten minutes to midnight. We have no time for finesse. Let's rock!" Belinda said.

They travelled quickly and silently through the criss-crossing streets and alleyways of Halloween town. The wind continued to howl as they moved stealthily under the full moon that cast faint and ghostly shadows. They soon arrived at the entry gates to the Freaky Fried Chicken Factory. An illuminated fibreglass figure of the Colonel loomed above the factory building, elevated aloft a rotating pole as if continually monitoring the whole town. The effigy looked sinister, and filled Belinda with a grim sense of foreboding.

They approached the wide double doors at the factory entrance and pushed them open then marched toward the service counter inside the lobby where two staff members sat. The first employee, an acne-faced teenage boy, was chatting animatedly about killing cats for sport. The second employee, an equally hideous young girl, was enthralled with the conversation and did not notice Joey and Belinda approach until they reached the counter.

An insipid muzak tune jangled softly in the background. *That seems appropriate*, thought Belinda. *Even the music in here is dead and soulless.*

"Oh, yeah. Cats are awesomely class," the acne zit-faced lad emoted to his co-worker. "Like, there's *totally* much better meat on a cat than on a dog. Dogs are too stringy for me."

They turned together to face Joey and Belinda. With a malicious grin, the girl asked, "Can I take your order?" Her fangs protruded as she spoke.

"Nothing for me, thanks. I already ate," Joey said. "But you can go and serve your master in Hell!" In a blur, Joe's arm shot out and struck the centre of the girl's chest. Blood gushed up his forearm and flowed over his fist that clenched the end of a sharpened stake.

The girl wailed in agony and fell backwards off her seat. The boy's facial pustules almost burst with shock and rage.

"They're norms! Kill them!" he shrieked as he leapt onto Belinda's shoulders and coiled his thighs around her neck. He gripped her ears and pulled his body forward, with his jaws open and ready for the kill.

Smelling the encroaching death breath, Belinda thrust a stake straight up above her head. The tip punctured the vampo's eye socket and burned through his skull like a red hot poker.

"Execution time vamp fudge wad! This is for the wee kitties!" Belinda roared in disgust.

He screeched in pure excruciation. Belinda reached up with her free hand, grasped him by his collar, and flipped him forward and headfirst onto the counter, cracking his skull wide open.

"And that's for all the wee puppies you butchered! Gah!" She shouted at his cadaver.

As the two dispatched vampires lay silently in pools of their own blood, the soft sounds of *The Girl from Ipanema* continued to gently waft through the foyer. For a moment there was no other sound.

"Oh, I love this song!" said Joey.

Belinda wasn't sure if he was being sarcastic. She jumped over the counter and got back to work. "Hurry, Joey. Grab these cooking pots!"

Each five-gallon pot was filled with cooking oil and weighed about fifty pounds. They lugged the pots all over the foyer, pouring the oil onto the floor, the walls, the service counter, and the two dead vampires. They placed a few of the remaining pots upright on the deep fat friers. They emptied one jerrycan of holy water into seven of the friers.

Joey and Belinda pushed through some swinging doors at the rear of the lobby and entered the main factory floor. It comprised a network of service galleys and tube ways where the meat was to be sliced, separated, and processed to be ready for grinding. The rumble of the grinding machinery could be heard coming from the next room.

"Okay, do you reckon that'll be enough for this room?" Belinda asked, heaving and sweating. Joey smiled and nodded.

An alarm sounded on the factory PA system. Six vampyres rushed in from the grinding room. They wore white aprons, black wellies[4], and wielded knives and meat cleavers. Belinda noted that they were not wearing hair nets, which was probably a food industry health code violation.

The vampyres launched themselves at Joey and Belinda, wailing for blood. Belinda drew her sword, and Joey joined the fray using his khanjali. An orgy of gore, violence and carnage then ensued.

"Who the fuck do you think you are, bitch?" the nearest vampo cursed at them. "*Buffy the Vampire Slayer?*" He brought his cleaver up to block Belinda's first strike.

"No, vamp-slag, I am the Northern Irish original!" She twisted her katana, blocking the meat-cleaver in a passata-sotto movement, feinting downwards and skewering the head of the vampyre.

"I am Belinda Auberon! Did *Buffy* ever do this?!" With all her might she cleaved the whole body across in an upper cut stroke, leaving only the torso, disembowelling the creature. She finished the vampo off by cutting out its heart.

"At your service!" she spat at his corpse.

The vampyres attacked Joey, but their numbers were no match for his skill. With a combination of flying kung fu moves; he struck terror amongst his adversaries, slicing off limbs with his dagger in a whirlwind of brutal destruction. Three were soon dispatched, impaled with stakes in their hearts.

---

[4] Wellington boots, known colloquially in Halloween town as Wellies, are large, waterproof rubber boots.

The two remaining bloodsuckers dropped their weapons and attempted to flee. Joey took a stake in each hand and threw them together with deadly precision. They hit their targets, skewering their hearts from behind. The vampos fell face first into a twisted heap.

Joey and Belinda ripped some of the clothing from the corpses, using them as wadding material and soaking them in the cooking oil.

"Let's go!" Belinda said. "To the meat-processing room!"

""This room has been pacified!"" Joey smiled, looking behind him, quoting his favourite comic book law enforcement hero.

"The alarm has been triggered, so they know we are here. I reckon the rest of the vampo-vermin will be ready and waiting for us!" Belinda said.

"We don't have much time," said Joey, "and it's only five minutes to midnight."

Belinda peered through the circular window in the swinging doors into the meat grinding room. They cautiously entered the room and splashed more holy water from the jerrycans onto the fryers, causing the scorching oil to react and spray all over the machinery. Angry geysers of blistering oil coated everything.

"Here they come!" yelled Joey. "You ready?"

Belinda held a balled-up rag from the dead vampyre and reached into her pocket for her lighter. She struck the lighter's flint to ignite a flame.

The lighter failed to spark.

"No!" She shook the lighter vigorously and tried again. Still nothing.

"Please God," she whispered. "And God said, 'Let there be light,' and there was light."

The rag kindled. Belinda's eyes grew wide in wonder.

"Suck on my haemoglobin, you soulless blood fuckers!" she shouted as she threw the lit cloth at the oncoming horde of vampos.

A huge torrent of flame erupted like a napalm blast through The Freaky Fried Chicken Factory, incinerating the approaching wall of vampyres. They squirmed, writhed, and screamed as they fell over each other, enwrapped in flames as the burning mix of holy water and cooking oil exploded their dark souls. The whole factory shook as the pans on the deep fat friers fulminated and detonated.

The growing flames enveloped the meat grinding machinery. The intense heat caused pipes to burst, and metal vents buckled and collapsed from the ceiling. Light fixtures exploded, and the backup lighting added an ominous red glow.

The emergency sprinkler system activated, but the inferno was fuelled by a burning oil that resisted being tamed. Pockets of fires continued to burn in the soaked floor, throwing a ghoulish glow throughout the factory. Belinda's and Joey's clothes were sopping wet and clinging to their skin.

The roaring sound of the flames abated. From the relative calm, a voice spoke from the gloom in front of them.

"So, this is Hung Fung Joey, the last of the Maguš Samurai, and Miss Auberon!"

The Colonel stepped forward from the darkness and into the centre of the floor. He nonchalantly looked around at the blackened mess that had been the core of his meat processing plant.

"Tut, tut! Just look what you have done to my place… and my staff!"

His voice rumbled, deeply, barely holding back a seething hatred.

"You were a good day worker here, my dear. You kept the place clean," he said, speaking directly to Belinda. "But look at all this unnecessary, wilful destruction. I am afraid I will have to deduct all damages incurred from your wages. But you have nothing of value, do you? Oh… except… your son, and his mortal soul!"

His voice grew louder.

"Bring out the boy, Raphael!"

Raphael stepped out from the space behind the Colonel and stood by his side. He was holding Ben's hand. Ben was holding the Soul Mask, and he moved is slow torpid steps, as if drugged or in a trance.

"Ah," the Colonel continued, "it is so good to have the family together, isn't it?" He flashed a wide, fake smile aimed directly at Belinda. "I'm very pro-family, you know," the Colonel said gleefully. "And, oh look, it's almost midnight!"

Above the Colonel the open end of a ruptured metal vent shook and wobbled. Out of the vent opening there was a spray of slime as Helvar the vampiric dolphin exploded out of the hole and lunged onto Colonel Godfrey Klunz's face. The force of the impact pushed the Colonel backward, stumbling into the machinery as Helvar's slithering tendrils coiled around his neck and began choking him.

"Fuck!" Belinda exclaimed. "I did *not* see that coming!"

Joey added, "Aye, I had totally forgotten about that… thing!"

Raphael ran from the mayhem, dragging Ben behind him.

The dolphin shrieked into the Colonel's face, spritzing him with slime and saliva. "Colonel Klunz!" Its voice was punctuated with high-pitched clicks and whistles. "Where have you put my body? And my penissss!?"

Seizing the opportunity offered by the distraction, Belinda punched the large red button to activate the grinder machinery. The gears rumbled to life. Although damaged by the fire, the slicing and grinding equipment still functioned. It snagged the Colonel and drew him into the machine's inner workings, with Helvar still attached to his neck.

"Sorry, Helvar — looks like no hand job for you today."

"No, Belinda!" the Colonel screamed. "Not the grinders!"

Both the Colonel and the disembodied Helvar screeched and shrieked as the meat grinders mashed and pulped their bodies together. The air was filled with the pounding sounds of the machinery, mixed with the screaming, cracking and snapping of bones, and a sickening sizzle as their flesh was fried, braised and cooked in a cocktail of holy water and frying oil. As the pressure inside the machinery grew, Joey and Belinda heard two loud popping sounds.

Belinda looked at Joey. "Yes," he answered before she could ask the question, "that *was* the sound of their skulls exploding. Do you feel like you're going to throw up again?"

"Ugh," replied Belinda. "Well, now we know the secret of 'The Colonel's Special Element!'" she said wryly, her mouth twisted to one side.

"Come on, let's find Ben!"

Joey and Belinda clambered over the strewn wreckage and headed into the corridors in the direction Raphael had fled. They zig-zagged through the building, searching. Then they heard a voice, singing.

I love a rainy night,
Mmmm, I love a rainy night.

They turned a corner in the corridor and saw the open door to the manager's office. The singing was coming from inside.

Raphael was waiting. Belinda and Joey entered. His sinister eyes shone and his fangs glinted in the moist air. Ben stood beside him, with the Soul Mask in his hands. It was two minutes to midnight.

"Stop right there!" Raphael commanded. "I could tear you both to shreds. It would take no effort at all. Do not doubt it, my love."

"I'd like to see you try," Belinda said through clenched teeth. She and Joey pulled out the crosses that hung around their necks, and thrust them forward toward the vampyre god.

"Get back!" they ordered.

Raphael flinched, retreated and hissed madly.

"I'll pay no heed to your trinkets; your innocent son is wanted below. We have a saying where I come from: 'You cannot live in hell, and not fight with Mephistopheles.' Look down at your feet. The time is upon us."

The Realm Way was beginning to open. A swirling vortex of light and shaped moved on the office floor as the portal between dimensions began to open.

"Wait, Raphael!" Belinda pleaded. "I have something here to bargain with… something you want more than anything else."

"What could you possibly have that I might desire, Belinda?" he scoffed cruelly at her.

Joey pulled the urn from his backpack and handed it to Belinda. Raphael eyed the urn with suspicion.

"Here! This contains the spirit of the one you desire," Belinda said as she proffered the urn. "We caught her with a spell and imprisoned her within. It is your eternal lover, Pandoria."

Raphael's eyes flashed with anger, then with lust. He fumed while he paused to consider. He had been under strict orders to deliver the boy. But the temptation was too strong, and he gave in to his desires.

"Very well, Belinda. You played this game with great sagacity. You can have your brat back, but I want that urn and my lover returned to me!"

Joey edged closer to Ben and reached out to take his hand while Belinda simultaneously stretched her arms out and holding the urn closer toward Raphael. They inched closer and closer, neither trusting the other, until Raphael at last could reach the urn. As soon as he had it in his grip, Joey pulled Ben away, still clutching the Soul Mask. Immediately, Raphael turned on them. He pulled the urn to his chest with one arm wrapped around it, then seized Belinda by the throat.

"You fools!" Raphael laughed at them. "I release my love, Pandoria Evǣfensang!" He raised the urn and prepared to hurl it toward the ground. Belinda reacted quickly and swung her katana with all her strength, striking it hard and cracking it open. A spray of holy water erupted from the split vessel and poured down over Raphael's head. As the water drenched his face and ran down his neck and torso, he instinctively dropped the shattered urn and released his grip on Belinda. He covered his face with both hands as scalding miasma streamed up through his fingers as his eyeballs burst and his face melted.

"Argh! You bitch!" he screamed through his hands.

He flailed around blindly, desperately swinging his arms in all directions, searching for Belinda as she backed away, always staying out of reach.

"What have you done to me?" Raphael slowed and dropped to his knees. Vapour continued to rise from his face as the skin dripped and tore off, landing in lumps on the floor around him.

"What have *I* done?" Belinda retorted incredulously. "Well, let's see. Since last night: I almost puked myself inside out; I've lost my best friend in the world; and I've had my son kidnapped by a depraved and evil night creature. Oh, but all these things pale in comparison to the fact that I haven't even had the time to get tampons from the chemist, you vile vampyre witch-fucker! I smell like hell, thanks to you!"

Raphael seemed paralysed. His head and shoulders were slouched forward and twitching.

Belinda removed her cross, and draped its chain over Raphael's head and rested the cross where his forehead had been. The silver melted as the holy water began dissolving into his bones. Raphael said nothing, but his flesh continued to hiss, and his throat gurgled.

Slowly Belinda reached for a stake. Striking through his crotch, she rammed the stake right upwards.

"Good bye, Raphael. You were such a bitter waste of time in my life."

Finally, to finish him off, Belinda clutched her katana tightly with both hands, then neatly lopped Raphael's head from his shoulders with one clean cut. His head bounced, and his body slumped down to the ground.

Belinda stared at the head for a moment. At last she could feel relieved. It was over. She and Ben were safe.

"Hurry, Belinda!" Joey yelled. "The Realm Way is opening!"

She pushed Raphael Diavolite's body into the swirling Charybdis between the worlds. For a blinding instant, a burning light enveloped the room, and the Realm Way was gone.

She rushed to hold her son. Ben was still in a trance. She unzipped her jacket.

"Ben, wake up! It's mummy! Look, here's teddy!"

Ben blinked.

"Mummy, I had a bad dream about daddy again… "

Belinda cradled her son in her arms, brushed a strand of hair from his forehead. She reassured him, "Yes, my son, I know you did. But your daddy has been dead for years. He is gone, and he is never coming back to hurt you or scare you ever again."

"Come now, Belinda Auberon — we must leave this place." Said Joey.

They all walked out of the crumbling Freaky Fried Chicken Factory. Joey sheathed his blade and carrying The Soul Mask, walking beside Belinda who still held her katana in one hand, the other hand held Ben while Ben held on to his teddy bear. All were dishevelled, bedraggled, smelled of gore, guts and blood.

They did not look back, even when a deafening sonic boom and a huge explosion ripped across the sky hitting the building, vaporising it. The revolving pole that held the Colonel's monstrous head collapsed into The Freaky Fried Chicken Factory.

"You have a lot of explaining to do, Mister," Belinda said to Joey, staring straight at the horizon. "So, you are a Maguš Samurai? I guess that's cool. But when we were at The Witches' Ball, how did you know which one was me? Pandoria had perfectly captured my likeness, my voice, and all my mannerisms. How could you still tell us apart?"

Joey was embarrassed. "Well, you did smell, a little."

Letting go of Ben's hand for a moment, she hit Joey hard on his forearm.

"That does it! Isn't there an all night chemist in this town?!"

Belinda noticed Ben staring straight up at the sky. Belinda looked up to where Ben was facing, and Joey followed suit. A glint in the heavens caught their eyes.

"Look, mummy!"

It was a shooting star, falling to earth. They all made a wish.

"Hey, Joey," Belinda said. "Do you have any of those Tic Tacs left?"

In the smouldering furnace of the impact crater where the factory had stood, something moved and began to crawl toward the surface…

*   *   *

The Reverend Zyne gave them sanctuary for a few days while an army of cleaners from The Running River Chinese restaurant cleaned Belinda's home. Joey himself took charge of the operation.

Saying good-bye to the reverend wasn't easy. He was in his study, sitting on his favourite chair and leafing through a book when Belinda knocked the door. She was rested, relaxed and felt both in body and soul, cleansed.

"Thrasymachus, I would just like to thank you again for all your help and hospitality."

The old man rose to his feet, shoving the book behind him.

"Not at all, my dear — that's quite all right. How is your young man? He will be a great warrior when he grows up."

"Talking of which," Belinda inquired, "may I ask a question? Joey revealed to me that he was the last of the Maguš Samurai, but that's not entirely accurate, is it?"

The Reverend harrumphed in his throat. He adjusted his pince-nez glasses, and stared at Belinda.

"Indeed not! As an old friend of mine once said, 'I cannot tell a lie.' I have travelled too long and far, and seen too much."

"I knew it! Ha!" She turned round, and began to pace back and forth. "It makes sense now. When Joey transported us from The Witches' Ball back to my kitchen, I didn't understand at the time how he had done that, but now I do. You and Joey are time travellers!"

"As you will be, one day."

When Belinda had left, The Reverend Zyne removed his glasses. He straightened and flexed his back muscles. He walked confidently to his cabinet on the wall of his study. He removed a small key that was hung around his neck. It was shaped like an ancient Egyptian Horus Ankh. He unlocked the tall cabinet.

Inside the cabinet, there where dozens of blades and mysterious magical daggers. In the front, arranged in a neat display, sat six Soul Masks.

He picked up one of the blades, and examined it casually. His mind drifted back — or was it forward? — to a time and a place connected to the sword. He smiled, and carefully set the blade back in its space, then locked the cabinet.

Joey was waiting for Belinda outside in the churchyard.

"Where is Ben?"

"He's resting. The poor kid has been through a lot."

Joey and Belinda returned to Zyne's crypt and removed the real urn containing Pandoria Evǣfensang's trapped spirit. Joey sealed the tomb again with a sepulture rite.

"What are you going to do with the urn and the Soul Mask? Do you think my Father is still trapped in it somewhere?" Belinda asked, eagerly. She flicked her golden hair from her face, and folded her arms while shivering in the slight chill of the morning air.

"I am unsure. When the Realm Way closed, powerful forces were trapped. The Soul Mask may just be redundant, but I will keep it safe in any case. As for the urn, we shall consign it to the ocean depths."

Joey continued, "Hey, did you see the paper this morning?"

He held his mobile phone up to show the headline from *The Halloween Telegraph:*

INFERNO!
No Survivors After Mysterious Midnight Meteorite Shower
Frags Freaky Fried Chicken Factory

"Huh. That's tabloid journalism for you. So, is that it? The end of the vampyres in this town?"

"Oh, no, there is still another you must face… the Mayor."

*　　*　　*

Germwarfilia Puckwudgie could not sleep. Her husband, Glargazop, was back at work. He had been hired as a trainee chef at The Running River, working the late evening shift. It was good, solid employment, and Glargazop was happy and grateful for it. Their son, Thrawgar, was still… Thrawgar.

At the end of a long shift, Glargazop wearily climbed the stairs to his bedroom. Upon opening the bedroom door, he saw his wife sitting bolt upright in bed, waiting for him.

"Aw, not now, woman! I'm exhausted after work, can't you see that?" He climbed in beside her, covering himself with the sheets.

"No, it's not that Glargazop. I have good news! Listen! Thrawgar is… well, how can I put this delicately…?"

"Go on, woman," he said gruffly. "Spit it out!"

"Thrawgar is going to have a little brother — and a sister!"

There was a pregnant pause, then a long wail of anguish from Glargazop.

*　　*　　*

The captain slowed the fishing trawler's engines and drifted to a stop amid the undulating swells of the northern fishing region about a hundred miles off the coast of Halloween town. Joey stood on the starboard side and looked down into the tempest. The spell he had cast was unbreakable — Pandoria would never be released from her prison. He cast the urn overboard and watched it sink deep into the ocean void.

He signalled to the captain, who gunned the engines and turned the vessel back toward port.

* * *

"Where are we going, mummy?" Ben asked his mother. Ben and Belinda were walking briskly side by side and hand in hand. He was looking up at her with eagerness. Belinda Auberon looked down at him with great affection in her eyes.

They walked down Samhain Lane in Halloween town. She halted, looking around. The busker was still there, playing his folk songs for all the beggars and all the kings and queens who ventured by.

"Nothing ever changes here."

There was an electronic cigarette shop she had noticed.

She was tempted to go in, but Ben pulled at her sleeve and her reverie.

"Mummy, where are we going?"

Her own house was still contaminated, and she did not consider it as her dwelling anymore. There were too many bad memories connected to the place: the history with Raphael; her dream encounter with Helvar, the vampire dolphin; and the bloody demise of her best friend, Fiona.

At the end of the lane stood *The Joker's Inn*.

Belinda hunkered down on one knee, and pulled Ben close to her.

"Well, young man." She pointed to the shop. "How would you like to live there, in the flat above your grandad's shop?"

"Oh, yes! Can we really, mummy?" was the enthusiastic reply. "It can be Halloween *every* day!"

"Then it's settled. We are going home."

OLD MACDONALD HAD A TIME MACHINE

Old MacDonald had a time machine,
E-I-E-I-O.
Bouncing 'round time like you've never seen,
E-I-E-I-O.
With a time slip here,
And a blackhole there.
Here a slip, through a hole,
Everywhere a worm hole.
Old MacDonald had a time machine,
E-I-E-I-O.

Old MacDonald had a time machine,
E-I-E-I-O.
Farming in the Cretaceous jungle green,
Prehistoric organs he a was harvesting,
Old MacDonald had a time machine,
E-I-E-I-O.

With a brontosaurus spleen here,
And a triceratops sphincter there,
Hear the chainsaw,
Smell the gore,
Every part he saw-sawed!

Old MacDonald had a time machine,
E-I-E-I-O.
Outside stalked meat eating dinosaurs,
With a Velociraptor here,
And a Tyrannosaurus Rex there,
Everywhere a hungry predator!

E-I-E-I-O.

See them charge,
Hear them roar,
Climbing walls,
With their claws,
Everywhere a claw-claw!

Old MacDonald couldn't reach his time machine,
E-I-E-I-O.
Then Old MacDonald grabbed his laser gun,
E-I-E-I-O.
"I'm gonna cook me some dinosaur scum!"
E-I-E-I-O.

Yes, Old MacDonald had a time-machine,
It was the purdiest darn thing you ever seen,
With a beam of light here,
And a blast there,
Hear his shouts,
As his battery runs out.
But Old MacDonald, he ain't there no more!
E-I-E-I-O.

OBLIVION OBSECRATION

In the graveyard, a marble seraph statue regarded the ghost with cold contempt. Her opaque limestone eyes smiled at him, mockingly. Eighteen tales were told, and turned into dust. The ghost was amused for an instant, his shrieking laughter disturbed the magpies.

The wind blew upon the gravestones. The cachinnation of the ghost's voice howled through the God's-acre. If someone outside the urn-field had listened, briefly, they would have sworn a banshee had wailed.

Rooks nibbled at the hanged corpse, fighting over the entrails of the cadaver. The rooks clawed and pecked at the rope, until it eventually snapped.

The body fell into the moss and earth.

Then he saw it!

His grave!

He mouthed the words that were inscribed upon the headstone. Then, a shockwave and a whirlwind whipped up in the graveyard.

He was powerless, someone had seized his soul. Twisting it, burning it in a maelstrom, sending it upwards, and downwards until —

There was nothing but oblivion. The ghost sighed. He had found peace at last.

Author Biography

Jonathan Fisher is a true survivor. He is the author of *August Always,* his memoir. The book has been cited by The Belfast Telegraph as "a triumph." The book itself took the author 17 years to write, a testament to Jonathan's endurance. In April 1992, age 22 he died — albeit briefly — from an undiagnosed Addisonian Crisis. Before then Jonathan had a full childhood and subsequent teenage troubles. Thanks to his parents intervention, he was rushed to the local hospital wherein Jonathan was comatose for three months. All these details are recorded in his self-published, heart wrenching memoir, the book itself sold out completely in the space of 6 months, leaving a Kindle version now available.

The doctors said it would be a mercy to turn off Jonathan's life support machines. Against all odds, Fisher moved his little finger to his mother's voice, proof of a semblance of life.

Later that year, Jonathan began the long, slow, hard road to recovery; a journey that would take him through many institutions and heartaches; spending time in the forge and on the anvil, a refining process that reshaped the author both mentally and physically.

Jonathan Fisher the author, remains a wheel-chair user, fiercely independent and he does not let his physical disability stop him from achieving his goals. He is a keen costume player and a member of the Emerald Garrison and Heroes Unite Ireland, professional costuming clubs who dress up as Super Heroes and Star Wars characters to support worthy causes.

Now he has crafted another masterpiece: eighteen short stories, from Fisher's dark imagination. With frightening tales of thrilling science-fiction, adventure, horror, fantasy, rich in satire and gallows humour.

Enter, if you will, to the spellbinding world of Halloween Town in Jonathan Fisher's latest book, *Ten Minutes On Mars.*